SPACE TRUCKERS 2

The Return of the Blue Eagle

Michael D'Ambrosio

Space Truckers: The Return of the Blue Eagle

ISBN
978-1-960197-85-6 (Paperback)
978-1-960197-86-3 (eBook)
978-1-964982-07-6 (Hardcover)

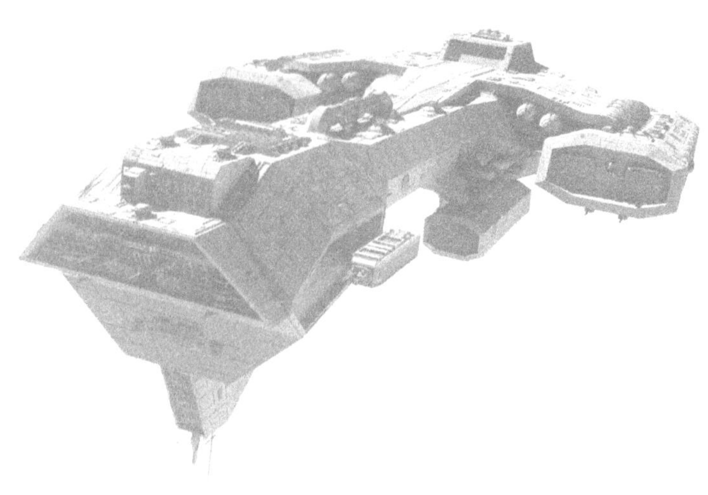

TABLE OF CONTENTS

CHAPTER 1

A DEBT TO BE PAID

Antwan and two of his thugs, dressed in muscle shirts and jeans, exited his office at Empire Shipping Headquarters. He looked weary and pale with a long beard and scraggily hair. As they approached the elevator on the fourteenth floor, five Kronos agents in dark suits stepped off and blocked his path. One of the agents instructed Antwan that he was to come with them to Kronos Headquarters. Antwan, sensing that his life was in danger, raised his hands in mock surrender. The agents were lulled into complacency, assuming he knew better than to defy a Kronos command. Antwan's men seized the moment, drawing their weapons first and firing at the agents. The agents drew their pistols and fired back, despite lethal wounds. Antwan dove to the ground and avoided the brief shootout as both his men and the agents lay dead or mortally wounded on the floor. He scurried to his feet and rushed back to his office.

With thoughts of fleeing, he frantically searched through the drawers of his desk for a fake ID chip and the tool to insert it under his skin. The 3-D monitor on the wall beeped. He froze, knowing it was too late. Reluctantly, he accepted the incoming message. A bearded man with a handlebar mustache stared grimly at him from the monitor. It was Carl Klingman, the CEO of Kronos Enterprises. Antwan greeted him politely as he sat at his desk. Sweat beaded on his forehead as he recalled the warnings the Klingman brothers gave him about failure when he was recruited. Jack promised him a luxurious lifestyle and a limitless budget to execute their orders. Carl was the quiet one of the two brothers and also the one to be feared most. His reputation for being ruthless bought him unquestioning loyalty from anyone who met him. He warned Antwan that his family would be held accountable for any failures he incurred but Antwan was confident that he had everything he needed to be successful – that is until Mike Colby entered the picture. That's when things went wrong.

"Antwan, you have failed us," Carl began. "Your incompetence has cost us dearly."

"But Sir," he pleaded, "I already have a plan in motion to deal with…"

"Enough!" interrupted Carl, showing his impatience. "The board discussed your situation and we have reached a decision."

Antwan knew that whatever punishment was coming would be horrific. "Please Mr. Klingman! I just need a little more time."

Carl shook his head in disappointment and stepped back. Antwan saw three children, a man, and a woman seated behind Klingman on the monitor. His eyes widened in horror and his worst nightmare materialized in front of him. It was his father, his wife and their three young children. Their eyes were filled with tears and their hands tied behind their backs.

"You've cost me a brother, Antwan," Carl reminded him. "Jack was part of my family as well as my partner. We had big plans and we trusted you to spearhead our efforts to achieve them."

Antwan broke down into tears. "Your brother is still alive. I've already heard from my sources," he tried to assure Carl. Humbly kneeling down in front of the monitor, he pleaded for mercy.

"Where are my men?" Carl asked, growing more irate. "I expected you to be in their custody by now."

Antwan knew there was no point in lying. Klingman already knew they were dead. When he didn't respond, Carl nodded to a woman in the corner of the room. Darra, dressed in a Goth-style, leather uniform with spikes in the shoulders and long, black hair, approached him.

"Show Antwan the remedy for his failure," he instructed her.

"No!" cried Antwan as he watched Darra slice the throat of his father. His heart broke as the man's life seeped from his body and pooled on the floor. Antwan's wife stared pleadingly for him to do something, but he was helpless. His son cried frantically as Darra held her blade to his throat. With a cold darkness in her eyes, she was no stranger to killing innocents.

"That was for not procuring the teleport module," chided Carl. Feeling some compassion, he informed Antwan that the girls would be sold into slavery and the boy imprisoned with other deviates who opposed Kronos. Antwan's wife cried as Darra escorted the children out of the room. The children pleaded for their mother to help them, but she was restrained.

"That was for allowing Gemini and Colby to ruin our plans to control all shipping in the galaxy," Carl continued. "You also failed to locate the renegade assassin Marina, who has set back our plans to possess the most dangerous weapon in the universe. And now, thanks to your incompetence, we have to begin again on a level playing field. This cost us significant money and resources. Fail us again," Carl warned, "and your wife dies next." He then walked over to her and brushed the hair from her eyes compassionately. Darra returned to the room and knew what Carl had in mind.

"In the meantime, we'll provide her with companionship," he assured Antwan and then burst into sarcastic laughter.

Darra looked with disgust at the bloody corpse that was Antwan's father, as it leaned forward, motionless. She kicked the chair over and the corpse fell to the floor, lying face up with a look of horror in the dead man's eyes.

Antwan's wife, Tia, now stared at Antwan through the monitor with hatred in her eyes. Antwan knew she would blame him for their children's fate. She warned him when he joined Kronos that this could happen. He wanted the luxurious life and she often emphasized that someday there would be a price to pay for it. He should have listened.

"I will take care of all of them," Antwan mumbled sadly. "This time they will pay."

Klingman chuckled mockingly at him. "You obviously can't handle all of this, Antwan. We overestimated your abilities."

Antwan knew things would only get worse. He waited silently for whatever additional punishment might come his way. Klingman again nodded to Darra and she approached Antwan's wife. "Darra will take care of Marina and perhaps your wife as well as a reward for her success."

Darra grabbed Tia by her hair and bent her head backward. She kissed her for what seemed like forever to Antwan. Darra then licked Tia's neck and gently ran her finger along Tia's breasts over her blouse. Tia cried as she lowered her head in shame. Klingman interrupted her and reminded her that she must succeed first in her mission or Tia would go to the men. Darra grinned fiendishly as she untied Tia's wrists.

Tia shouted at the monitor to Antwan, "I hate you! You arrogant son of a bitch!"

Darra stood her up and proceeded to kiss her unwilling victim with unbridled passion in front of the men, adding to her humiliation. Klingman shrugged his shoulders at Antwan and quipped, "C'est la vie." He ended the transmission and the monitor went blank.

Antwan paced the room like a rabid animal with tears streaming down his cheeks. He cursed Colby, Gemini and the rebel known as Marina, whom he disregarded as someone his men could handle easily. "They will all pay," he cried out as he punched the walls and flipped the furniture over. "And one day, Klingman will pay as well," he swore aloud to himself.

Tears streamed down his cheeks. In desperation, he activated his wrist transmitter and sent a group message that posted a sizeable bounty on both Gemini and Mike Colby's head. After contemplating for a moment, he sent out another for a bounty on the mysterious Marina. Antwan then boarded his shuttle with five of his thugs. He needed to find a certain assassin for assurance that the job would get done. Colby needed to pay for destroying his life.

The next day, Antwan's shuttle arrived on Gamma-5 and docked. Gamma-5 was one of the smaller trading stations in the galaxy. It was a critical lifeline to the settlers in the 1st sector. Established to handle the overcrowding on planet Earth, it was the first and closest colony to be inhabited on a permanent basis.

Antwan exited his shuttle and left three of his men at the hatch for security. The other two followed from a distance for his protection. He searched left and right for anything or anyone suspicious. Content that no one recognized him, he continued down to the end bay. A mercenary, armed with a pulse rifle and two daggers, guarded the entrance to the bay. When Antwan approached, the man targeted him with his rifle. "State your purpose quickly or die," he ordered.

"I'm here to meet with Borath," Antwan replied, unconcerned by the guard's threat. The man whispered into his transmitter and then allowed Antwan to pass.

Antwan handed over his pulse pistol to the guard and entered the bay. Four well-armed men exited a large cruiser docked at the platform. They split off to either side of Antwan in pairs. Exiting the cruiser next was Borath, a tall, muscular man with a thick main of hair and a pointed beard. His expression was imposing as he approached Antwan.

"I hear things are not going so well for you, Antwan," he commented in a cynical manner.

Antwan became uneasy, knowing his credibility was in question. "I made the mistake of hiring incompetents to handle a problem."

Borath gestured for him to follow him on board the ship. They entered the main cabin and sat at the conference table. One of the men brought a crude decanter of wine and two wooden goblets. He poured the wine and placed the goblets in front of each man. Borath raised his goblet in a toast and announced, "To good hunting and better business."

Antwan raised his goblet and echoed Borath's words. The two men sipped from their goblets. Borath maintained a stare while Antwan looked down in shame. "This is humbling," Antwan started. "I don't have to tell you that Kronos is unforgiving of failure."

Borath chuckled and countered, "What made you think it would be easy doing their bidding?" Antwan didn't respond. He sipped again from his wine. Borath grew impatient and questioned him about what he wanted from him and how much he had to offer.

"I have three problems," Antwan answered, nervous. "Each needs to be dealt with permanently."

"I'm listening," Borath remarked, curious as to what kind of challenge this would pose.

"Five hundred thousand credits for obtaining the *Blue Eagle;* the executions of a mercenary Mike Colby and Gemini, the Sysco CEO from Taurus and a rebel named Marina from Yord," Antwan revealed, determined. "But I need it done soon. Soon as in three cycles."

Borath scratched his beard and finished the wine. He stared intently at Antwan, pondering a counteroffer. "One million if I do this in less than three cycles. Five hundred thou if it takes longer."

Antwan's jaw dropped. A million would deplete his entire budget from Kronos. "I can't do that!" he blurted.

Borath stood and activated a holographic emitter. "Perhaps this will help," he remarked. The holograph illustrated several symbols. Borath waved at one of them and stepped back. An image formed of Antwan's wife in a sex video with Darra. Darra looked up at the camera and grinned as she indulged in Antwan's wife. Antwan was horrified. Borath then informed him that copies of the video were used by Darra to settle some old debts.

Antwan paced the room in a panic. This was so humiliating and he could do nothing about it. "All right! One million if you take care of it in less than one cycle."

Borath laughed at him and countered, "Two and we have a deal."

Antwan considered for a moment how he could raise that kind of money. Then he realized that Kronos would be happy to help if the problem was solved. The men shook hands and Antwan stormed off the ship.

On Taurus, in Gemini's 11th floor conference room, Dax sat across the table from Gemini and Julian. He was fully recovered from his abdominal wound, but his survival was kept secret for his own protection. Everyone fully expected Kronos to come for him, looking for either revenge or leverage to get the designs for the new engines and fuel management system.

Captain Tieg sat at the end of the table and observed the signing and backdating of the contract for the disposition of equipment and product from Hellfire Fuels to Sysco Galactic. Both Gemini and Dax were pleased with the transaction and what they could accomplish together. Gemini toked on her perfora until the signing was done; an indication of her impatience. At this point, she sat back and sipped from a glass of bourbon.

Julian activated the monitor on the wall and displayed the Sysco organizational chart. He discussed several personnel moves at the executive level with Dax to assure his inclusion on executive matters. Julian then informed Dax that Gemini's sister Sara and her team from Galactic Security Services would handle all external station security while supporting Capt. Tieg and his team internally on Taurus. This was to alleviate concerns by

Tieg's men that they were being replaced by GSS, and to dissuade his men from selling them out.

Captain Tieg was uneasy about the arrangement, fearing that they didn't have the resources on Taurus to handle the responsibility but, sensing his concern, Gemini interceded and clarified that Sara's team would hunt Empire's spies both arriving on Taurus and departing. Captain Tieg and his men were responsible to handle any situations inside Taurus. In addition, she assured him that there were now resources to increase his manpower and weaponry. The two groups were expected to interface with each other and share information to eliminate threats to the corporation.

Julian then informed Captain Tieg that his new position was to act as the liaison between the two security groups and a promotion in rank to Major. Tieg was reluctant at first, but then realized what his responsibilities would be and was satisfied. With a change in attitude, he gratefully accepted his promotion.

Concerned about the export of corporate secrets by employees, Tieg questioned the vetting of the engineers and technicians from both companies. Dax reminded him that all his employees involved in the new technologies had chips installed in the back of their necks and on their wrists. The wrist chip accessed secure doors while the second chip was a locator, designed to release a fast-acting toxin through the base of the brain if the employee was identified in a suspect area to ensure no one fled Taurus with the intent of selling their trade secrets. The toxin could also be released if the employee was under duress. Gemini added that her employees would be chipped as well. Julian suggested that Tieg's security team receive the same chip as assurance of their loyalty. He promised Tieg that he would consider a financial incentive for their commitment.

Tieg inquired as to the logistics of the *Blue Eagle* since so much was riding on the success of its mission. Julian explained the reason for the secrecy was due to its new, long-distance capabilities and revealed that the ship was on its first run with the possibility of winning them at least one lucrative contract for shipping to the outer rim. He refused to reveal neither the cargo nor the destinations for security reasons.

Satisfied that everything was under control, Gemini poured glasses of bourbon for Dax and Julian, while refreshing hers. They toasted to the completion of the liquidation of Hellfire Fuels' technologies to Sysco and the wealth to come with it for both of them. Tieg was bored with the theatrics and excused himself from the room.

Gemini took the *Blue Eagle's* new role as a long-distance transporter to the edge of the galaxy very seriously. This was a lucrative business that no one had been able to successfully operate in until now. Pirates, hostile aliens, fuel management and ship maintenance were major issues in the past. Also a problem for them were the unknown variables such as asteroids and cosmic storms, associated with long distance travel. She felt that they now had the ability to overcome those issues, using the *Blue Eagle* as a blueprint for their future.

Despite Gemini's ambitions, GSS through Sara proposed that Sysco Galactic use only the *Blue Eagle* with the new engines until the rest of the industry had something comparable. Then Sysco's other ships would be upgraded as well. There was great concern by Sara and her peers that rivals would go to great lengths to procure the technology if installed on multiple ships. Any single ship could be commandeered and the engine technology would then be reverse-engineered. Sara also reminded them that additional ships wouldn't have Colby on board to mitigate those attempts. Thus, the new technology should be restricted to the *Blue Eagle* for now, where they had strict control of it. Gemini agreed to postpone any additional upgrades for now but they were on the table for a later date.

After Julian left the room, Dax remained to speak with Gemini. He suggested they find a way to contact the manufacturer of the teleport module and propose the purchase of several more of them. Gemini smiled, pleased by his ambition and revealed that she, too, hoped for that same goal. They both stood at the same time and, after staring into each other's eyes briefly, Dax made his move. He embraced Gemini in his arms and kissed her. Gemini was pleased, but informed him that she won't be an easy conquest. He assured her that he would prove himself to her and win her heart. She kissed him back and wished him luck with this endeavor. With that, she left the room. Dax sighed and grumbled, "Women." He couldn't help but wonder if that attitude is what drove Colby away.

On the bridge of the *Blue Eagle*, Tisch and Wilmer studied the service manuals for the new upgrades. They recently completed the maintenance and operations courses for the new engines installed on the *Blue Eagle* and were excited by the advantages they gained with them. These engines were designed to function more efficiently with an advanced fusion propulsion system and a fantastic new process, unique to Hellfire Fuels, which would replenish spent fuel using high-frequency pulse lasers. Originally it was designed to be used on-line but a later modification that wasn't revealed allowed for off-line replenishment. For this reason, Dax and Gemini felt the merger would leave them with the most powerful ships and a corporation that could control all the valuable long-distance trade routes in the galaxy and beyond. Unfortunately, their successes in galactic shipping also made them the prime targets for Kronos Enterprises and other criminal elements around the galaxy.

Safety systems, weaponry, life support systems, navigation and control systems on the *Blue Eagle* were all replaced with state-of-the-art technology developed by Sysco Galactic's own engineers. Despite being an older vintage freighter, the *Blue Eagle* was the first of its kind. Modifying an older freighter made for the perfect camouflage as few outside of Taurus would suspect the *Blue Eagle* as the recipient of this technological upgrade. From the bridge, all the controls looked the same. The new modifications were integrated into the existing control panels, distribution panels and circuitry panels. Unfortunately for Tisch, her crew's success often brought unwanted attention, as their past history showed.

Mike entered the bridge and took a seat next to Tisch. They discussed the upcoming stop and cargo transfer. This was expected to be a quick stop with one container off-loaded and the contents swapped. Once the new cargo was staged inside the container, the container would be reloaded for a later delivery at another location. Mike questioned the value of a small load swap for a ship like theirs. Tisch reminded him that the extra stops were to give him and Wilmer practice with the new onloading systems. Mike groaned and left the bridge. He felt it was an unnecessary risk with all that they encountered with Empire and Kronos already, plus it was boring.

Geezer, with long gray hair tied back in a ponytail and a long beard, briefed Zenith on the docking practices at various stations and what to expect when they reached Vega. He eavesdropped on Tisch's conversation with Mike and was surprised that it was all business. Zenith, dressed in jeans and a tee-shirt with short, dark hair, took notice as well but said nothing. Everyone expected that, at some point, there would be another flare up between Mike and Tisch.

Bored with the ship's routines, Mike entered the fitness room for a work out. Dust covered the weight machines and the small refrigerator, staged for water, was empty. The shelves were bare of towels and a full-length mirror leaned against the wall, still boxed. He wondered why no one on board ever used the room. While doing crunches on a mat, he enjoyed the silence and pondered his relationship with Tisch. It was lacking of emotion even though she denied it was a problem.

Wilmer and Shannon walked down the corridor hand-in-hand and noticed the open hatch to the fitness room. With his confidence up, Wilmer was clean-cut with cargo pants and a collared shirt. Shannon, likely from her time on Taurus, always dressed professionally. They paused at the hatch, surprised to see Mike inside, and then entered. Mike took a break between sets of leg-lifts to chat with them.

Wilmer admitted that he had never seen the inside of the room before and was impressed. Mike recommended that he spend some time in there to get back into shape. Shannon elbowed Wilmer playfully in his side. Then Mike questioned Wilmer about his thoughts on the ship's current status and how he felt about it.

Wilmer admitted that he enjoyed the stability of the crew and did not miss the drama. Shannon commented that she felt the crew was developing a chemistry. They both noticed Mike's saddened expression. When pressed to explain, Mike confessed that things changed between him and Tisch. It seemed that she was all about the business with no time for him. Shannon touched his arm compassionately and assured him that it was temporary. They returned to the bridge, allowing Mike to resume his workout.

The *Blue Eagle* approached its first destination, a small hub called Vega. While Shannon called ahead to obtain a gate to dock, Geezer sat next to Zenith and coached her on the problems that they often encountered during their stops. Tisch, wearing black jeans, a white blouse and long, dark hair, stood alone on the bridge, proudly watching her crew perform. This was her dream and they were like her children. *But at what price,* she often wondered, realizing her relationship with Mike was fading.

Mike and Wilmer sat on the floor in the power distribution compartment. They had just completed the installation of the teleport module in a discrete portion of a power panel and were soaked in sweat. Mike high-fived Wilmer and thanked him for his help. The two stood and leaned back against the wall, fatigued from the arduous task in an energized panel. Satisfied with the results, they left the compartment for the galley. On the way, Mike informed Tisch over the intercom that the 'item', in reference to the module, was taken care of. They both felt that there was no need for the others to know what they were up to, nor where the module was. Mike preferred that they believe it was lost or destroyed in the fighting. The module was like a curse that haunted him. He would never lead a normal life so long as it was in their possession.

Wilmer sat at the furthest table from the door and exhaled with relief that their workday was done. Mike unlocked a cabinet in the corner of the galley and took out a bottle of rum. He displayed it to Wilmer and took two glasses from another cabinet. Wilmer joked that beer would have been adequate, but since the four cases they procured were on Gemini's tab, it was worth it. Mike poured two drinks and set them down on the table. He plopped into a chair across from Wilmer. The two tapped their glasses and drank.

With no one else present, Wilmer questioned Mike about his handling of his relationship with Tisch. Mike shrugged his shoulders and replied, "I wish I knew what to do. She says we're fine but we're hardly ever together." Mike revealed his expectations since her words to him after he rescued her from the Scrat ship. She wanted him then and was anxious for a relationship.

Wilmer considered his response and asked, "Do you think she's holding back her feelings over the confusion on Taurus during the siege?"

Mike stared at his glass for a moment and then responded, "She says the job comes first and we have a lot on our plate. In other words, when she gets around to me, then we'll see."

Wilmer realized that Tisch was probably looking for a nice way to end it with Mike, but didn't want to hurt him. He hoped that Mike was smart enough to see that. After another sip, Mike confessed to Wilmer that he felt as though he lost his mojo. Then he mentioned that perhaps he should have gone through with his resignation on Taurus when he had the chance. Wilmer suggested that he take it easy for a while and see how things played out. Mike agreed, realizing that he had no other choice.

CHAPTER 2

ROADBLOCKS

When the *Blue Eagle* approached Vega, Zenith was instructed to shut down and await further instructions. She complained to Geezer that they were supposed to dock in Bay 5, but there was a freighter in the way. Geezer grumbled and contacted the transport supervisor to request another bay. The transport supervisor informed him that the ship had mechanical problems and would be departing shortly. Zenith questioned Geezer if this happened often. He explained that normally a disabled ship was towed and moored off-site until repairs were made. "If Vega did things smartly," he explained, "then the *Blue Eagle* would be able to get in and get out without delay and the bay would be available again. Overhearing the issue, Tisch grew concerned about meeting their schedule and summoned Mike to the bridge.

In the galley, Mike complained to Wilmer, "If she's on the bridge, then this is no booty call." Wilmer burst into laughter and the two men finished their drinks. Mike locked the bottle up in the cabinet and rinsed the glasses. Wilmer noticed that he was in no hurry to respond to Tisch's command. This was never a good sign for the crew when the two of them didn't see eye-to-eye. Finally, Mike left the galley with Wilmer following close behind.

When they arrived on the bridge, they could tell right away that Tisch was in a bad mood. She informed them of the problem with the stranded ship and requested they go down to the transport control center and see if they could expedite things. Mike was more than happy to get off the ship and escape the boredom that ailed him.

Wilmer didn't share his enthusiasm and was reluctant to leave the ship without Shannon. He immediately pretended to be involved in a navigational issue at her station. Mike quickly realized he was on his own and felt that perhaps it was better that way. Before he could leave, Tisch ordered him to stay in contact with her. Mike agreed and departed the bridge.

It was a short trip to the station and there was ample room for his shuttle to dock in the smaller bays. When Mike's shuttle approached, he was surprised at how small Vega really was. Vega had five bays for large ships and three smaller bays for shuttles. All the large bay doors were closed, indicating the bays were sealed and pressurized. Two shuttle bay doors were open and he received instructions to take the last one, number 8. He thought to himself, *What a crappy way to treat the crew that's going to increase their commerce and revenue.* Looking to make an impression, he docked the shuttle and donned his long coat and boonie hat. "Just like old times," he muttered to himself. "Just me and... no one else!"

When he exited the shuttle, three dockworkers awaited his exit to inspect him for weapons. They informed him that Vega was a 'no weapons' station and violators would be fined and imprisoned with their ship impounded indefinitely. Mike allowed the men to search him and when they were satisfied he was unarmed, he was instructed to follow them down the long corridor to the transport supervisor's office.

Mike noticed as he reached Bay 5 that the ship was in cold shutdown and there were no technicians working on its exterior. Interior repairs could be performed offsite, arousing Mike's suspicions. He entered the bay and approached the ship. The three men behind him continued past the bay to the supervisor's office at the end of the corridor. One of them hollered back to Mike and warned him that he should stay with them. Mike assured them that he wouldn't be long. When he approached the open hatch to the freighter, the ship's captain stood in the entrance. "Can I help you with something?" he asked politely.

Mike questioned him about his ship and why it was delayed leaving the bay. The captain informed him that they were placed on hold due to a cosmic storm by the transport supervisor. Mike found that strange as Tisch wasn't informed of any impending storms. He thanked the man and then continued down the corridor to the supervisor's office. His transmitter beeped until he turned it off. He knew it was Tisch and she couldn't wait until he had something worthwhile to report.

Inside the office, a bearded, old man sat at a desk and studied a large monitor. "Quite a ship you have there," he remarked to Mike. "I see you have the new Titan engines that disappeared from Hellfire Fuels."

Mike realized that the man just finished a scan of the *Blue Eagle* and he now knew that this was a trap. Mike suggested that they could return later when the bay was available if that was okay with him. The transport supervisor slid his chair back and stared at Mike. "Did you know there's a hefty bounty on your head?" he inquired. "And one on your ship, I might add."

Mike was surprised and responded, "And who would care so much to put a bounty on my head?"

The man chuckled and informed him that there was quite a reward for anyone who turned in either him, Gemini and/or the ship. Now Mike was really concerned. He wondered what resources were staged on Vega to apprehend them.

"You might want to consider the source of the offer as this man has reneged on several bounties already," Mike bluffed and then mentioned that he and Antwan were on a first name basis. "He needs my help and I won't make time for him," he lied. "So, you can understand why he's a little peeved."

The man laughed and instructed Mike to take a seat while he contacted Antwan. Mike complied as he contemplated an escape plan, not just for him but for the *Blue Eagle* as well.

On board the *Blue Eagle*, Tisch became irate over the delay as they crept closer to Vega. She ordered Wilmer and Shannon to take the shuttle that once belonged to Griff and Topa to find out what's going on. Zenith scanned the station with the short-range sensors and displayed the results as an overhead three-dimensional image. "Tisch you might want to look at this before sending them out," she suggested.

Inside four of the bays, ships were powered up and their weapons systems were energized. Geezer commented, "If I didn't know better, I'd say they plan to open those bay gates and blast us." Tisch agreed and instructed Zenith to get them out of there.

"What about Mike?" asked Zenith, fearing that they were abandoning him.

"We'll figure something out and come back for him," she responded.

Wilmer paced the flight deck and then his eyes widened with excitement. "We should have the firepower to damage those gates so they don't fully open," he suggested. Everyone looked at each other and then at Wilmer, wondering about his suggestion.

"Can we do that?" Tisch asked. Wilmer explained that they could damage the frames that the gates slide on with short blasts; just enough to damage them and not blow them apart.

"What are the risks?" Tisch questioned.

"If any gate opens before we blast it, they will be firing. If we damage the gates, not only can't they leave, but they can't exit their ships for repairs without environmental suits. It'll take them quite a while before they can leave the station. I say we go for it."

Tisch considered Wilmer's idea and then recalled that Zenith fired the cannons with Mike before. She explained to Zenith what they were targeting and instructed her to take the lower turret. "When I give the order," she informed her, "you take Bays 3 and 4. I'll take 1 and 2." Zenith, anxious to prove her reliability, rushed from the bridge to the lower turret. Tisch then instructed Wilmer and Shannon to take the second shuttle for a rescue mission.

As soon as they were in position, Tisch gave the order to fire on the bay gates. The gates had just started to open when they were targeted with light cannon fire. First the left frames on the selected bays were targeted and then the right frames. Two of the freighters in the bays attempted to blast the gates off their frames but only worsened their problem with warped metal protruding in dangerous positions around their ships.

The gates ceased moving and were only partially opened. The shuttle raced from the *Blue Eagle* to one of the shuttle bays. As soon as they docked, the gate automatically closed and sealed. Wilmer and Shannon exited the shuttle, armed with pulse pistols. As they hurried down the corridor, they were relieved that no one could leave the ships in the damaged bays to confront them due to the loss of bay integrity to space. Shannon complimented Wilmer for his idea and the two tapped knuckles in a friendly gesture. "Maybe we're the next dynamic duo," quipped Wilmer. Giggling, Shannon agreed with him.

Inside the transport supervisor's office, Mike was tied up by one of the men. The supervisor watched in horror as the *Blue Eagle* pummeled his gates. He instructed his men to prepare their shuttle for a quick escape.

"Mr. Colby, you are proving to be an expensive investment," he complained. "I may not have the *Blue Eagle,* but Antwan's going to have to up the ante if he wants you."

"Antwan's not going to pay you squat," Mike warned. "Kronos leaves no loose ends and is suffering from severe budget constraints after their recent run of losses."

"What would you do if you were me?" he asked Mike.

"First, get that ship out of Bay 5. He's not involved in this. Then get Antwan to show up in person to discuss the swap," suggested Mike. "We'll help you lay out a trap in case he screws you over." The man grumbled that he still wouldn't get paid if Mike was right. Mike kidded that he would be alive at least.

Three men approached Feeling confident in himself, Wilmer and Shannon with pistols drawn. They held their hands up innocently and requested help in procuring some supplies. When the men were within reach, Shannon grabbed one man's pistol and used it to shoot the second. Wilmer kicked the gun from the third man's hand and chopped him in the throat. He and Shannon both grabbed the first man by his belt buckle and lifted him upside down in the air. After a quick glance and a smile at each other, they drove the man headfirst into the floor, snapping his neck.

"Not bad," remarked Shannon. Wilmer pulled her close to him and kissed her forehead.

They stepped inside the transport supervisor's office and startled the transport supervisor. Mike was pleased to see them and kidded, "Fancy meeting you here."

Wilmer countered, "Maybe things are reversing around here. Now we're saving your ass for a change." Shannon untied Mike, while Wilmer tied up the man.

"I'm not complaining," Mike responded cheerfully. He pointed to the computer system and mentioned that the transport supervisor scanned the *Blue Eagle*.

Shannon quipped, "We can't have that now. Can we?" She then fired several pulses from her pistol and destroyed the entire computer bank and its peripheral components.

The transport supervisor, now fearing for his life, pleaded with them not to leave him like this. He dreaded that he would be killed for failing Antwan. Mike asked for one reason why they should spare him. He explained that their cargo was staged in Bay 5 if they still wanted it. Mike untied the man and then ordered him to assist them in docking the *Blue Eagle* and coordinate their cargo transfer. After that, he recommended that he leave the station as quickly as possible, until things settled down.

The freighter staged in Bay 5 was authorized to depart and freed up the bay for the *Blue Eagle*. Mike contacted Tisch with an update and she informed him of the damaged bay doors. He suggested they dock the *Blue Eagle* since there was a legitimate load to be picked up, but they should do it fast. Then they departed the station in Mike's shuttle and docked inside the *Blue Eagle*.

Inside Bays 1 through 4, several men emerged from each ship in environmental suits, equipped with welding packs. They promptly began the task of removing the metal impediments. The damaged gates were significant and would take days before any of the ships could exit.

On board the *Blue Eagle*, Tisch was glad to see them return. The Bay 5 gates on Vega opened and the freighter departed, allowing the *Blue Eagle* to dock. Once the bay gates secured, Mike quickly executed the cargo container offload, using the old method. Vega was not equipped to move containers with automated equipment to and from the ship.

Wilmer operated a mini-crawler to remove the crates from inside their container and transported them through an automated gate to the receiving compartment. Shannon operated another mini-crawler and retrieved their new cargo from the staging compartment and deposited it inside the container. These two compartments were essential for storing cargo away from the freezing temperatures and vacuum of space when the bay gates opened for a ship's passage.

Mike promptly inserted the container back inside the ship. Wilmer and Shannon parked the crawlers inside their designated compartments and hurried back on board the *Blue Eagle*. Mike gave Tisch the okay to request the transport supervisor open the gates for departure. Soon the *Blue Eagle* was on its way.

Everyone met on the bridge to discuss the events that transpired on Vega. Tisch updated the log with the details as they spoke. Mike related what he knew about the bounties. Shannon offered to contact Sara with an update. Meanwhile, Tisch contacted Taurus to inform them of their situation. Mike shook hands with Wilmer and Shannon and thanked them for rescuing him. He explained that he couldn't escape on his own until he had more information and then had to find a way to warn them about the ambush.

Tisch proudly placed her hand on Zenith's shoulder and told Mike how she thought to scan the station. Mike was impressed. Excitedly, Zenith revealed how she discovered the ships in the bay were energizing their weapons systems and preparing to fire when the gates opened. Mike and Tisch were both pleased with the crew's performance under pressure. Tisch then felt compelled to question Mike about why he didn't respond to her transmissions. Mike frowned and countered, "Why do you think?" Frustrated with her mistrust, he left the bridge.

Wilmer politely asked Tisch, "Why do you think Mike didn't respond?" She replied that he could have responded before he exited the shuttle and immediately after, but he didn't respond at all. After that, he probably had a legitimate excuse. Wilmer begged her not to go down this road again with him. He pointed out that Mike may have been protecting them while assessing the threat.

"What should I do, Wilmer?" she inquired. "I thought we were past this."

"But are you?" he countered. "The two of you hardly ever talk anymore." Realizing he was right, she left the bridge to speak with Mike.

Mike went to his quarters and sat on the bed. He didn't know what to feel, regarding Tisch. Just when he thought they established an understanding, she tuned him out. He wondered how to tell her how much he loved her and if it even mattered anymore to her. Frustrated, he undressed and laid down in his bed. Perhaps, he considered, that he should leave when they return to Taurus. Some things were inevitable.

Tisch stopped outside his quarters and knocked on the wall three times. Mike gestured for her to enter. She ogled him as he sat up on the edge of the bed. "What's up?" he asked.

Tisch sat next to him and massaged his shoulders. Mike missed the feel of her touch and savored it. She apologized for neglecting him, but she emphasized that her role as captain of the *Blue Eagle* has expanded much since they first met. Realizing that things weren't going to get easier, Mike asked her what she wanted to do about it.

After contemplating their situation, she recommended that they put their relationship on hold. She couldn't handle a relationship and her responsibilities right now. She also worried how their relationship would affect her crew. Mike lowered his head, knowing that this was the end. Tisch kissed his cheek and departed his quarters. Frustrated, Mike dressed and stormed off to the fitness room. After working out for over an hour, he considered that he was back on his own again – a loner with no responsibility.

The next morning, Mike went to the engine compartment and studied the new fuel regeneration system until he knew it well. He was interested in using the regen system to replenish the fuel in the shuttle. When he finished, he ate alone in the galley and then studied the data that Julian supplied, regarding the amended schedule. Then he had an idea. He summoned Shannon to the galley to speak with him – in private.

When she arrived, Mike questioned her about her communications with Sara. Then he requested that she contact Sara and find out who provided the orders for the scheduled stops that were added to their schedule. Shannon questioned him about his intentions, should he learn the source of the orders. He confessed that he didn't have an answer yet but then their conversation was interrupted by Tisch's voice over the intercom, summoning Mike to the bridge. When he arrived, she spoke with him to make sure they were okay. He assured her that he understood her wishes and would move on. It broke Tisch's heart to end their relationship, even though she called it a "pause", but she felt it was necessary for her to maintain control of her crew and her ship.

On Taurus, Sara met with Gemini and Julian to discuss the *Blue Eagle's* issue on Vega and what they learned from their visit with one of her sources. Before starting, she received a call from one of her officers, Tariq, with information about the *Blue Eagle's* stop and excused herself to speak with him in private. Gemini was pleased that Tisch's crew still made the pickup and delivery, despite the mercenary interference. Julian was impressed as well, but emphasized that the root of the problem was the bounties. They attracted people who, up until now, had nothing to do with the *Blue Eagle* and its crew.

Sara returned to the room and took a seat. Gemini and Julian suspected that something of importance was discussed, based on Sara's grim expression. Gemini immediately got up and went to the bar. Sara rolled her eyes at Julian as they knew she would become volatile. Gemini returned with three glasses of bourbon and set them on the table. "Go ahead, Sara," said Gemini as she sipped from her glass. "Hit me."

Sara explained that the stop on Vega was legitimate, but the bounties on the ship and on Mike compromised the station's personnel. Julian stared at his glass but refrained from speaking for now. Sara took a sip from her glass and continued, "The *Blue Eagle* was in play for the capture of a high value target."

Gemini's face turned beet-red as she chugged the rest of her drink. "Let me guess," she said sarcastically. "The *Blue Eagle* was bait for this fiasco."

Sara nodded and finished her drink. She slid her glass across the table to Gemini for a refill. Julian remained calm and passed his glass to her. Sara took another swig and sighed. Gemini couldn't pass on the opportunity to remind them how she felt when they kept things from her and she had no control. Frustrated, Sara accepted the fact that this was now bigger than them. Gemini then inquired, "Does Tisch or Mike know about this?"

Sara shook her head and finished her drink. "I'll see what I can find out," she assured her and left the room. Gemini tapped her fingers on the table as she tried to regain her composure. Julian reminded her that the alliance knows what the *Blue Eagle* is and they'd never risk losing her. Gemini confessed that she now knew how Mike felt, every time she hung him out to dry on a job. Julian offered to maintain contact with his source for information as well and see what else he could find out. He was concerned that there was no high value target at Vega and that the real trap might be the upcoming stop. Of course, they wouldn't know until after the fact. He left Gemini and returned to his quarters.

Antwan sat at his desk with his head in his hands. He was just informed that his plan on Vega failed. Realizing this might be his last chance, he made arrangements to travel to Archimedes-9 as a backup plan in case Borath failed. This would be his last stand. The monitor on the wall beeped. Fearing what was to come next, he accepted the incoming message. Carl Klingman's face appeared on the monitor, looking irate. He said nothing and only stared, disappointed in Antwan.

Antwan informed Carl about the traps on Parris-5 and Archimedes-9. He assured Carl that he would soon have both Colby and the *Blue Eagle*. Carl requested that he watch the monitor as he had something to show him. The monitor then displayed the bedroom in Darra's apartment. As the camera zoomed closer, Antwan realized that, once again, Tia was in bed with Darra. Both girls were nude and involved in intense sexual relations. Carl's voice greeted Darra and mentioned that Antwan was watching as well.

Antwan cussed at Tia, calling her a tramp. Tia shouted back, "Now I have someone who will take care of me and respect me. You failed Kronos and you failed your family. Your children will curse you whenever they think of you." Antwan cried, knowing she was right.

After a long, wet kiss, Darra commented that Tia was well-worth the time she invested in her. She and Tia then kissed again and their transmission ended. Carl suggested that Antwan do something right before it was too late. When his transmission ended, Antwan screamed in rage and stormed out of his office.

In an apartment overlooking Marina's palace on Yord, Darra maintained an exotic lifestyle. Every day she watched, hoping that Marina would return to the palace, making her job that much easier. Unfortunately, Marina hadn't been seen in many months.

Darra informed Tia that she had to go away for a while to take care of Marina. She gave her access to an account for food and supplies as a reward for her growing loyalty to her. Tia had given in to the fact that her children were gone and she had nowhere to go, since Kronos confiscated Antwan's residence. Having someone like Darra to care for her at least kept her from becoming homeless and working the streets for survival. She swore that if she ever saw Antwan again, she would kill him.

CHAPTER 3

PRECAUTIONS AND LIMITATIONS

When the *Blue Eagle* docked without incident on Parris-5, Tisch was relieved. The advantages of a large space station, as designated by the number after the station name, were significantly better compared to what they experienced at their prior stop. On Vega, they were forced to unload a container's contents and reload the new cargo on the dock. Vega had no number after its name which indicated it was small and lacked proper facilities for cargo transfer. It was also an ideal location for black market materials to pass through. The -5 after Parris indicated that it had some state-of-the-art equipment and could handle large ships in numbers. Unfortunately, there wasn't much traffic in the region... yet.

Mike became proficient with the new onloader system. With the interface link active, he used the control device strapped to his wrist while wearing the glove which was an integral part of its control functions. With this new device, he could point and squeeze a small module in the palm of the glove to operate the system in any one of the four bays. The control pendant was no longer required. New cargo containers within the system were designed to be explosion proof and immune to temperature changes. The only operator interface with the container storage and retrieval was to scan the manifest on the container with the glove.

In addition, the new system would automatically retrieve a container from the crawler and place it in a designated location in the ship's storage section. The location was determined by a QR code on the container's manifest and the programmed destination to allow for an efficient on or off-load. There were two cargo bays on each side of the ship so multiple containers could be loaded or unloaded at one time. To maximize the system, each bay would require an operator with a gloved device. This was optimal when time was of the essence. The ship held a total of twenty-four containers when fully loaded. Ten containers were designed for cargo with special requirements like temperature control or energization, while the other fourteen were standard issue for cargo.

Satisfied with the operation of the system, Mike stowed the control device on board and then entered his pass code to exit the bay. When the cargo hatch to the bay slid open, two men bull-rushed him and pushed him back inside the bay. They wore dark uniforms like Kronos' agents on Zim with no identifying patches. One of the men held him at gunpoint, while the other tied him up. The first man spoke into his transmitter and announced that they had Colby in custody.

The inner hatch opened for the transfer of a container into the bay on a crawler. A fair-skinned man, Jonas, and a blonde woman, Margot, escorted the crawler toward the *Blue Eagle*. Both wore denim jeans and tank tops with IDs dangling from cords around their necks. The couple saw the men tie Mike up and approached to question their presence in the bay. One of the men ordered them to mind their own business. Margot informed them that they needed to leave immediately, drawing a laugh from the men. Mike was grateful for the help, but realized that neither were armed nor physically capable of taking on his assailants. This wasn't going to end well.

Twelve more men entered the bay in dark uniforms. Four surrounded Jonas and Margot, while the others approached the personnel hatch of the

Blue Eagle. Mike panicked as he had no way to warn his friends on board. Then a mysterious woman entered the bay, disguised in a hooded cloak. Undaunted, she called out to the sentries and warned them to stay away from the *Blue Eagle*. Now, Mike was really baffled. None of this made sense. Fourteen of these mercenaries against him and three unarmed strangers.

Margot taunted the closest men, warning them that they should have heeded her warning and left. The leader of the sentries ordered one of his men to close the inner bay hatch to ensure no one witnessed what was about to happen. The mercenary left, but never returned. A dozen armed men and women in plain clothes then entered the bay and gunned down the mercenaries nearest the ship with pulse fire. The cloaked woman hurled two daggers at the men closest to Mike. They fell to the ground, one dead and one badly wounded. Margot untied Mike and escorted him toward the cloaked woman. Jonas joined the others and assisted in removing the mercenaries' bodies from the bay for identification.

When the personnel hatch on the ship opened, Tisch and Wilmer appeared and were surprised by the corpses and the strangers. Mike chided them, "Thanks, but I'm just fine now. You can go back inside." Tisch became annoyed, knowing that, once again, she had no clue as to what was going on. She and Wilmer approached the group.

"Thanks so much for helping me out," Mike commented and shook hands with Margot. She smiled coyly and gestured toward the cloaked woman, who was responsible for his rescue. The woman dragged the wounded survivor to them and dropped him on the floor. A dagger was embedded in his chest, just above his heart. One twist and he would die. The man was frightened as he suspected who she was. Only the infamous Marina could throw a dagger with that kind of accuracy. Mike, meanwhile, still had no idea who she was under the cloak.

Tisch demanded an explanation for what just occurred. Margot again pointed toward the cloaked woman and introduced her as Marina, leader of the rebel alliance. Marina slid the hood back and removed her cloak. Mike was stunned to see her again. Tisch quickly backed down and apologized for her tone. Wilmer was amazed that this was the woman who knocked out Mike.

"I need to interrogate him," Marina announced to them.

Tisch offered the use of the bridge or her quarters for the interrogation. Marina accepted her offer, but paused to stare down Mike. "Well, Mr. Colby." she remarked cynically. "It seems we meet again."

Humbly, Mike requested a brief, private conversation with Marina. The two stepped aside from the others. Marina inquired if he still wanted to go another round with her. He surprised her with an apology for his poor judgment at the pirate haven on Zim. He admitted that he was now aware that this is far from a one-man operation and wanted to pledge his loyalty to her.

Marina was pleased to hear that and then inquired if he would have a problem taking on a mission with Margot. He was interested, but expressed his concern about leaving his position on the crew. Marina's plan was to have Jonas take his place on board the *Blue Eagle*, while he and Margot would lead an effort to kidnap someone of importance. Mike was eager to help and under the circumstances, he was happy to leave the *Blue Eagle* on a temporary assignment. He mentioned that he needed to discuss it with Tisch.

"We can help with that," replied Margot.

On the bridge of the *Blue Eagle*, Marina and Margot performed the interrogation of their prisoner. Mike was amused as Margot grabbed the man's wrist and gripped his shoulder near his neck while twisting the wrist. The man screamed in pain and wasted no time revealing their purpose on Parris-5. "We were sent to kill Colby and some courier from the fringes. Now please, stop!" he blurted.

"I want more," Margot demanded as she placed her hands against the prisoner's head and squeezed the temple area. The man cried out, "Someone from Empire put out a bounty on Colby and their ship. We saw an opportunity and thought it would be easy."

Margot turned her attention to Marina and suggested she do the honors. Marina kicked the man behind his left knee, staggering him. She then slammed him to the ground on his back. She placed her boot on the man's groin and threatened to crush his manhood if he didn't continue his cooperation. "Where is Antwan?" she inquired.

The man refused to answer until she increased the pressure on his groin. His eyes grew wide and he pleaded for mercy. "Do I hear something of value," she taunted and twisted the man's leg. "Antwan's going to Archimedes-9 to make sure Colby is dead and the *Blue Eagle* is in his possession!" he blurted. "Please stop!"

Mike saw the opportunity to intercede and get answers to his questions. "What is Kronos to Empire?" he demanded to know, while pressing both of the man's temples. Tisch was appalled at the techniques used by all three on the mercenary, but said nothing.

"Empire is a subsidiary of Kronos!" he shouted and squirmed desperately. "Kronos runs everything!"

"Where do we find Kronos," Mike asked.

"We don't know that information," answered the prisoner.

Mike glanced at Marina and Margot for their next move. "I believe he's spilled everything he knows," Margot relented.

"When you cross Kronos, you usually end up dead," the prisoner warned, weakened by the abuse he received.

Mike remarked to Marina, "Kronos probably already knows what happened here. They have eyes and ears everywhere." He exited the ship and stood by the inner bay doors, wondering what the consequences of accepting the mission would be with Tisch. Margot exited the ship and joined him. "We've heard that your ship is special and is designed for long-distance hauls," she mentioned.

"And what else have you heard?" Mike inquired, suspicious. "I sense you know more than you're letting on."

"I know Kronos has deep pockets and that's one hefty bounty they put on you. It got Marina's attention for sure."

"So, what's to keep you from killing me and claiming the bounty?" Mike kidded. Margot held her pistol to the back of his head. "I should have known," grumbled Mike.

She stepped in front of him and stowed her pistol. "If I was after the bounty, you'd be dead," she chided. "And then I'd take your ship for bonus money."

Jonas joined them and introduced himself. Mike recalled what happened on Zim with Marina and asked why he should trust them. Jonas reminded him that they didn't have to interfere with the Kronos mercenaries and that they weren't for hire. Margot added, "We still have our integrity and you are one of our own."

One of our own, he pondered her comment as he considered they might have once been Special Forces. He kidded her about her relationship with Jonas. "You two come as a package or something?"

"We're siblings," replied Margot playfully.

"I was thinking more of your background – military, mercenary, or whatever."

"You ask a lot of questions, Mr. Colby. Be patient," she suggested. Mike folded his arms and studied the two of them. They seemed harmless, but he knew better. If they worked with Marina, then they can fight.

Jonas left them and boarded the *Blue Eagle* for his introduction to the crew. Margot invited Mike to join her at the pub to get acquainted. As if on cue, Marina exited the *Blue Eagle* and departed the bay. Mike was baffled, thinking that she was going with them. Margot reminded him that Marina had much to do in preparing the alliance for their big move on Kronos and, in addition, couldn't risk being seen with them. Disappointed, Mike hoped that he would learn more about this alliance from Marina.

On the bridge of the *Blue Eagle*, Tisch introduced Jonas to the crew. Everyone was stunned when they heard that Mike was replaced. They fretted that Tisch might have arranged for him to leave. They also suspected that, if she had no input in the change, then perhaps Mike volunteered to get back into the battle against Kronos. Jonas was pleasant and promised to do his best to fill in until Mike returned. They appreciated the fact that he knew he was only a temporary replacement. Tisch reminded them that they have a job to do and needed to get at it.

Wilmer used the opportunity on Parris-5 to train Jonas, Zenith and Shannon on the use of the onloader. They delivered five containers of supplies, while picking up three new ones for a later delivery. The mood was somber as things weren't the same without Mike.

Tisch met with the owners of the station and discussed the cargo manifests and future shipments. The owners were pleased to have Sysco Galactic handle their parts and supplies. Their business was mining ore from the nearby asteroid belt and it was very expensive for them to ship across multiple stations to their destinations, as their ships had neither the fuel nor the cargo capacity for extra fuel. They were ecstatic to learn that the *Blue Eagle* with its new engines could haul their ore as well as fuel cartridges and supplies, which were sorely needed. Then the question came up about the teleport module. The station owners were curious to know if Sysco planned to incorporate *more* into their fleet. Tisch became uneasy and claimed to have no knowledge of such a module.

Mike sat with Margot at a table in the back corner of the pub on Parris-5. She noticed his distant expression and questioned why the dour look. "It's complicated," he remarked. Then Margot inquired about his relationship with Tisch. He responded that it was purely business at this point. Sensing that this pleased her, he countered, "So, what is it you're looking for?"

Margot confessed that she heard of Mike's daring escapades and, despite his first encounter with Marina, was anxious to meet him. He admitted that his boldness got him a real ass-whooping by her boss. The two laughed over the incident and drank beer. Margot assured him that Marina respected him, despite the incident on Zim. If she didn't respect him, he'd be dead or wishing he were.

Margot grew curious as to what Mike hoped for, now that he was included in the battle plan. He stressed that he needed to understand what was going on, especially with intel that Marina's rebels might have on Kronos. Before she could answer, Mike received a message that the cargo swap on the *Blue Eagle* was nearly finished. Reluctantly, they ended their conversation and returned to the ship.

Wilmer closed the last cargo hatch and waited, hands on hips. "If you came to help, you're too late," he kidded.

"I've been voted off the island. Remember?" Mike replied. Margot and Wilmer chuckled over his humor.

All eyes were on Tisch when Mike and Margot boarded the ship. Everyone was anxious to see how Tisch reacted to Mike teaming up with Margot. Margot informed Tisch that they would meet them on Archimedes-9 with someone very important to transport. She and Mike then left the bridge to board his shuttle. Tisch watched them with a vacant expression as the bridge hatch closed behind them. Her face did little to indicate how she felt about Margot and Mike working together. With the cargo swap completed, the *Blue Eagle* departed for Archimedes-9. Mike's shuttle was released from the shuttle portion of the cargo bay and proceeded ahead to the next stop.

Tisch noticed the dismal mood among the crew and called for a meeting. Everyone assembled on the bridge, well aware of her intent. Tisch started by thanking them for a great job in meeting the schedule on Parris-5 and Vega, despite the *distractions*. Then she raised her concern about the moral on board the ship. She confessed that losing Mike wasn't her doing, but she did miss him already.

Geezer pointed out that the two of them have been distant, where they used to be the core of the crew. Zenith added that they were at their best when they were together. Wilmer chose to refrain from any comment. He felt that Tisch already knew what he thought.

Shannon commented that her interest in joining the crew was their chemistry. They were like family, even with the squabbles. She revealed that she never had a family and was rescued from an orphanage by Sara when she was a teenager. Sara had a lot of responsibilities with GSS and was more of a mentor than a mother. She admitted that Sara did well with her under the circumstances, but it wasn't the same as having a family.

Tisch admitted that it was difficult for her to be in charge, while having a relationship with one of her crew. Then Wilmer suggested that Mike shouldn't be a crew member anymore. Everyone looked at him with baffled expressions, wondering why he would say that. Wilmer elaborated that perhaps Mike should be their on-board liaison with GSS and the alliance as a security officer. He could still help out, but officially he would no longer be one of the crew. Jonas' only comment was that they were known as the best among truckers and were well-respected for their accomplishments.

Shannon added that they knew Mike would be pulled from time to time, as a liaison, to deal with security items, so the only real issue was Tisch's interaction with him. Wilmer indicated that it was a simple solution if she really did want Mike to be involved with them. If not, then they all need to move on. Tisch promised to consider their suggestions and talk to Mike.

Margot admired Mike as he piloted the shuttle away from the *Blue Eagle*. With her curiosity piqued, she inquired as to why his shuttle was named *Self-righteous*. Embarrassed, Mike related the story about his history with Gemini. After a lengthy discussion, he suggested they alternate for sleep for the duration of the trip to Archimedes-9, since there was only one rollaway bed on the shuttle. Margot wanted to know more about Mike and was disappointed when he elected to rest first.

When Mike awoke and returned to the pilot's seat, Margot was eager to talk more and inquired about his experience with the Scrat. Weary of the conversations about him, he suggested she get some rest. When Margot stripped down to a sports bra and panties, Mike couldn't help but glance back at her. She noticed and smiled before climbing into the bunk.

After docking his shuttle on Archimedes-9, Antwan contacted one of his field marshals at Empire's headquarters and instructed the man to arrange an all-out assault on Taurus, regardless of his success on Archimedes-9. He then authorized payment of whatever funds he had left to fund the attack. When he finished the transmission, he retrieved a near-empty bottle of whiskey and finished its contents. He smashed the bottle against the back wall and cursed Colby. "Why couldn't you just take the damned money and leave?" he cried out.

Antwan washed his face in the basin at the rear of the shuttle and regained his composure. He departed the shuttle and met with the transport controller to learn what arrivals were scheduled over the next few days. The man informed him that the *Blue Eagle* was still two days out and hadn't called in yet for a berth. Antwan mentioned that he expected some associates on the next shuttle in and arranged to pay him if he notified him of any modifications to the schedule. As soon as Antwan left, the controller contacted Marina and informed her that Antwan was onsite.

A shuttle with twenty high-priced mercenaries was due in a few hours and their instructions were to take out the crew of the *Blue Eagle* permanently and hijack the ship. It would be bittersweet for Antwan but at least he'd have some measure of revenge on Colby and Gemini for ruining his life. One way or another, this was all going to end soon.

Mike's shuttle approached Archimedes-9 and received permission to dock. From the rear of the shuttle, Margot awoke. Rubbing her eyes, she sat down in the copilot's seat. "Hello, sleepyhead," Mike teased. She looked good to him, even after waking up with her hair tossed wildly. Margot crooned playfully as she nestled against his shoulder. Mike was surprised by her affection, unsure of how to react.

The transmitter beeped for an incoming signal, interrupting their moment. Mike nudged Margot away. "Duty calls," he grumbled. Margot got up and retrieved a container of water from the cooler. When he accepted the transmission, Wilmer's face appeared on the monitor. "Hey, buddy! How are you doing?"

"Not bad," replied Mike. Margot finished her water and stood behind him, massaging his shoulders. Wilmer was wide-eyed with surprise, realizing that the two of them were getting along quite well. "How are things going?" Mike asked. "Miss me yet?"

Wilmer laughed at his question, as he should know better because of Tisch. He informed Mike, "Your friend Marina arranged to obtain the parts Creeg needs on Vega to complete the repairs to his ship."

Mike was impressed and realized the importance of the pickup, especially after the ambush. He told Wilmer that they'll be on Archimedes-9 about eight hours ahead of the *Blue Eagle* and should have their *business* finished before the ship's arrival. Margot knelt next to Mike and inquired, "How is Jonas doing?"

"He's doing well," answered Wilmer. "The crew have adapted to his friendly disposition and positive attitude." Tisch's voice was heard in the background, shouting for Wilmer. "I have to go. Momma calls," Wilmer kidded discreetly. Mike and Margot wished him well and ended the transmission.

CHAPTER 4

PULLED STRINGS

As Mike piloted the shuttle, Margot commented, "You and I have more in common than you know." Mike was taken aback by her openness. He questioned her about her past and why she was so trusting of him. She mentioned that she was married once and also had two partners that were killed in the line of duty. Then she revealed that one of them gave up valuable intel under duress that led to her husband's death – at Antwan's hands. Marina and her brother were the only people she trusted and neither one was what she needed. Now it made sense to Mike. She wanted revenge on Antwan and needed Mike to help her get it done.

"I know what you're thinking," she commented, disappointed. "You think I'm using you." Mike mentioned that the thought did cross his mind. Margot lowered her head and confessed that she was lonely and wanted someone to fill that void in her life. She admitted that, in their line of work, she feared that she might die alone.

Mike leaned toward her and kissed her softly. She placed her hands on his face and responded in kind. Suddenly, Mike pulled away and howled. "What's wrong?" she asked, frantic over his reaction.

"A back spasm!" Mike jumped up and stretched in several different positions. Finally, he breathed a sigh of relief. "Sorry about that."

Margot leaned across and hugged him. "I really hope we have more than just this one mission together," she remarked, while gazing at him. "I really do enjoy your company.

"Me, too," blurted Mike, wondering if he should have admitted that without vetting her further. He was enamored with her, but was concerned about Tisch. Even though he was justified in moving on, part of him didn't want to.

Both were surprised when the transport supervisor contacted them to inform them that a shuttle for a person of interest was already there and that others were arriving soon in a second shuttle. Mike warned Margot that they'd have to work fast. She questioned if he had a plan, but he already decided that they'd improvise on the fly. Margot suggested they contact the *Blue Eagle* and delay their arrival, but Mike was concerned that a change in the schedule would arouse suspicion. They still didn't know who they could trust on Archimedes-9 and might be walking into a trap. Mike requested from the transportation supervisor to dock in the bay that was scheduled for the second shuttle. The supervisor agreed and assured them of privacy.

Archimedes-9 was a ten-tier, cylindrical station with a rotating magnetic wheel around the outside of the station. The wheel generated artificial gravity on the station as well as the power for the station to function. There were bays for thirty-five large ships and fifteen bays for shuttles and small haulers. The station didn't get much traffic as of yet and was usually a staging point for cargo to Parris-5 or to one of the smaller colonies.

None of the ships in this part of the galaxy had the range to travel the whole distance to other stations like Taurus for trade. Every haul was a series of hops. Each of these stations was stocked with limited fuel cartridges as well. The time it took for their ships to make a long-distance run was limited by their access to the fuel cartridges. The lack of fuel rods at the stations abbreviated many hauls and, when available, those ships lacked the storage capacity to carry the extra fuel cartridges needed to complete the route.

The station was designed proactively so that one day larger ships like the *Blue Eagle*, would make them profitable. When the owners learned that the *Blue Eagle* had that capability, they were ecstatic that their hopes might finally be realized.

After docking their shuttle on the upper tier of the station, Mike instructed Margot to loiter in the main corridor outside the bay entrance. He expected that Antwan would be there soon to meet his mercenaries. When Antwan arrived in the corridor, Margot was to lure him into their bay, requesting his help. She needed to convince him that she was blocking an incoming shuttle and needed to vacate as soon as possible.

They exited the shuttle and left the hatch slightly ajar. Margot took her position in the corridor while Mike was further down, past the elevator. A short time later, the elevator bell rang and the doors slid open. Mike immediately recognized Antwan and pinged Margot's transmitter once. She responded by pacing back and forth, looking frantic.

When Antwan approached, she pleaded for him to help her with the shuttle's hatch. He realized the importance of the shuttle's departure and followed her into the bay. She fretted that the manual over-ride lever was stuck and she couldn't get the hatch to fully open. Anxious to meet his reinforcements on the arriving shuttle, he didn't give a second thought that it might be a trap.

Antwan briefly studied the lever and the position of the hatch. He pulled the lever out and rotated it ninety-degrees. As soon as the hatch operated smoothly, he realized he was set up. Before he could react, Mike grabbed him from behind and dragged him inside the shuttle. Margot closed the hatch while Mike tied him up with a tether line. He set his pulse pistol to 'stun' and aimed it at Antwan. Margot stepped between them and demanded that she be the one to shoot him, even if it was only to stun him. Mike was happy to comply and handed her the pistol. Antwan warned them that they were as good as dead when his men arrived. Mike responded that he and Margot had great plans for all of them. He was going to pay many times over for making this personal with Mike.

Antwan taunted them and announced that the crew of the *Blue Eagle* would be dead before they even docked at the station. Mike immediately tried to process what they could do to execute such a plan. He gloated at Mike and bragged that, no matter what, he won. Mike reminded him of his warning the last time they spoke. "Antwan, you made this personal with me. That was your big mistake."

Margot placed the pistol against Antwan's head and grinned fiendishly. Antwan inquired as to why she was so passionate about killing him. She revealed that he killed her husband at the pirate haven when he first brought his thugs in to monitor the occupants, just to set an example. Antwan laughed at her and boasted that he killed a lot of people. Her husband was just another insignificant casualty of their operation. Margot's face turned red and she pistol-whipped him several times until Mike stopped her. Antwan lay on his side, unconscious and bloody. Margot then burst into tears and dropped the pistol on the floor. Mike held her in his arms and comforted her. When Margot regained her composure, she apologized for losing her temper. Mike seemed disappointed and shook his head at her. She was embarrassed, until he confessed that he wanted to beat him like that. She was relieved, knowing that he understood her feelings.

"Stun him, anyway. Will you?" Mike urged, displaying a sense of compassion. He picked up the pistol and handed it to her. "Just to keep him quiet for a while." Margot smiled and fired two stun pulses into Antwan's body. He shuddered while urinating in his pants and then remained still. She kissed Mike's cheek and then kicked Antwan's head for good measure.

"We have to figure out what their plan is before the *Blue Eagle* arrives," he informed her. She recommended that they speak with the station engineers or the maintenance technicians for more information. In agreement with her,

Mike took Margot by the hand and led her off the shuttle. She was pleased with the respect and attention she received from him.

Inside the station, they stepped off the elevator and entered the maintenance department. Two technicians sat at a table, while on a break. They were surprised to see strangers enter their area, especially when Mike requested their help in preventing a terrorist attack on the station. He explained what Antwan said about the *Blue Eagle's* crew being killed before they even docked and wanted some theories on how that could happen, assuming that the *Blue Eagle* was clean of explosives or sabotage.

One of the technicians, Damon, considered a breach of the bay doors after containment, but they would have to be docked for that to affect the crew. The second technician, Samson, suggested that, should the ship's hatch open with the outer bay doors open, the crew would be killed almost instantly and sucked out of the ship toward space.

Mike then inquired how someone could get into the bay with the outer doors open to plant an explosive on the ship. Damon explained that a person could wear an environmental suit and enter through the overhead maintenance hatch for that bay. He added that explosives wouldn't necessarily be required if the outside manual release of the hatch was activated. "The airlock would likely be disabled in a docking evolution to allow for egress from the ship," explained Samson. "That's where the danger lies."

Mike informed them that he was going to execute that feat on the mercenaries before they could use it on the *Blue Eagle*. He requested they give him a suit and show him how to access the bay. Margot contacted the transport supervisor and verified the new bay assigned to the mercenary shuttle. Meanwhile, Damon displayed the bay on a monitor. There were several catwalks across the ceiling of the bay and several ladders down the walls at evenly spaced locations. He pointed to the ladder that Mike would use to approach the arriving shuttle. Damon suggested using a tether but Mike insisted he could handle the task without one, based on a prior experience with Special Forces.

When Samson questioned Mike that he could be the terrorist, Mike explained the situation and that the mercenaries were well-armed. He assured him that he could prove these men were coming to inflict damage on the station. Damon mentioned that Kronos was notorious for sending teams of mercenaries into facilities just like this and taking control of them. He expressed his concern that Kronos could ruin the future they were building at the station for freight transportation in and out of their region. Then he mentioned that everyone knew the *Blue Eagle* was the key to long-distance hauling for them. Mike informed him that Kronos wanted his ship and their station to take control of the region, thus convincing the men to help them.

Damon led them to another floor and into a smaller maintenance shop. He explained that this was the access room for their designated bay that they used when maintenance was required with the outer doors open. Samson brought two suits for them but Mike only wanted one. Margot was surprised and insisted she go with him. He ordered her to stay put, fearing the risk if something went wrong.

Damon revealed that there were two personnel hatches with an interlock between their location and the bay. The inner hatch couldn't be opened unless the outer hatch was secured. In addition, the inner hatch was vertical while the outer hatch to the bay was horizontal, mounted in the floor of the airlock.

Margot received a message from the transport supervisor that the second shuttle would be docking shortly. She stood in front of Mike and pleaded to accompany him. He insisted that, if something went wrong, she would know what to do. She watched helplessly as he suited up.

When Damon opened the inner hatch for Mike, Mike gave them a thumbs up and entered the airlock. Margot paced back and forth with concern and then instructed Damon to suit her up in case Mike needed help. He and Samson assembled the second suit and dressed her. Samson attached a tether to her shoulders and instructed her to tie off if she had to retrieve him. He cautioned her that she only had twenty-five feet of line to work with. They watched the monitor, concerned for Mike's safety.

Mike crossed a catwalk and then descended a ladder down to the deck of the bay. The shuttle had just entered the bay, drifting through the channel toward the dock, from Mike's left to his right. Mike lunged at it and attempted to grab the pitot tube for the long-range sensor, which was mounted forward of the hatch. His plan was to grab the tube with his right hand and then pull the manual over-ride lever with his left as the shuttle drifted past him. In this manner, he'd be clear of the hatch when it ejected.

Mike panicked when his glove slipped off the pitot tube. His left hand waved frantically and missed the manual over-ride lever as well. In desperation, he grabbed the lever with his right hand while his body was positioned in front of the hatch. With the outer doors open and the bay depressurized, the hatch blew off toward the wall, taking Mike with it. The hatch struck the bay wall with Mike absorbing the impact in front of it. Unconscious, his body drifted aimlessly toward the open bay doors. Margot and the technicians watched in horror on the monitor. Margot shouted, "I'm going in now!"

Samson opened the inner hatch and Margot entered the airlock. Frightened, she looked back, knowing the risk she was taking, as he closed the hatch behind her Three seconds elapsed and the airlock depressurized, allowing her to open the outer hatch. She emerged from the outer personnel hatch and dropped down the short, five-rung ladder onto the catwalk with the tether in hand.

Bodies ejected from the mercenaries' vessel with arms flailing helplessly and then were still. One mercenary saw her and, as a last desperate act, attempted to aim his pulse rifle at her but died before he could shoot. Margot felt horrible, watching them die. Yes, they were enemies but they were human beings as well. *Was it murder, self-preservation or something else?* she wondered.

Margot hurried as fast as her feet would allow her in the suit across the catwalk until she was nearly above Mike. After latching the tether to the catwalk railing, she climbed over the rail and pushed downward toward him. A feeling of nausea swept over her from the weightlessness and she shuddered at the sight of open space ahead. If she missed Mike, he would drift into space and die a horrible death.

As she drifted closer to him, she realized that the tether line was barely long enough. With her arms outstretched, she reached desperately for his motionless body. When she grabbed him, the tether went taut and jerked her backward. With her gloved hands slipping off his suit, she instinctively turned her lower body toward him and wrapped her legs around his waist. Pain shot through her shoulders from the impact of the tether as she pulled with one hand on the line.

Back in the maintenance room, Damon and Samson watched the camera's monitor in horror. Mike's face plate was cracked and the white mist spraying from the crack indicated that oxygen was seeping out. They were helpless to do anything but watch.

Margot strained with every bit of strength in her arm while holding onto Mike with her legs. Her right arm was useless from her injured shoulder. Her left shoulder throbbed with intense pain but she could still use it to pull. Her legs cramped as she maintained a lock on Mike. Finally, she made it to the catwalk and pulled Mike over the rail. Then she saw the leak in his faceplate and panicked. After all her efforts, he could still die on her. Frantically, she pushed him ahead of her toward the ladder. She could barely stand when she reached the ladder, but was able to shove him upward into the airlock. She heard a pop and then saw the shards of glass from Mike's faceplate drifting away from him. She knew she had to move fast or he would die from exposure.

Damon stood by the wheel for the inner hatch, ready to open it as soon as the outer hatch locked. Margot leaped up and into the airlock, striking the ceiling. Stunned from the impact, she bounced back down toward the hatch. Fortunately, she grabbed the outer hatch and pulled it closed. With little strength left, she turned the wheel to secure the hatch. It felt as if it never moved but then she heard the airlock pressurize and knew she closed it. Her head dropped and she closed her eyes, exhausted and hurting. Her fears had overcome her, as she knew Mike could be dead. Her first mission with someone she cared for and he could already be a casualty.

Damon opened the inner hatch and Samson rushed inside. He pulled Mike out and laid him on the floor. Damon was behind him with Margot in his arms and laid her next to Mike. He hurried around the shelves to the alarms on the wall. There were two knobs above the work bench. One was for "fire" and the other for "medical" emergencies. Damon slapped the medical alarm, which alerted the med-techs where to go.

The door to the shop burst open and a woman in a black uniform entered with a pulse rifle. She only saw Samson standing over Mike and Margot. "Get out!" she ordered. Samson raised his hands and hurried past her. Damon hid behind the tool rack and searched for a weapon. The woman targeted Margot with her rifle and told her she would die for what they did to her team in the bay. Margot was helpless to move and Mike appeared unconscious. Damon picked up a piece of conduit and threw it at the woman.

Mike opened his eyes and, seeing the woman target Margot, he instinctively rolled over on top of her. As the woman fired, the conduit struck her in the head, but a second too late. She fell to the ground unconscious. A burst of energy struck Mike in the back and left a smoldering black spot on his suit.

Damon rushed to Mike and pulled him off of Margot. He examined the wound to Mike's back and laid him on his side. The suit minimized the impact of the energy pulse but still inflicted damage to his back. Margot cried as she thought Mike died, not once, but twice.

Three med-techs arrived in a flat-bed cart outside the shop. They entered and examined Mike's face, neck and back. Damon helped Margot out of the suit and saw her right shoulder was badly dislocated. He informed the med-techs immediately. They brought in a scissor-scoop stretcher for Mike and moved him onto the cart. Margot was ushered by the third med-tech onto the cart as well. They drove off to the infirmary, while Damon contacted security to remove the unconscious assailant from the shop.

Margot sat on a gurney in the infirmary and watched sadly as the med-techs removed Mike's suit. His face appeared like that of a zombie, gray and decomposed. A deep wound to his back between the shoulder blades had a deep crater, cauterized by the heat from the pulse fire. She explained to the med-techs how Mike was smashed by the hatch against the wall.

A doctor entered the quarters and, after examining the damage to Mike's face, neck and back, instructed the technicians to insert him into a grafting chamber. They lifted Mike onto a tube-like device at the rear of the examination room and closed the glass cover on him. A yellow beam of light scanned his face and neck for over an hour. Over time, Mike's skin slowly transformed back to its original color. The flaking, decomposed patches took on a normal texture once more. Mike groaned in pain during the process as he drifted in and out of consciousness.

Tears streamed down Margot's cheeks as she watched. The doctor peered at her right shoulder and walked behind her. He gently felt around the shoulder joint and then yanked, nearly sending Margot to the floor. When her shoulder popped back into place, Margot cried out in a short yip and then sighed with relief. "You could have warned me," she complained.

He ignored her comment and probed her left shoulder with his fingers. "Just a bad sprain on this one," he informed her. "We'll put a sling on your arm for a few days." The med-tech instinctively took the hint from the doctor and retrieved a sling from one of the drawers. As he positioned Margot's arm into it, she asked, "Will Mike be okay?"

"We'll see," the doctor replied and turned his attention back to Mike. The grafting machine completed its cycle and the glass cover opened. The doctor instructed the med-techs to move him into another machine for further evaluation. They placed him on a sliding table, which then inserted him into a larger tube. Fifteen minutes later, the table with Mike slid out of the tube and the machine shut down. The doctor studied the information that scrolled on the machine's display for several minutes.

Damon and Samson entered the infirmary. Damon informed Margot that security extended their thanks for preventing a terrorist attack on the station. Samson apologized for doubting them at first. Damon then inquired if they were Special Forces as he had never seen anything like what they did in the bay. Margot cracked a smile. "We're just ordinary people who want an end to Kronos reign and their criminal activities," she replied.

The maintenance techs shook her hand and thanked her for saving the day. She pointed to Mike and explained that it was his plan. They watched anxiously, waiting for the doctor to speak. Finally, the doctor turned to them and related the extent of Mike's injuries. He had a concussion, a sprained neck with minor inflammation, minor lung damage from his exposure to the cold temperature of space, and significant bruising on his shoulders and knees. The grafting machine healed his skin, throat and his back, but there would be some soreness and itching for several days. He expected Mike to make a full recovery and should be conscious soon.

Damon and Samson high-fived Margot and then left the quarters to return to their work. The doctor assured her they would both be fine and then he left the quarters. Margot rested her head on Mike's chest and held his hand in hers.

The *Blue Eagle* docked and began transferring cargo. The transportation supervisor requested that Tisch report to the infirmary on the sixth floor at once. Tisch feared that something went wrong with Mike's plan and took Wilmer with her. The others remained to work the loads.

Tisch and Wilmer left the elevator on the sixth floor and hurried to the infirmary at the end of the hall. When they entered, Mike was asleep on the gurney. Margot looked up and greeted them. She explained what happened to Mike and relayed the doctor's prognosis. Margot then burst into tears and blurted how Mike saved her life.

"He has a habit of doing that." Tisch mentioned calmly. "He's a good man." She suggested to Margot that they get something to eat and talk about what happened. Wilmer offered to stay with Mike in the meantime.

The women went to the pub and ordered food. Margot remarked, "I need something strong after this." Tisch ordered two Wild Dog Whiskeys for them. Tisch related everything about Mike and her past with him. She told her of how Gemini broke his heart and then she did as well. "If he gives you his heart, please don't break it," pleaded Tisch. "I don't think he can handle another one."

Margot burst into tears again and related her story to Tisch. After four drinks, both women felt better about how things turned out. A woman with long, auburn hair entered the pub and approached the table. She introduced herself as Rebecca, the station manager. Tisch invited her to sit with them.

Rebecca praised her for their success in making their run to all three stations. Then she complimented Margot for the job she and Mike did in apprehending Antwan. Her security team moved Antwan from Mike's shuttle and placed him in a cell until they were ready to depart. Margot inquired as to what Antwan's fate would be. To their surprise, Rebecca revealed that he would be transported on the *Blue Eagle* to Murgatroyd's Oasis and wait for their contact.

Tisch was surprised and mentioned that they were banished from the pirate haven. Rebecca chuckled and then explained that Kronos has withdrawn most of their resources from the sector, especially after losing so many high-priced mercenaries. She warned them that there would likely be one more attack on Taurus, funded by Antwan's remaining resources. After that, Empire should be easy pickings and they could focus solely on Kronos.

Concerned, Tisch responded that her job was to transport freight. "What happens to Empire is Gemini and Sara's problem," she remarked.

Rebecca then inquired, "How do you feel about keeping Jonas on as a crew member to replace Mike?"

Tisch grew concerned. "What will happen to Mike?"

Rebecca explained that she spoke with Marina and she would like to keep them together – on the *Blue Eagle*. Tisch grinned, knowing that she had hoped for that anyway. Rebecca then instructed Tisch that she was to remain on Archimides-9 for four days before leaving so they could coordinate Antwan's transfer at the pirate haven. Tisch was more than happy to accommodate her and give the crew some down time. Rebecca thanked them again and departed.

Mike awoke and strained to open his eyes. When he did, he was surprised to see Wilmer. "Where's Margot?" he asked frantically. Wilmer assured him that she was nearby and then complained that he was just as good-looking as she was, drawing a chuckle from Mike. Mike got up from the gurney and rubbed his head gingerly. "What the hell happened to me? I feel like I got shoved through a sausage machine."

Wilmer shook his head at him and suggested he speak with Margot about it. Mike rubbed his face again and groaned, "I feel like I'm wearing a mask." He struggled to sit up and then tried to stand. "Am I okay?" he asked nervously.

"Now you are. A few hours ago, not so much."

"Let's get a drink, buddy," he suggested and walked to the door. "I can tell this was a bad day."

Wilmer saw the burnt hole in the back of Mike's shirt and the star-shaped scar from the graft. "Geez, Mike! What the hell did happen to you?"

Mike looked back and frowned. "If I remember correctly what happened, then this is going to take some time to get over – and more than a few drinks."

Wilmer suggested he change into another shirt but Mike didn't care. Damon stopped in and tossed Mike a shirt. "I figured you might need one of these. It's the least I can do for you."

Mike thanked him and then man-hugged him. Damon shook Mike's hand and then left. Mike held the shirt up and declared happily, "Problem solved." He swapped shirts and threw his burnt one into the disposal.

Wilmer complained that he felt left out as they walked down the hall since he was the one who always accompanied Mike on these dangerous escapades. Mike reminded him that he elected to stay with Shannon on Vega. Wilmer was embarrassed as Mike was right and said no more. Rebecca approached from the other direction and instructed them to follow her. Mike and Wilmer glanced at each other, unsure of what to expect. Mike feared that he screwed something up and he was about to get his ass chewed out.

When they entered Rebecca's office, she had the video of Mike's incident with the mercenary shuttle on her wall monitor, displaying footage from all four cameras in the bay. Mike was embarrassed by his ineptitude, but had no idea how he made it out of the bay. She replayed it from the beginning for them to see. Wilmer was impressed with the plan until Mike missed his hold on the pitot tube. Mike cringed when he saw the impact his body took from the blown hatch. Then he saw his body drifting toward space through the open bay doors. "Holy crap!" blurted Mike. "That's not good!"

Wilmer was amazed at how quickly the mercenaries were sucked out of the shuttle. Rebecca was pleased with how things went. Mike's plan made perfect sense for what they needed to do. No station damage; no casualties to station personnel or their crew; and twenty less mercenaries to worry about. Then they watched in awe as a second person appeared and rescued Mike. "Who was it that saved my ass?" Mike asked.

"I believe that was your partner, Margot," kidded Rebecca. "You two make quite a pair." Mike was stunned by the extent that Margot went to save him.

Rebecca then selected a different video from the maintenance shop. Mike and Wilmer watched as the female mercenary entered and shot at Margot. He didn't remember rolling onto her to save her, but was glad he did. He was also impressed to see Damon knock the woman out with the conduit. "Wow! I owe that guy a drink," he uttered, surprised by the unexpected help. Wilmer requested a copy of the video for the ship. Rebecca smiled and promised to take care of it. Mike frowned, knowing where this was going.

Rebecca then informed him of the discussion she had with Tisch about his status. She also mentioned that the teleport module should be installed on the shuttle, if it wasn't already. Realizing that she was part of the alliance leadership, Mike expressed his concerns about knowing details of Kronos' organization. He also inquired if the alliance had any information about how Kronos was able to wipe out two Scrat worlds while sustaining very little damage to their forces.

Rebecca admitted that they knew there were five Kronos bases and one of them was already in alliance hands, thanks to Marina. She also mentioned that they believed Kronos used Federation cloaking technology that was thought to be lost years ago, to destroy the Scrat. It was only a theory as they had no proof yet. She added that any pertinent information would be filtered down to him and Margot. With that, she thanked him for his assistance.

Mike and Wilmer went down to the pub to catch up with the crew. Wilmer prodded Mike and teased about Margot's concern for him. Mike blushed and claimed it was nothing to get excited about.

Everyone was thrilled when Mike arrived. He was surprised to see Tisch and Margot sitting together, smiling no less. Geezer sat on the other side of Tisch. Shannon, Zenith and Jonas also sat at the table. Everyone was relieved to see him on his feet.

Margot stood and rushed to him. "I was so worried about you!" she exclaimed. Mike gazed at her, unsure of what to do. *How do you thank someone for saving your life like she did?* he thought. A slow song played and caught his attention. He took her left hand and led her to the dance floor.

Ever the opportunist, Jonas stood at the table and requested a dance with Zenith. They, too, danced. Shannon glanced at Wilmer, a hint for him. He eventually caught on and led her to the dance floor as well.

Geezer leaned toward Tisch and asked if she was okay. Tisch smiled and answered, "I'm more than okay. I'm glad for Mike." Geezer kissed her cheek and praised her for making such a hard decision about Mike. She confessed that she knew she couldn't have him and a crew. She chose her crew and she broke his heart. Geezer knew the ship and crew were always her dream. He was pleased that she finally knew what she wanted and accepted the price. When the song ended, Mike kissed Margot. She blushed and asked, "What was that for?"

"You have to ask," he responded and kissed her again. She embraced him as tightly as she could with the sling in the way. Mike was surprised to see Wilmer and Shannon kissing, while Jonas and Zenith embraced. Everyone returned to the table.

Mike was concerned and asked Tisch, "Are you okay?"

Tisch smiled and nodded her head. "I think everyone has what they wanted most; even me."

Mike understood and felt relieved that their breakup wasn't personal. He took Margot by the hand and announced that they were retiring for the night. Rebecca had provided accommodations for them inside the station and secured their ship. After they left, Geezer told Tisch that he was happy that he completed his job – helping her overcome her demons. Tisch told him that she would always need him, no matter what happens. He smiled and left for the night.

The next morning, Mike and Margot arrived for breakfast. Everyone looked sad and teary-eyed at the table. Tisch looked up and told Mike that Geezer passed away during the night. His body was cremated and a service would be held after lunch. Mike expressed his condolences and sat at the next table. Margot went to the counter and got a breakfast meal for each of them. When she returned to the table, Mike jotted several questions on a napkin.

Expecting that Mike was plotting his next move, Wilmer crossed over to his table. Mike looked up innocently at both of them. Margot commented to Wilmer, "You sense he's up to something, too?"

Wilmer nodded and folded his hands, staring with a sinister smile at Mike. Margot turned her chair to face Mike and stared as well. Finally, Mike put his pen down and responded to them. "I have a theory about what happened to the Scrat."

Everyone listened, wondering why his sudden interest in the Scrat worlds. Tisch leaned over Margot's shoulder and whispered, "Can't you do something to occupy his mind at night?"

Both women erupted into laughter. Margot kidded that the two women together might not be enough to keep him out of trouble. Tisch was amused by her comment and remarked that they might have to consider that option. They high-fived and then turned their attention to Mike. He frowned at them and explained his revelation.

Mike intended to take the shuttle to the Scrat world to the location where he and Creeg previously landed. He was interested in the two Kronus ships that crashed on the planet's surface. Tisch folded her arms and inquired, "And what, pray tell, do you expect to find there?"

Mike explained that there was a reason those two ships crashed and none others. He mentioned that he didn't recall seeing any indication that they were shot down, although he only saw them from a distance and from a single angle.

Margot commented that this was a long shot that they would find anything conclusive and there was also the risk that Kronos was monitoring the area for any surviving Scrat activity. Mike was insistent and promised that it would be less than a day to get his answers and they still had a few days before they departed. Tisch agreed to speak with Rebecca after the service about it and get permission so they don't piss off any more of the alliance's leaders. Mike reluctantly accepted her terms. "By the way," she added, "take your module and install it in the shuttle. Rebecca's orders."

"Yeah, we already got the Rebecca briefing," he grumbled. Mike was pleased with the outcome. Initially, he feared that Tisch would never agree to a mission in the Nebula Galaxy just to investigate two shipwrecks. Wilmer commented that it was a risky plan but it may be worthwhile if they find anything. Shanna and Zenith were excited to go, but Wilmer chided them about their responsibility to Tisch and the *Blue Eagle*. He added that this was what caused problems in the first place, as Mike was not their boss. Mike felt bad, knowing that Wilmer was right. Tisch appreciated having their support, another sign that things were evolving well.

The service for Geezer was short and solemn. Mike mentioned how Geezer was the wise man who always knew what to say in any situation. Tisch recalled how he was like a father to her and reeled her in when she went off the rails over her father's death. Wilmer commented that he was a good friend and a great drinking buddy. Tisch took his loss especially hard. Mike hugged her and expressed his sympathies. He also told her that he was always there for her if she needed someone to talk to. Tisch was grateful but assured him he'd regret that offer. He expected nothing less.

After the service, Tisch spoke with Rebecca privately about Mike's suggestion. Margot pressed Mike to reconsider his plan. She feared that they had no backup if something went wrong. Mike quipped that it's a given that something would go wrong. "It always does," he joked. Margot didn't appreciate his lax attitude about the trip and told him so. He suggested that she could remain on Archimedes-9 and he'd be okay by himself. She was disappointed that he would even think she'd abandon him.

When Rebecca left the chapel, Tisch approached Mike and Margot. "Rebecca's okay with it," she informed him. "Tomorrow, you can make your fantasy run." Mike thanked her and followed the others out of the chapel.

Wilmer walked with Mike. He complained that he would like to return with him and investigate some of the weaponry on the Scrat and the Kronos ships, but Tisch wasn't likely to let him risk his life. Mike understood the circumstances and knew he was chasing this theory on his own.

Tisch asked Margot if she had any idea what brought this on with Mike's interest in the Kronos ships. Margot had no idea and mentioned that he was distant from her last night at the bar and said little. Tisch warned her that he can be moody. The women both knew that Mike was born for combat, whether he was fighting for the military or taking down mercenaries. Each understood what a challenge it was to handle him but they both realized how their friendship formed and grew as a result of him. There was no competition for Mike and both seemed to see eye to eye on everything. Margot informed Tisch that she was going with Mike, even though he expected her to stay at the station. Tisch supported her decision and assured that it's the right way to handle him. Don't ask. Just do.

Wilmer accompanied Mike to the *Blue Eagle* and dismantled the teleport module from the power distribution cabinet. They returned to the shuttle and installed it as it was before. Mike thanked him for all his help and hoped that this new position for him eased the tension on board the ship. "Speaking of tension," Wilmer commented. "What gives with you and Margot? Is this serious?"

"Why do you ask? Is it obvious?" he responded.

Wilmer pointed out that they seem to be in sync and don't argue over every decision. Mike agreed with him and admitted that she is special. Wilmer wished him well with her.

CHAPTER 5

WHO'D HAVE THOUGHT

When Mike boarded the shuttle the next morning, he was surprised to see Margot, Wilmer and Tisch seated at a table in the aft section. "What the hell's this? An intervention." he asked cynically.

Tisch explained that Rebecca's one condition for the trip was that she and Wilmer accompany Margot to keep him out of trouble. Mike wasn't thrilled about it but relented. When Margot informed him that they were leaving at the first sign of trouble, Mike threw his hands up in frustration and waited for Wilmer to say something. Wilmer shook his head. "I got nothing, buddy. It's their show or no go."

Mike took the pilot's seat and started the shuttle's systems. Margot sat in the copilot's seat and arranged for their departure with the transport supervisor. Tisch watched as Wilmer programmed the module for the Nebula Galaxy. She inquired how Wilmer knew so much about it.

"I'm an engineer," he responded defensively. "That's what I do." Tisch smiled and rubbed his shoulders. She appreciated what he could do, when he was sufficiently motivated.

Mike piloted the shuttle out of the bay and into space. When they were distant from the station, he instructed Wilmer to activate the module. Wilmer pressed the 'start' sequence and waited for Mike's response. Tisch approached the front of the shuttle and leaned over Margot's shoulder to see what happened next.

Margot questioned Tisch about her prior teleporting experience. Tisch replied that the only time was during their escape from the Scrat warship and she had no idea what happened. Margot then asked Mike what to expect when they teleport. "We're there already," he announced. "We're starting our descent." Tisch and Margot stared at each other, surprised by the simplicity of the process.

Mike located the two Kronos wrecks and then found a place to set the shuttle down. Everyone was appalled by the destruction on the short-range monitor. When Mike shut down the ship's systems, he instructed them that they would split into two teams. He would take Margot and Tisch would take Wilmer. Each would take a ship and see what they could find out about the weaponry and control systems.

When they exited the shuttle, they climbed over the wreckage on the way to the ships. Tisch hated to admit that Mike was right, but she noticed that there were no indications of cannon fire on the hull of the ship and the front section appeared to be crushed as if it collided with something. Tisch and Wilmer reached their ship first and crawled through the busted hull. Wilmer instructed her to see if she could scavenge anything from the ship's instrumentation on the bridge. He descended a ladder to the lower level and searched for the navigator's station.

Tisch noticed a panel assembly on the rear wall. There was a large selector that was marked 'cloak', 'force field' and 'off'. She followed the wiring harness to a cable tray behind it until it passed through the wall. She left the flight deck and attempted to enter the next bay. The hatch was labeled 'Inverter Area – High Voltage'. Tisch tried to force the hatch open but with no success. She climbed down the ladder to inform Wilmer about what she had seen.

Wilmer opened a small panel on the side of the station and attached his pulse pistol to a terminal block, set for stun. When Tisch approached and eyed him curiously, he explained that he hoped to power up the database and see where the ship came from. Tisch doubted that his idea would work but watched patiently.

Wilmer pressed the trigger and energy streamed from the pistol into the work station's power terminals. The station came to life and the monitor illuminated. Tisch anxiously accessed the system through the touch-screen and watched as information scrolled. After thirty seconds, Wilmer released the trigger on his pistol. They were pleased to see that the station stayed active. Wilmer assumed that the backup system charged with enough power to run the station for a short time. They were amazed to see the coordinates from the ship's source. "We know exactly where they came from!" he shouted excitedly. "Now, if we can only find out how they got here unnoticed," he remarked.

Tisch told him of the panel on the bridge and led him to it. When Wilmer saw it, he exclaimed, "Mike was right! This cloaking mechanism is what helped Kronos destroy the Scrat so easily."

"What happened to the ship that it crashed?" questioned Tisch

Wilmer explained that the Scrat must have narrowed the sources of the cannon fire to two small areas and then sent their ships out to ram them. "Mike's a genius! In 'cloak' mode, they no longer had force fields to protect them!"

Tisch grumbled, "I hate when he's right. I'll never hear the end of it."

Wilmer chuckled and attempted to enter the Inverter Section next. They used a broken piece of conduit to pry the hatch open and enter. Two of the four inverters had broken off of their base bolts and leaned against the hatch and wall. Wilmer was able to push the one inverter back on its base, allowing them clear access through the hatch.

"We need to find the ion generator that they used for the force field," he blurted excitedly. Tisch enjoyed seeing Wilmer like this, full of emotion. He was always so quiet and laid back. They followed the corridor to the aft of the ship and descended two decks to the engine compartment.

The ion generator was an add-on piece of equipment and stood out. About the size of a large suitcase, its temporary power cables indicated that it was installed in a rush or borrowed from another ship. Wilmer promptly disconnected the cabling and removed the generator's restraints. He and Tisch carried the ion generator and the control assembly back to the shuttle in two trips.

Mike and Margot approached the second ship and paused to inspect the outer hull. The stern was caved in and torn as if it was rammed by another ship. Margot now understood Mike's suspicions. As they circled the ship to gain entrance, the ground gave way and they dropped into an underground tunnel. Bruised from the drop, they got up slowly. The tunnel was dark and they couldn't see anything. Mike looked up at the hole in the ceiling and complained, "I told you that stuff would go wrong. It always does."

Margot took a small flashlight from her belt and turned it on. They were shocked to see Scrat soldiers standing around them with pulse rifles. Margot shrieked in fear, but Mike placed his arm around her and assured her that it was okay. He advised her to keep the light on as the Scrat can see in the dark.

The Scrat raised their pulse rifles and targeted them. Mike made an image of a box with his hands and pointed to the closest Scrat. He pointed to himself and then to the Scrat. He explained that they needed the box to talk. Margot was surprised that the Scrat soldier understood Mike. The soldiers led them to another area where they met a Scrat officer.

Mike again gestured for a box to communicate. A Scrat soldier arrived and handed a small translating box to the officer. He placed it around his neck and questioned Mike about who they were and why they were there. Mike mentioned that they knew Creeg. The Scrat were surprised at the mention of Creeg's name. He introduced himself and Margot as allies in the war against Kronos. The officer commented that they would be punished for killing Creeg and the other Scrat on his ship. Mike informed the officer that Creeg and the others on the ship were alive and well. He explained how Kronos attacked them as well but they worked together to repel them.

The officer inquired about the fate of General Asher. Mike informed him that Asher was defeated in battle and Creeg assumed command. The officer introduced himself as Gendry and revealed that Creeg was his brother. One of the soldiers, Tybus, interrupted arrogantly and informed him that his friend Carnak warned him about Mike and that he was responsible for the destruction of their bases several years back.

Gendry stepped back for the two to resolve their differences. Tybus threw a punch to Mike's jaw that staggered him backwards. Mike stepped up to Tybus and stared him down. "As I told Carnak, this ends the same way every time," Mike stated boldly and floored him with an uppercut that left Tybus humiliated. He got up and came at Mike again but Gendry ordered him to stand down. Tybus then mocked Mike for bringing a woman with him and questioned her resolve to fight. Not one to be shown up, Margot threw an uppercut and decked Tybus again. The other Scrat were amused and mocked Tybus. He snarled and left them.

Mike stared at Margot, speechless. "What?" she asked innocently.

Mike informed Gendry that he was there to find out how Kronos was able to defeat the Scrat so easily. Gendry explained that some of Kronos' ships were cloaked. The only chance they had was to fly at the source of the cannon fire and hope to collide with their ships. He claimed that they damaged several but only brought down the few that caused the most damage. He mentioned that they had many ships staged elsewhere to follow Asher's lead when they were summoned. As a result, they still had an armada of ships in the mountains. "We can still fight," Gendry assured him, "when the time is right."

Mike asked if they would be interested in joining the alliance against Kronos. Gendry responded that they would but only if he received his orders from Creeg. Then he would know that Mike was telling the truth. Mike promised to contact Creeg and arrange for them to meet.

Then the question came up about a module that would allow them to transport their fleet over great distances. Mike calmly answered that it was destroyed during a battle on the bridge of the Scrat warship, thanks to Asher. Gendry agreed to let them leave but swore that if Mike was lying, he'd hunt him down. Mike assured him that Creeg would vouch for his credibility. Gendry instructed his troops to show Mike and Margot to the surface. Mike thanked him and left.

When they reached the surface, the Scrat turned back. They were on the other side of the wrecked Kronos ship from where they fell. Mike paused and stared at Margot. She grew uneasy and asked what she did now to annoy him.

"You decked a Scrat," he uttered in amazement.

"So?" she responded. "That could be you next time, if you don't lose the attitude."

Mike realized that he offended her by requesting that she stay at the station. He apologized and promised not to do that again. She gave him a death stare and walked away. "Damn, I love that woman!" he exclaimed to himself.

When they reached the Kronos ship, they encountered Wilmer and Tisch exiting with the control assembly from the bridge. "Where the hell were you, two?" Tisch shouted, concerned by their absence.

Mike pointed to the hole and said humbly, "Long story."

Wilmer blurted to him how they found the cloaking system and removed the components from the first ship. Mike was eager to remind Tisch that he was right once again, while Wilmer kidded Margot that they suspected the two were having an alone moment somewhere. That's why he and Tisch removed the components from the second ship for them. Margot responded politely to Wilmer that they weren't at that point in their relationship – yet. Mike was anxious to leave with the information they had. He carried the ion generator over his shoulder for them while Wilmer took the control assembly.

With the main components for two cloaking systems on board, they closed the hatch and departed the planet. Wilmer taunted Mike that they had something to show for their efforts and wanted to know what he had. All he would say is that they wouldn't believe it.

Wilmer knew that this meant something epic happened and Mike wanted a crowd before he revealed it. Tisch looked to Margot for some indication of what happened. Margot complained that, unfortunately, Mike was right. Whatever he does, something will go wrong. It's a given. Tisch pressed her for more but she said that it's Mikes story to tell. Wilmer laughed as he was familiar with that scenario in the past.

Wilmer explained that the cloaking system used by Kronos is the old technology used by the Federation. It was believed to be lost in the last war as only two ships had it and the factory was destroyed along with the technology. He believed that it worked in parallel with the force field generator and that only one of the two can be used at a time. That's why the Scrat could ram the two ships. Their shields were down. Mike grew excited and asked if the system could be integrated into the shuttle or the *Blue Eagle*. Unfortunately, when cloak mode was selected, there was no force field available. Wilmer was sure that it was an easy installation based on the temporary install that Kronos did on their two ships. "But why the big deal if it's easy?" questioned Tisch.

"It's a combination of two technologies," explained Wilmer, "that no one would think to try."

Mike wondered aloud if they shouldn't reveal that they had the actual components for the cloaking technology. "Now that we know it really wasn't anything innovative," he surmised, "why risk sharing something that can be so dangerous to civilization?" Tisch agreed to disclose only that they took some components off the Kronos ships to get a better understanding of their weaponry and nothing about the cloaking system.

The shuttle teleported back to Archimedes-9 and docked. Tisch contacted the *Blue Eagle* and instructed the crew meet them at the pub. She then contacted Rebecca and requested that she join them for an update.

The crew congregated at a table in the back of the pub. The bartender brought over a tray of drinks and placed them on the table. Tisch requested that Mike wait for Rebecca to arrive before debriefing the mission. Mike was pleased that his jaunt was referred to a mission after the mockery he put up with from everyone. Tisch kidded with Margot that Mike's head will get even bigger than it already was. The two tapped glasses and chuckled as they drank. Wilmer noticed their camaraderie and elbowed Mike in his side. Mike nodded, well aware that they mocked him again for his 'astute' intuition about the Kronos ships.

When Rebecca entered the pub, Tisch waved and caught her attention. She approached and took a seat with them. "So, am I to assume that Mr. Colby came through with another of his amazing epiphanies," she said wryly.

"It pains me to say that he did," kidded Tisch as she motioned for Mike to speak. He started with the details of the Kronos ships and how they used stealth technology to overwhelm the Scrat. Then, he announced that a good portion of the Scrat military did survive the onslaught and are hiding underground until they have a plan to retaliate against Kronos.

Rebecca gestured for him to stop and walked over to the bar. She returned with a glass of Scotch whiskey. "I have a feeling I'll be needing this before the story is finished." Tisch and Margot both nodded to her in agreement.

Mike explained how he convinced the Scrat to work with the alliance, pending a meeting with Creeg to prove that the details about their relationship were credible. Rebecca was pleasantly surprised but grew suspicious and asked, "What did they say about the teleport module?"

Mike informed her that, when the topic came up, he told them it was destroyed on Creeg's ship during their battle. Rebecca was relieved, knowing that any change in leadership by the Scrat could quickly alter their relationship. "Did you learn anything about the stealth technology on the Kronos ships?" she inquired.

Wilmer interceded and explained that their investigation was limited by the arrival of the Scrat. He detailed how he identified that their force shields can't be used while in 'cloak' mode which may have led to the intentional collision of the Scrat ships with theirs. Rebecca then inquired about a return to the Scrat planet for more information. Mike rejected the idea, knowing that the Scrat would be suspicious and possibly investigate the Kronos ships on their own.

Wilmer expressed his confidence that he could eventually solve the operation of the cloaking system but it would take time. Knowing that the cloaking system was interlocked to the defense shields, he had some ideas.

Rebecca was pleased by the information and promised to relay it to Marina as soon as possible. She also intended to speak with Julian on Taurus about arranging a meeting between Creeg and the surviving Scrat military. Margot mentioned that it was vital to keep the Scrat on board with their plans to prevent any mistrust between them and the alliance.

Mike requested that he join Creeg when the meeting occurs. He believed they could narrow down the location of the Kronos base in that region if they worked together. Margot added that knowing the second location of the five bases could be a turning point and put Kronos on the defensive. Mike contemplated aloud that, if this worked out, Kronos might be led into making mistakes.

Tisch then prodded Wilmer to speak. Rebecca inquired, "Is there something else?"

Wilmer handed her a note with coordinates on it. She glanced at it and then at Wilmer. He informed her that it was the location where the Kronos ships came from and likely one of their bases.

Mike was dumbfounded. "You didn't tell me about that?"

"Long story," Wilmer teased.

Rebecca handed the note back to Wilmer and suggested that this might be a nice present for Mike's Scrat friends. She thanked them for their efforts and left the pub.

Shannon asked Margot about her impression of the Scrat after her experience with them. She smiled and commented, "Pussies." Tisch then asked if she really punched one of them in the face. Mike clarified that she knocked him to the ground with an uppercut just like his. Wilmer kidded that they were two of a kind, her and Mike. Tisch advised Mike that he should watch himself, now that he knew what Margot was capable of. Careful to be respectful, he responded that he already knew what she was about. Wilmer and Shannon excused themselves to begin work on the cloaking equipment.

Tisch was pleased with the way things worked out thus far and expressed her appreciation to Mike and Margot for working with her. Mike reminded her that he was a work in progress and was doing his best to be a positive influence. Zenith was grateful as well that the drama was behind them. She announced a toast to their good spirits. The others were happy to drink with her on that fact.

Mike worked out in the fitness room on board the *Blue Eagle*. He liked his time alone and the workouts helped him think. With one more night on Archimedes-9, he pondered what else he could accomplish before they departed. After working up a sweat, wearing only his gym shorts and sneakers, he stopped to finish his container of water. Then it happened. Tisch and Margot both entered the fitness room wearing shorts and sports bras. Mike was surprised to see them and unsure why they had to intrude on him. "What's the deal?" he asked.

The girls each started their own workout, while Mike watched. He sensed that they were determined to distract him and tried not to get aroused by their appearance. He placed his hands on his hips and reminded them that he was waiting for a response.

"We're here to keep you from coming up with any more crazy ideas," Margot teased. "Seems that I can't keep your interest at night so I brought Tisch in to help me."

Tisch paused from her reps and warned, "Don't even think about it, Colby. We're here to work out. Nothing more."

Mike groaned and resumed his workout. Nobody ever used the room before and now that he used it as a place of solace, the girls chose to use it as well. He did his best to ignore them but they continuously teased him about anything they could think of from the size of his feet to the shape of his nipples. Finally, Mike gave up. He grabbed his towel and went to shower in the lavatory. Tisch and Margot high-fived and then continued with their new workout. Tisch commented, "I don't know why I never thought to use this equipment before. It's great for stress relief."

Margot mentioned that she needed to work out when she started training in hand-to-hand combat to build up her endurance. Tisch praised her for having the strength to knock out a Scrat. Margot confessed that she saw where Mike struck the Scrat and realized it was a tender spot. "That's why I chose to throw an uppercut and strike the Scrat just like Mike did," she explained. "The only difference between us was that Mike is right-handed and I'm left-handed."

Tisch laughed and commented that the Scrat must still be hurting on both sides of his face. Margot admitted that she feared the Scrat would have retaliated against her if she didn't get the same result as Mike. Tisch felt even more respect for her, knowing that she was brave enough to try it, even if she could have been hurt. Margot asked her to keep her secret about her knowledge of the Scrat's weakness from Mike. Tisch laughed and promised her that it wouldn't be a problem. She enjoyed that Margot could keep Mike back on his heels.

The next morning, Mike awoke with Margot sitting nearby and staring at him, grim-faced. He immediately suspected that this wasn't going to be pleasant. "You're leaving me for Tisch," he said somberly. "Why not? It's about time to break my heart again." He sat on the edge of the bed.

Margot reached out and held his hands. "How could you even think that after all we've been through?" Mike then realized he just made an ass of himself. She reminded him that she worked for Marina and could be summoned back at any time. Mike questioned why she brought it up now and was stunned by her response. She explained that they were at a crossroad in their relationship and they needed to understand the consequences, if things changed. She was falling in love with Mike and feared what would happen if she did have to leave.

Mike was grateful for her concern and asked her thoughts on leaving the alliance to stay with him. She countered by asking if he could leave his friends. Aware of Mike's hesitation, she pointed out that this was why they had to address it now. Mike was curious as to how she wanted to approach the situation. Margot responded that she didn't want to break his heart if she had to leave. She felt he suffered much more than she did in that area. He realized she was right and there could be consequences. Margot waited patiently for his response.

Mike accepted the fact that she could be recalled at any time and reminded her that their work is dangerous. They could die at any time as well. He revealed his feelings for her and that he would rather have her to love for a short time than not at all. Margot smiled and kidded, "So friends with benefits is out of the question."

Mike chuckled at her. "Loyalty is priceless. I've been in love where there was no loyalty. I'm willing to take the risk with you." Margot leaned forward and hugged him.

CHAPTER 6

DANGEROUS WORK

Morning came and the crew assembled in the station's cafeteria. When everyone was settled with a meal, Rebecca entered and joined them. "I've been instructed to have you leave the cloaking technology with us," she ordered Mike. "Our people will reverse-engineer it and replicate it for our ships to use."

"I expected as much," commented Mike. "Wilmer and I will bring it to you after breakfast."

"I assume it's just one system you managed to procure," Rebecca commented.

"Just one," Wilmer responded. "The other ship was too badly damaged to access its equipment."

Rebecca smiled, knowing that they likely had another operating system. She directed them to return to Taurus and work with Creeg to get his ship repaired. "We may need it as a prelude to a meeting with the Scrat," she postulated.

"We?" questioned Mike.

"Either Marina or myself will join you for this meeting," she informed him. "We will need to develop a plan of attack with the Scrat as well as a means of locating the remaining three bases with your help."

Mike high-fived Wilmer and Margot. "Now we're talking!" he exclaimed.

"Just don't get into any trouble before then," Rebecca advised. Then she turned her attention to Tisch and Margot. "My security team will deliver Antwan to your ship. He's been sedated so I don't expect him to give you any trouble until you get to the pirate haven. I'm counting on the two of you to make sure everyone stays alive and no one draws any unnecessary attention to you."

Tisch assured her that she and Margot would work together to ensure their success. Mike frowned at Wilmer, knowing that the women were putting the cuffs on him, regarding his search and discover missions. Wilmer shrugged at him once again, accepting the fact that it was their show now. Tisch stood and addressed the crew. "We're leaving in an hour. I know you all have a lot to do before we return to Taurus so let's get to it."

Rebecca reminded Mike and Wilmer to drop off the cloaking equipment and wished them well as she departed the cafeteria. "I expect that from Mike, but you Wilmer? I'm surprised," quipped Tisch regarding his omission about the second cloaking system.

"Hey, we earned that equipment," complained Wilmer. "She's lucky we're giving her one system to play with."

Tisch glanced at Mike, expecting a sarcastic remark. Mike smiled and said nothing. That bothered Tisch more than a comment. She worried that he had something else up his sleeve.

After breakfast, they returned to the ship. Sedated, Antwan was delivered to them and placed in a container in the cargo bay for security reasons. The crew started their preparations for take-off, excited to get underway once again.

Mike and Margot went to the galley to discuss their options. Mike took two beers from the cooler and set them down on the table. He sat down, feeling pleased with himself. Margot leaned back in her chair with folded arms. "So, what do we do for an encore?" she inquired coyly.

Mike contemplated their situation and suggested that he and Wilmer should get the cloaking device implemented on the shuttle before they arrived at the pirate haven to deliver Antwan. Margot agreed and offered to help.

Once the *Blue Eagle* departed and was out of range of Archimedes-9, Tisch left the flight deck in search of Mike and Margot. When she arrived in the galley, Margot briefed her on their intentions with the cloaking device.

"What's the urgency?" she asked, curious, and took a beer from the cooler.

"I don't think we should bring the *Blue Eagle* to Murgatroyd's," Mike mentioned. "With the bounty on the ship – and me, it's quite a temptation for pirates."

Tisch considered his words and, to his surprise, agreed. He promised to include her in the plan, especially for their departure, before they arrived at the pirate haven. Tisch offered Wilmer's help in making use of the cloaking system on the shuttle if Mike wanted. He was happy to accept her offer. Content that everything was under control with Mike, Tisch returned to the bridge.

The *Blue Eagle* took a week at full speed to reach Murgatroyd's Oasis. During the trip, Mike and Wilmer completed installation and testing of the cloaking system on his shuttle. They met with Tisch and Margot in the galley to discuss Mike's plans. He requested that Tisch continue on to Taurus, while he and Margot delivered Antwan in the shuttle. Tisch was apprehensive until Mike explained that they would arrive cloaked and deliver Antwan to Korick.

Margot was concerned, as it was a pirate haven and Mike did have a bounty on his head. Mike believed that they were safe so long as the *Blue Eagle* wasn't nearby. The bounty was much higher for both of them together. Tisch agreed, knowing there would likely be a trap waiting for them if her ship appeared.

Mike and Wilmer stuffed Antwan's unconscious body into a peanut oil drum and stowed it inside the shuttle. He and Margot bade the crew farewell and departed from the *Blue Eagle*. With the shuttle cloaked, they hovered outside the docking bays at Murgatroyd's Oasis for hours waiting for a ship to depart. When one of the bay doors opened for a departure, Mike quickly guided the shuttle into the empty bay before the outer doors closed again.

Once they docked and the engines shut down, Mike breathed a sigh of relief. Margot was impressed with the plan so far, but wondered how they'd get out when the time came. The two rolled the drum through the personnel hatch into the main corridor and then used the service elevator to move the drum to the second floor. Mike sought out Korick, the owner of the station but no one had seen him. When they arrived in front of Korick's office, Mike picked the primitive lock and opened the door. They stashed the barrel inside and locked the door once more.

As they descended the stairs on their way to the pub, Mike noticed a small ball above them. It was one of many security probes implemented by Kronos's sentries to monitor for rebel activity. With Kronos' sentries gone now, Korick accessed the system only to identify problems. Mike turned the corner at the bottom of the stairs and was met with a fist to the face that left him stunned. Borath, a half-cyborg assassin hired by Antwan, grabbed him by the neck and slammed him face first into the wall. Margot kicked Borath in the back of the knee several times until he spun and grabbed her by the throat. With incredible strength, he carried the two of them down the stairs to a storage area in the lower level. They struggled but to no avail.

Kellen heard from his peers that Mike was seen at the station and sought him out. He approached the hatch, leading to the ship bays in time to witness Borath taking his friends down the stairs. He panicked at the sight of the assassin and hurried off to find help.

The abandoned room was filled with broken furniture and scaffold pieces. Borath tossed Margot over a scaffold rack into the wall with little effort. She crumbled on top of the rack, barely conscious. He slammed Mike's head into the wall several times and then dropped him in a chair. Mike was dazed and unable to move. Borath tied Mikes hands to the armrests and then picked Margot up once more. She pleaded for him to spare them but he choked her until she nearly passed out. Content that she wasn't a threat, he lifted her over his head and threw her to the ground. Laid out flat with one eye barely open, all Margot could do was watch in pain.

Borath questioned Mike on the *Blue Eagle's* whereabouts. Each time Mike refused to answer, he belted him. Frustrated, Borath saw a box with 6-inch nails and a scaffold hammer on the floor by the door. With a sly grin, he approached Mike and asked once more for the *Blue Eagle's* whereabouts.

"Why do you care?" asked Mike weakly, hoping to stall for a miracle. Borath revealed that he was there to rescue Antwan, while capturing Mike and the *Blue Eagle* for the bounty. He was concerned why Mike was there but the *Blue Eagle* wasn't. Mike forced a smile, angering the cyborg. Borath drove a nail through each of Mike's hands into the armrest. Mike screamed in pain but still refused to answer Borath. Margot was teary-eyed and helpless as she witnessed Mike's torture.

Borath grew impatient and grumbled, "I can't kill you yet, but I can kill your friend." Mike panicked, knowing he would do worse to Margot.

Borath grabbed Margot by the back of the neck and held her against the wall with his back to Mike. He took a ten-inch dagger from a sheath on his belt and held it to Margot's face. "Anything you want to say, Colby, before I remove her pretty face?"

Mike knew that no matter what, Borath would kill her. Borath, with his back to Mike, uttered, "I didn't think so." He cut Margot's face from her ear down to her chin and warned, "I can carve the rest of her face if you don't answer me."

Margot wept and pleaded for Borath to kill her and end her suffering. Mike, in a desperate attempt to save her, stood and dropped backwards, ramming the chair into the floor. When the chair shattered into pieces, Borath released his hold on Margot, letting her drop to the floor.

Mike was free but with his arms still tied to the broken armrests and the nails sticking through them. He rushed at Borath and slammed the two slats against the sides of his head. The nails pierced Borath's ears and penetrated his brain. Borath fell to his knees and groaned in pain. Mike backed away as Borath frantically clutched the sides of his head. He stalked Borath and smashed one of the slats into his face, the nail penetrating his right eye. Borath moaned and attempted to stand. Mike quickly pounced on him and smashed the other eye, rendering him blind. Borath got to his feet briefly and then fell to the ground dead. Mike fell next to him and passed out from the pain.

Korick and Kellen rushed down the stairs and burst into the room. They were shocked to see all three of them covered in blood. Korick summoned help from the corridor at the top of the stairs. Several men rushed to their aid. They carried Mike and Margot up to Korick's office and set them side by side on a table. He sent one of the men to find the doctor.

Kellen tried to comfort them, wiping the blood from their faces with a wet rag but they were unresponsive. Korick saw the drum marked peanut oil and grew curious. He was surprised to find Antwan's body inside it, still unconscious from the drug he was administered prior to departure.

The doctor arrived and did a quick evaluation of the two. He informed Korick that Margot had a damaged larynx and many broken bones, aside from her torn face. When he inspected Mike, he shook his head at Korick. "They're both in really bad shape," he said somberly. "I'll do what I can but we don't have the resources here to help them." He then requested that Korick help him with Mike. The two wrestled with the slats until both nails were removed from Mike's hands.

Mike groaned and became responsive. "Where's Margot?" he mumbled weakly. "Is she okay?" Korick informed him that she was hurt badly but there with him. When Mike reached out for her, Korick placed her hand in Mike's. The doctor and Korick noted with concern that Margot was unresponsive.

The door opened and Marina entered, cloaked as usual to escape detection. She saw them and immediately questioned Korick about what happened. Standing over them with a saddened expression, she listened while he explained their encounter with Borath. Then she turned to him with angst, fearing that they lost Antwan. Korick lifted the cover off the drum and pointed inside. Marina was relieved to see Antwan's limp body.

The doctor stitched Margot's face back together, while the others watched. Marina informed him that they were her most valuable assets and she needed him to save them. He confessed that, other than the stitching, there was little he could do and their prognosis was grim. Marina paced the floor and then asked Korick, "How did they get here? Is the *Blue Eagle* here?"

Korick looked befuddled and replied, "I don't know how they got here. No ships arrived, even for a brief stop."

Marina knelt by Mike and spoke softly into his ear. She questioned him about their ship and that she needed to take them where they could be helped. Mike turned his head slightly and mumbled, "Bay seven. Cloaked."

Marina left them and rushed down to the personnel hatch for Bay 7. She entered what appeared to be an empty bay and walked toward the center. Suddenly she bumped into an invisible object. She ran her hands across the side of the shuttle until she felt the manual release for the hatch.

"That slick son-of-a-bitch," she uttered. Grinning, she hurried back to Korick's office.

Kellen inquired if she found what she was looking for. She nodded and ordered them to move Mike and Margot down to Bay 7. Korick was baffled by her mention of Bay 7 but before he could ask, Marina cautioned him that the less he knew, the better. Korick stepped back and said no more. He and Kellen moved the drum down to bay 4 to Marina's shuttle. There, her crew awaited their human cargo.

Inside Bay 7, Marina located the invisible manual release for the hatch again and pulled on it. The hatch opened and the interior of the shuttle was visible. Marina gestured for them to hurry. After the men set Mike and Margot inside, Marina instructed Kellen to pilot the ship. She searched the panels in the rear of the shuttle until she discovered the teleport module. On the opposite side was another panel with the selector switch for cloak/force fields/off. With her hands on her hips, she was impressed with what Mike accomplished with both the cloaking system and the teleport module.

Kellen immediately started the engines and ran the diagnostics. When he contacted the transport supervisor to open the gates, the man became suspicious. "There's nothing in Bay 7. It's empty." Kellen grew impatient and complained that they'd better fix their cameras then because they were leaving out of Bay 7. The outer bay doors opened and they departed.

Once they were clear, Kellen contacted the transport supervisor and said apologetically, "My bad. I meant Bay 8. Back on maintenance hold, though, so scratch that request." They supervisor laughed it off and verified Bay 8 had a ship docked inside, which was Borath's ship.

The *Blue Eagle* glided toward Taurus at three-quarter speed, awaiting word from Mike's shuttle. Tisch became edgy and pressed Wilmer to make contact with Mike. Shannon and Zenith had already tried several times but with no response.

"I'll bet he's playing games again," complained Tisch. "When will he ever grow up?"

Shannon replied, "The shuttle's receiver is active, Tisch. It's like there's no one on board."

"Could something have gone wrong?" questioned Jonas nervously.

Tisch paced the flight deck with her hands on her hips. "I don't know. Continue on to Taurus at full-speed." She explained to the crew that their primary responsibility was to get Creeg his parts and then discuss with Sara how to proceed. Everyone understood, despite their concern for Mike and Margot.

Marina programmed the teleport module with the coordinates for Taurus. As soon as they were clear of all traffic, she activated it and instructed Kellen to request a docking location. Kellen was amazed at the site of Taurus on the monitor when they appeared to be in the middle of nowhere. "Can I ask where the heck this space station just came from?"

"No!" replied Marina tersely. "Just get us docked and request emergency medical personnel." She turned off the cloaking device and then focused her attention on Mike and Margot. She was proud of what they accomplished but felt guilty for the price they paid. Marina always feared that one day she would encounter Borath and knew she would lose to the cyborg. To know that Mike and Marina took him down in a blood fest was an honor to have two people like them on her side.

When Kellen called in to the transport supervisor, Sara was present at the transport control center and interceded. "Colby, is that you?" she shouted. Kellen responded and explained their situation. Sara rushed to arrange help for them.

Within a short time, Kellen docked the ship. Marina rushed out of the shuttle and directed six med-techs inside. They promptly moved Mike and

Margot onto their vehicle and rushed them to the hospital on the third level. Sarah arrived right behind them with Gemini and Julian shortly after. Kellen completed the shutdown of the shuttle and joined them.

No one spoke as they waited anxiously in the corridor for the med-techs and the doctors to return with any news. Finally, Sara questioned Marina about her identity and purpose. She was stunned to finally meet her. "I need to be briefed on what happened," she informed Marina. "I'm responsible for all security in this sector."

Marina assured her that they had plenty to discuss before she would leave the station. Sara inquired about what happened to Mike and Margot. Marina revealed that, thanks to Mike and Margot's heroics, Antwan was in the alliance's custody and a very dangerous assassin named Borath was terminated.

Julian was stunned by her words. "You said Borath?"

Marina nodded and continued, "The *Blue Eagle* avoided Zim and continued their course. Had they not, Borath and his men would have surely taken control of the ship."

Sara looked baffled by the concern for the assailants. Julian explained that Borath was a cyborg assassin from the planet Polaris. The human portion of him was genetically engineered in a lab. "He is very expensive to hire and never failed…until now," he explained.

"You seem to know a lot about this, Julian," Sara remarked cynically.

"I do," he replied somberly. "Borath came to Aurora during the regime change to 'eliminate' obstacles. When we saw what he could do, we surrendered. That's how I wound up in prison."

Marina revealed to them the details of how they found their two friends and why she chose to bring them to Taurus. She requested they discuss an urgent upcoming matter once the *Blue Eagle* arrives. Gemini inquired as to the success they had in reaching their stops, despite the obstacles.

"They exceeded all our expectations, both commercially and strategically," Marina announced. "Those two in there (Mike and Marina) are by far my most valuable assets and I'll do whatever it takes to save them." Sara was impressed by the praise Marina had, especially for Mike, considering their auspicious beginning.

The doctor emerged from the infirmary and informed them that Margot had brain swelling from head trauma and a shunt was inserted to drain fluid. Her lungs were punctured in three places by broken ribs and were being repaired surgically as they spoke. Mike also had head trauma and a fractured skull. His hands were badly damaged and were also being repaired surgically. The doctor cautioned them that, emotionally, both were likely to suffer severely from their experience - if they survived at all. Marina thanked him and offered any assistance they required. Sara received a message on her transmitter, informing her that the *Blue Eagle* was now docking. She informed the others and departed.

Tisch ordered the crew to unload the cargo while she inquired about Mike and Margot. When Sara intercepted her at the elevator, Tisch questioned her if they heard from Mike. With a grim expression, Sara answered, "He and Margot are here, as is Marina."

"Oh, shit," blurted Tisch. "What did Mike do now?"

They stepped on the elevator and waited anxiously as the doors closed. Then Sara explained, "The two of them may have saved us all from a very bad day."

"I don't understand. Why didn't Mike respond to our calls?" Tisch asked, feeling there was more to the story.

"He couldn't," answered Sara. "Nor could Margot." Tisch feared what she meant and trembled. Sara placed her hand on her arm to calm her, sensing she already expected the worst.

They exited the elevator and approached the Red Room on the seventh floor. The sentries immediately opened the door for them, skipping the security protocol for access. Inside the secure room, Marina, Kellen, Julian and Gemini sat at the table, looking devastated. Tisch entered with Sara and took a seat at the table. Marina immediately briefed them on the condition of Mike and Margot. She related how Borath arrived with a crew to capture Mike and the *Blue Eagle* but failed.

"Shit!" blurted Tisch. "We've all heard the myths about Borath. He's the Grim Reaper of the universe."

"Not anymore," remarked Marina somberly. "Mike killed him."

Gemini inquired, "Did you get the parts for Creeg's ship?"

Tisch affirmed that they did and that they were being offloaded. As if on cue, Creeg arrived and joined them. He was saddened by the news about Mike.

Marina pressed Tisch to reveal what they discovered on the Scrat world. Creeg was surprised when he realized they returned to his worlds without him. Tisch related Mike's suspicions about the Kronos' ships and their attack on the Scrat. She informed them that much of the Scrat military was still intact and led by someone named Gendry. Creeg was ecstatic by the news. Tisch then explained that Gendry had doubts about Mike's information about Creeg and his forces. He was reluctant to commit to joining the alliance, but agreed that if Mike was truthful, he would only take orders from Creeg.

Creeg asked anxiously, "When can we meet with them?"

"Soon," Marina assured him. "We're making plans as we speak."

Wilmer barged into the room and interrupted, "I just heard that Mike and Margot are in critical condition! What happened?" Tisch instructed him to sit and be quiet. Embarrassed, he realized that something serious was being discussed and he interrupted them.

"I believe there is another valuable piece of information here," mentioned Tisch and she nodded to Wilmer. Surprised by his unexpected inclusion in the discussion, he retrieved a note from his pocket and handed it to Creeg. At first, Creeg was baffled by its meaning. Then he realized what it was. "You found the Kronos' base!" he exclaimed.

Marina's eyes widened with joy over the thought of knowing the location of the second of five bases. "Are you sure about this?" she questioned him.

"Absolutely," Wilmer replied. He explained how they extracted the information from the Kronos ships' data bases using his pulse pistol to energize the backup system.

Marina then spoke of the cloaking system on the shuttle. She revealed that there were only two such systems and they were designed for the Federation for two specific deep-space reconnaissance vessels that were believed to be destroyed. She was concerned how Kronos got their hands on them. Creeg surmised, the Scrat were smart enough to isolate where the cannon fire came from and, in a desperate defensive measure, sent their ships toward the two areas to ram them before they destroyed their entire fleet. Uncloaked ships likely followed to ravage the planets' surfaces. He added that the surviving forces were likely part of Asher's invasion force and were away from the planets, awaiting transport by the module through Asher. "Lucky for all of us, that it didn't happen," he remarked cynically.

Marina revealed that one more attack on Taurus was likely, since Antwan surely would make a last desperate attempt to get control of Taurus. Sara expressed her concerns over traitors and depleted resources but was determined not to go down without a fight.

Marina insisted on speaking with Mike before they departed. Once that was done, they would set out on board the *Blue Eagle*. Creeg questioned what Marina's plans were for the Kronos' base. Marina thought the Scrat would appreciate handling it their own way. Creeg appreciated the gesture and assured her that they would. With that, the meeting ended and everyone departed for the hospital level.

When they arrived, the doctors and med-techs had just completed surgeries on Mike and Margot. Marina and Tisch were allowed into the recovery room but were cautioned to let Mike and Margo rest. Zenith, Shannon and Jonas arrived, concerned and anxious to hear what happened. Before Wilmer could speak, Zenith peeked through the doorway and saw Margot. She burst into tears. Shannon and Jonas looked past her. When they saw the line of stitches down Margot's face and the shunt inserted into her skull, they cried on each other's shoulders. Jonas' heart broke to see his sister in that condition.

Marina and Tisch approached Mike and Margot, devastated by the injuries they sustained. Tisch held Mike's arm while Marina held Margot's hand. Tisch commented softly, "We can't even make Borath pay for this. He's already dead."

"I know who is going to pay for this," stated Marina. "Kronos is going to feel my wrath now."

Mike stirred and whispered, "Where's Margot?"

"She's asleep next to you," Marina answered somberly. Tisch was surprised to see tears stream down Marina's cheeks after witnessing her badass act at the pirate haven. "We're all here for the two of you. Get well, my friend," Marina uttered sadly and then left the infirmary.

Tisch squeezed his arm again and then held Margot's hand tightly. "I'll help you get through this, Margot," Tisch whispered between sobs. "I'm here for you no matter what." She rushed out of the recovery room past everyone with tears streaming down her cheeks.

Gemini requested that Wilmer join her for a briefing on new stops for their next trip out. Julian, standing alone, waited until everyone was out of sight. He entered the recovery room and pulled up a chair between Mike and Margot. He placed his hand on each one's leg and spoke to them as if they could hear him. With tears in his eyes, he recalled how Mike helped turn his life around. He also spoke of how he was envious of Mike's courage and his ability to get important things done while under pressure. Then he turned to

Margot and got sentimental. "And you, you little vixen. You did what no one else could do: you got Mike under control." He told her how he admired her courage as well and how she gave Mike what Tisch couldn't. After another tearful pause, he swore to both of them that he would do whatever he could to help them. With nothing more to say, he stood to leave. "Julian, what has Gemini done to you?" Mike mumbled weakly.

Stunned, Julian sat back down and smiled at Mike. Tears streamed down his cheeks. "How do you feel, my friend?" he asked.

Mike closed his eyes and sobbed. "I'm okay, but what about Margot. All I hear is that she's here with me. Is she okay?"

"We don't know yet. We're really concerned about her head trauma."

Mike cried and blurted, "I couldn't protect her and look what happened."

"The two of you took on the baddest son-of-a-bitch in the universe, a bio-engineered cyborg, and killed him," Julian said proudly. "Marina admitted that she feared the day that she might go up against him."

"A lot of good that did," muttered Mike.

Margot opened her eyes slightly and sighed. "Will you two please stop whining?"

Mike tried to sit up and see her but Julian held him down. "Talk but don't move," Julian ordered him. Mike attempted to speak with Margot but she gestured with her hand that she didn't want to. The doctor entered to check on them and was pleased to see both were responsive. He added a sedative to their IVs and warned them that they needed to rest. Julian wished them well and left the room. As soon as they were asleep, the doctor left as well.

Several days elapsed and things returned to normal. Mike and Margot's conditions were upgraded to stable. Mike took medication for migraines and was expected to limit his time on his feet to a few hours a day. Margot required a wheel chair due to breathing issues until her lungs were fully healed. In addition, she had soft casts on her ankles and elbows.

Marina met with Sara, Gemini and Tisch in Gemini's conference room to discuss their plans. Marina had already briefed Sara on the status of the alliance and their plans. She revealed that she needed to return to Murgatroyd's Oasis on Zim, where her ship would rendezvous to pick her up.

Tisch agreed to take Creeg to Archimedes-9 where they would work with Rebecca to meet with the Scrat leadership. They expected to be without Mike and Margot indefinitely and planned to move on without them. Marina requested time with Wilmer to understand the cloaking system as well as what he and Mike planned to do with the teleport module. It had little value to her as she was working with General Lennox of the Space Federation to install portals in key locations to eliminate the need for the module. They all agreed it was too dangerous in the wrong hands, so it needed to be kept a secret.

The door opened and Julian entered, followed by Mike. Julian stepped aside and everyone's jaws dropped. They were stunned to see Mike on his feet. "I should have known you'd all forget about me," Mike quipped.

"Get back to your bed, you fool!" shouted Gemini. "Are you trying to kill yourself?"

"I just wanted a glass of that fine rum you have," he joked.

Everyone shouted in unison, "No!"

"All right, then. My next point is I'm going with Creeg and Margot to meet with the Scrat command," he stated adamantly. "They removed the shunt from Margot and she's responded well."

"Absolutely not!" Tisch exclaimed.

"I gave Gendry my word and I will be there to make sure he knows I held up my end," Mike stated, determined.

Marina considered for a moment, but then replied, "Margot isn't going anywhere in her condition."

Mike stepped aside and Margot appeared in the doorway in her wheel chair. "Mike's right," she said firmly. "We need to be there to show a sign of good faith to Gendry."

Tisch was dead set against it and looked to Marina for support. Marina sighed and shook her head. "It's probably the stupidest thing the two of you could ever do, although Colby has done several other things that rank up there as well. However, you do have a valid point. We need this alliance with the Scrat and Creeg will need to prove his camaraderie with Mike and Margot to the others to earn their trust."

Gemini gestured to Julian for a drink. When he picked up a glass, she shook her head and gestured for a bigger glass. When he picked one, she nodded in approval. He filled it with bourbon and brought it to her.

Marina emphasized that it was critical for the Scrat to succeed if they attack the Kronos base in their sector. With only three bases left, Kronos would be considerably limited in their range of influence.

"What about Taurus?" Gemini inquired. "What if we aren't able to defend it if Empire launches a desperation attack?"

Sara suggested that Creeg leave someone in charge of his ship while he's away and to expect an attack by Empire. "If Creeg's command ship is still here, we should be okay," Sara suggested. "It might be enough to deter them."

"And if it's not?"

"Then we might have a problem. We'll take significant damage, win or lose."

Mike questioned Marina if she had resources to launch an attack on Empire's headquarters before they attack. She admitted that they were light on support in this sector and most of her support had come from Mike's antics. Mike blushed as everyone stared at him, knowing his ego would inflate.

"I need to speak with Korick," Mike declared. "He might be the key to putting away Empire for good." Everyone stared at him, wondering if he lost his mind or if the medication was affecting his logic. Marina agreed, however, to arrange it when they reached the pirate haven.

Mike explained that he had a plan. He recommended that Creeg move twenty of his fighters into some of the bays on Taurus. When repairs on the ship were completed and Empire's ships are deployed, they should move the command ship away before they arrive for a surprise appearance at the right time. His logic was that Empire's freighters will think they have easy pickings when they attack.

"How will they know when Empire deploys their ships?" Marina asked.

"I'll take care of that," Mike assured them. "We got this."

Gemini agreed to provide five bays which were adequate for four fighters each. Creeg liked the plan and would brief his men what was expected, since he wouldn't be there.

Julian stepped to the head of the table and spoke confidently about Mike and Margot. He indicated that their ability to change their plans on the fly were key to their successes and they more than proved their commitment by putting their lives on the line against Borath.

"Then so be it," announced Marina. "We leave as soon as the *Blue Eagle* is ready."

"One more thing," Mike mentioned. "Since I beat Borath, does that make me a bigger badass than you, Marina?" Everyone laughed.

"Don't make me kick your ass again and embarrass you, Colby. You did good, but don't get cocky."

"I'm happy being number two to you, Marina," he confessed. "I learned my lesson." Again, everyone laughed. The meeting ended and they dispersed.

Mike and Margot, with assistance from Kellen, boarded the *Blue Eagle*. Everyone cheered for them as they formed a circle around them. Jonas knelt next to Margot and held her hand, while nestling his head against hers. Zenith emphasized to Mike how worried they were and feared losing both of them.

Tisch mentioned to Mike that, thanks to Kellen, they were able to watch the security footage of their fight with Borath. Mike lowered his head, saddened by the thought of the assault. Zenith complained that no one would tell them what happened or how badly they were injured until much later. Shannon blurted out how brave they were and that she could never do what they did. Wilmer turned away and said nothing. Mike noticed, but understood his feelings. Wilmer was always there for Mike until Margot came along. Now he felt the guilt of wondering if he might have made a difference.

Margot admitted that, whenever she closed her eyes, she felt Borath's knife cutting her face and would wake up in a panic. Mike was concerned by this and feared how long it would last. Then Zenith asked the question everyone wanted to hear. "When will the two of you be joining us again?"

Mike forced a smile and replied, "How about now?" Everyone stared at them as if Mike and Margot were crazy. Mike explained that they needed to rest and would be in their cabin if needed.

Jonas pushed Margot in her wheelchair to a cabin. Mike was escorted by Kellen and walked slowly behind them. Kellen mentioned to Mike how he saw Borath ambush them and when he arrived with help, it was too late. He felt horrible and couldn't speak to either of them until now. Mike assured him that he did all he could. "It was just a shitty situation," he remarked. Then Mike requested that Kellen join him in his meeting with Korick on Zim as it might very well involve him. Curious, Kellen agreed.

When they reached their cabin, the men helped Mike and Margot into their bed. Mike thanked Kellen and Jonas for their help and assured them that he and Margot would be fine. Margot rubbed her hands together nervously, knowing that she'd never get over what happened to them. Shortly after, the two were fast asleep.

Several times Margot cried out in her sleep and Mike would whisper softly to her and calm her. He considered if bringing her was a bad idea, but they both needed each other to get through their ordeal. Eventually Mike got up and went to the shower. He had recurring dizzy spells but at least the medication helped with the migraines.

On the bridge, Shannon and Zenith piloted the ship. Creeg slept for the trip's duration as Scrat could go long periods with and without rest. Jonas took inventory of their medical supplies and staple items. Tisch sat with Marina in the galley and they spoke of their families' pasts, including Tisch's father, John Mallory. After a few beers, Marina retired to her cabin to rest. Tisch remained and considered everything that happened recently. Her heart broke for the pain that Mike and Margot suffered.

Zenith was startled when an alarm came in on the alarm annunciator panel for Emergency Airlock Access. "Shit!" she uttered. "That can't be good."

Shannon called Tisch on the intercom and informed her of the unusual alarm. The emergency airlock is the only airlock that can be used to exit the ship while in space. With an interior and exterior hatch, both are interlocked to prevent a breech of atmosphere. Tisch had a horrible feeling and rushed to the airlock on the lower-level port side of the ship, just behind the cargo bay. When she arrived, Margot was inside the airlock with her hand on the exterior hatch release lever. With tears streaming down her cheeks, she stared out the thick plated glass at the stars.

Tisch pleaded with her through the speaker not to do anything rash. Margot blurted, "I can't take it anymore! The nightmares won't stop."

Tisch begged her to let her help her but to no avail. She reminded Margot how Mike would be destroyed if she killed herself. Margot, with her hand still on the lever, dropped to her knees, distraught. "I can't stand it anymore, Tisch," she cried. "I can't."

When Mike returned from the shower, he panicked when he arrived at an empty cabin. He paged Zenith and asked if Margot was there. She informed him about the alarm and that Tisch was looking into it. Mike rushed down to the emergency airlock where Tisch tried to coerce Margot to come out. Tisch warned him to choose his words carefully with Margot.

Mike scanned the interior hatch and pulled two wires from a limit switch mounted above the door. "What the hell are you doing?" shouted Tisch.

"It's an interlock," he replied. "The inner hatch won't open if the outer hatch handle is off the normal position."

"So now what?"

Mike operated the inner hatch and opened it. "Close this hatch immediately," he instructed Tisch. "If you don't and she pulls the lever all the way, you know what happens to your ship." Tisch nodded, fearing what might happen to all of them.

The hatch closed behind him and he approached Margot. She turned to him and released the handle. He lifted her in his arms and asked calmly, "You were going to leave me without saying goodbye?"

"I want to die, Mike," she said tearfully. "I can't take it anymore."

Mike thought for a moment and then replied, "Then we'll die together."

Margot was baffled by his response. This isn't what she expected to hear – no argument, no conflict. "You can't die," she told Mike. "You are too important."

Mike reached for the lever to the outer hatch and pulled it halfway. "If you don't want to live, then I don't want to live without you. Let's do this."

Tisch was mortified as she watched the monitor. She wanted to scream out to them but she trusted Mike. Margot shook her head at him and confessed, "You don't understand. I'm losing my mind right now. I feel the stitches in my face. I'll never look normal. I keep reliving the moment when that psycho cut my face. I just can't live with that anymore."

Mike kissed her gently and hugged her. "Neither can I," he said somberly. "I failed to protect you. I never felt so helpless as when Borath did that to you. I lost my mind and went nuts. That's how I broke free of the chair and stabbed him with the nails. That was insanity you saw."

Margot looked surprised by his revelation. "How do feel about it now?" she asked.

"Like shit," he admitted. "I lost control of the situation and it almost got us both killed. I have to live with that every day for the rest of my life. I'm tired of fighting bad guys, Margot. I'm... I'm just tired. Somedays death seems like a good idea but it's permanent." Margot reached for his hand and took it off the lever. The two embraced.

Margot knew that there was something strong between them but she couldn't remember what. Obviously, Mike cared about her a lot and what he revealed made their relationship sound like love. She recalled the battle with Borath but nothing before it. Perhaps, she wondered, her memory was gone and with it, a beautiful relationship. Tears streamed down her cheeks and she felt lost.

Outside the hatch, Tisch breathed a sigh of relief. Unaware of their conversation, she assumed everything was okay. She had no idea how Mike really felt. When they returned to the cabin, Tisch requested that Mike let her spend some time with Margot. Reluctantly, Mike agreed and left. On his way past the galley, Marina intercepted him. "What the hell happened? Is Margot okay?"

Mike shrugged his shoulders and replied, "For now." He continued past her and went to the galley. Marina followed and sat with him. "If we're going to have an intervention," he kidded, "then we're going to need something stronger than beer." He unlocked the cabinet and returned with a bottle of rum and two glasses. He and Marina discussed their pasts and Margot's current dilemma for over two hours. They felt each other's pain and understood what Margot was dealing with. Mike suggested that the medical technology used on Archimedes-9 might be able to help Margot if she can keep it together until then. When he held up the empty bottle, he muttered disappointedly, "I guess this session is over, doctor."

Marina chuckled and hugged him. "Don't give up on Margot. She's strong and she's very important to me."

"She's special to me as well," Mike replied somberly. "I don't want to lose her. She and I are the perfect couple, in love and in war."

Marina giggled at his words and paused at the hatch. "You want to tell me what's going on with Korick?" she asked.

"Nah, not yet, "answered Mike. "Besides, you'd never believe me."

"You're full of surprises, Colby."

"As are you, Marina," he responded playfully. Marina departed, leaving Mike alone.

Tisch sat with Margot and revealed how she suffered since witnessing her father's death. Margot was amazed to learn how it inhibited her from having a serious relationship, especially with Mike. Tisch always used the ship and crew as an excuse, but it was her father's murder that haunted her. She mentioned how she hoped to one day avenge his death by Kronos' operatives and wondered if it would bring her relief. Margot questioned her about contemplating suicide and if she ever considered it at any time in her life. "On several occasions," replied Tisch somberly. "Geezer understood me. Whenever I was on the brink, he always brought me back."

"Do you regret not going through with it?" Margot asked humbly.

"Not at all. That shadow over me is a temporary thing that passes. It comes back but the good things I've experienced outweigh the bad." She explained to Margot how special she must be for Mike to trust her after what Gemini did to him and how she ended her relationship with him.

"Does it get easier?" asked Margot.

"I don't know," answered Tisch. "I just take one day at a time and make the best of it."

"What was my relationship with Mike?" Margot asked, embarrassed.

Tisch looked surprised by her question. "What do you mean?"

Margot struggled to find the right words and then explained, "There's a lot I don't remember. I went along with the conversations we had but I don't remember much about us."

Tisch was stunned. "Memory loss could be a short-term thing," she explained. "Let's see what happens."

"Please don't tell him," pleaded Margot. "I need time to figure this out without hurting him."

Tisch hugged Margot and promised to be there for her anytime she needed someone to talk to. Margot promised to try and deal with her nightmares.

CHAPTER 7

DECISIONS

On board the *Blue Eagle*, Mike and Margot shared a cabin and rested until they approached the pirate haven. Several times, Margot awoke, screaming and startled Mike. He comforted her until she calmed down and slept again. He was concerned about the frequency of the panic attacks and wondered if it would affect their ability to accomplish the mission.

Marina stopped in and informed Mike that Korick would meet with them when they arrived. She warned Mike once more that he'd better take care of her girl, Margot – and himself as well. Mike was flattered that she exhibited concern for him. Marina then explained that once the plan is set in motion and the Scrat defeat Kronos at their base, then Mike and Margot were to take a long vacation. Margot said little but smiled at the idea.

Mike and Kellen moved Margot and her wheel chair into the shuttle in preparation for their visit to Murgatroyd's Oasis. Marina and Creeg joined them and closed the hatch.

The trip was quiet, which concerned Marina. She attempted to speak with Margot about what she and Mike accomplished but Margot gave vague answers. Finally, Marina questioned her about her memory and if it would affect their mission. Margot explained that she was good going forward. She just couldn't remember the past. Marina urged her to be patient and to trust Mike. Margot inquired about their relationship, both as partners and as lovers. Marina admitted that she knew they were a dynamic team and saved each other's lives on more than one occasion. She revealed that she could tell they were in love, but her time spent with them was limited so she was short on details. Then she recommended that Margot have this discussion with Mike. Margot promised she would try when they had a chance. Right now, she was still weak and needed time to heal. The two hugged and then Marina left.

Later, Margot stepped onto the flight deck and requested that Mike meet her in their cabin. Concerned that something was wrong, he hurried after her. Inside the cabin, the two sat next to each other on the bed. Margot admitted to Mike that she was having memory issues but she was still a functional and reliable partner. Mike was relieved to know that there was a logical reason for her vagueness.

"After all the discussions I've had with everyone about Kronos and Empire, I have a plan of my own."

"And I am anxious to hear it," Mike replied.

"First, I have to know something," she informed him. Curious, Mike waited for her to speak. She surprised him with a passionate kiss. Then they embraced and lay across the bed. When they finished, Margot smiled at him and commented, "I can tell there is a lot between us. I'll find a way to remember what it was."

"Just don't give up on me," Mike requested and kissed her again.

The two discussed Margot's plan until she tired. Mike urged her to rest and he returned to the flight deck. Margot was pleased that Mike understood her memory issue.

On the flight deck, Mike and Kellen had several discussions about how the pirates did business and if they could be incorporated into a legal arrangement if the conditions were favorable. Mike revealed that there was great opportunity in the long-distance hauling business, especially if the Federation installed portals at key locations. Then Kellen surprised him and inquired about Margot.

Mike related how concerned he was for her health and how he felt like he failed her. Kellen reminded him that, in their business, this was always a possibility. He then commented that they survived and Borath didn't. That, in itself was a miracle. Mike admitted that he was looking forward to getting out of this mercenary/rebel business and living a normal life.

Kellen burst into laughter and replied, "You can never walk away from what you are. There will always be someone or something to pull you back in."

Mike feared he was right. There would always be someone else out there to piss him off. Unfortunately, Margot was affected by his decisions. Then Mike mentioned that Margot didn't seem right. He pointed out how she acted strange when he spoke with her. Kellen grew curious and inquired how.

"She doesn't remember important things about us," he answered, somewhat embarrassed. "I don't want to ask her about us and then find out I made things worse."

"The best thing you can do is give her space but be there for her," Kellen recommended.

They approached Zim and received permission to dock at Murgatroyd's Oasis. Kellen piloted the shuttle into the designated bay and docked. The hatch opened and they prepared to disembark.

Margot insisted on standing out of pride and limped off the shuttle without her wheelchair. Mike placed his arm around her waist and urged her to take it easy. Marina cringed, watching the two of them struggling, beaten but still pressing forward out of a sense of duty. Kellen joined Mike in helping Margot off the shuttle. Marina admired the way everyone respected Mike and Margot. That can only be earned, not given.

Korick greeted them at the personnel hatch to the bay and was pleased to see them. They proceeded to the elevator and then to his office. In anticipation of their meeting, he arranged for a table and several chairs to be set up. When everyone was seated, Korick commented, "Knowing you, Colby, this ought to be really interesting. What can I do for you?"

Mike made his first request and asked if Korick could provide someone to monitor Empire's headquarters and let them know when they launch their freighters toward Taurus. Korick questioned why one of Taurus' security people couldn't handle it. Mike smiled at him and asked if he ever considered expanding his business beyond Murgatroyd's Oasis. Amused by the question, Korick countered as to where he might expand to.

Marina suddenly realized what Mike was getting at. She glanced at Margot, wondering if she was part of this. Margot cast a sly smile at her. Marina was pleased that her most valuable assets may have come up with yet another game-changing ploy against Kronos.

Mike explained that there was a plan in place to defend Taurus but he had a better one that would give Korick and his men possession of Empire headquarters as either a new or a second pirate haven. Now he had Korick's attention. Korick inquired as to why Taurus security or GSS would allow pirates to occupy a base that they could control themselves. Mike stood and paced around the table, beaming. "And now for the punchline," he announced. "I want you and your men to send ten armed ships to Empire after they launch their force to Taurus. Then you'll send the remainder to ambush Empire's ships from behind after they start their attack on Taurus."

Korick laughed at the idea and questioned why he would do this. Mike revealed that the ambush they have for Empire was enough to handle the attacking force but Korick's presence in support of them would give him credibility in possessing Empire's base. Mike assured him that he and Marina would back him up in regards to GSS and Taurus.

"Think of your ships as an insurance policy that Taurus is victorious. Minimal casualties, if any, and you look like heroes supporting the alliance and Taurus. Korick turned his attention to Margot. "Isn't there something you can do at night to occupy his mind? He's insane!" Margot shrugged her shoulders at him. Marina burst into laughter, much to everyone's surprise. No one had seen her laugh before. Korick turned his attention back to Mike and replied, "I love it. So long as I have both your assurance and Marina's that you'll back me in taking ownership of Empire's base."

"You have my word," Marina assured him, "but I have one demand that must be met."

Mike and Korick were both curious as neither expected Marina to intervene in their discussion. "I want you and your men to pledge your loyalty to the alliance and support us if needed."

"What's this 'if needed'?" countered Korick. "We aren't rent-a-cops, you know."

"Your only responsibility is to assist if needed in defeating Kronos. After that, you are released from your obligation."

Mike suggested that he employ Kellen to maintain the current pirate haven for those who aren't comfortable trusting the Federation or GSS. Korick considered the idea and then asked Kellen what he thought.

"Damn! I didn't know I was part of this negotiation!" he blurted. "Of course, I'd love to do it."

Korick stood and stared for a long moment at each of them with a somber expression. "I believe we have a deal," he replied and burst into laughter. Kellen leaped up and shook his hand.

Mike continued, "There's one more thing."

Korick quipped, "I knew this was too easy." He took his seat again and waited, curious.

"Borath's body," Mike announced. "I want it."

"What?" blurted Korick, shocked by the request. Margot turned toward Mike and glared at him. Marina and Kellen were speechless.

"I may need our dead cyborg friend for leverage in a future endeavor," Mike revealed. "It's personal."

Korick considered his request for a moment and then responded, "I thought about selling him to the Federation. General Lennox has a keen interest in cyborg technology."

Marina interjected, "I'm sure Lennox won't mind if it's at my request. We're pretty tight."

Mike was surprised that Marina would back his request. He thanked her and then waited for Korick's decision. "Well, since you are offering me an opportunity to turn an Empire base into a pirate haven, I'd be hard-pressed to say no. I would like to get that dead bastard off my station though. He gives me the creeps."

"Copy that," Margot remarked. "I'm not a fan of this so I hope it's worthwhile, Mike."

Mike promised her that it would help solve a big problem for both of them. With no further issues to discuss, the meeting ended. Korick mentioned to Mike how his initial opinion of him had changed drastically. Mike remarked that he's heard that a lot lately. Korick then assured him that they would make contact when Empire launched their force toward Taurus and they would be there to back them up during an attack as well. Mike instructed Korick to have his man contact Sara on Taurus when the time comes. They shook hands and Korick left the room.

Marina complimented Mike on one hell of a plan and that he made a wise choice in requesting Borath's corpse, although she didn't say why. She admitted to being surprised by the whole thing.

"Will we meet again?" Mike asked, curious.

"I'm sure we will," Marina replied pleasantly. "I'll be checking in to make sure you're taking care of Margot – and to see what you screwed up next."

"Don't worry. Whatever it is, it'll be interesting," he joked.

"I'm sure it will," she said and then hesitated.

Mike noticed and commented, "Looks like you forgot to say something."

"Yes, and no," she answered reluctantly. "I know someone who might be able to help Margot with her nightmares. Dr. Lowell on Sargassa in the Nigus star system. She helped to develop a machine that saved my father's life. Unfortunately, it also had to something to do with his death."

Mike grew hopeful that there was a chance to heal Margot. "Thank you, Marina," he replied appreciatively. "I owe you."

"No, you don't," she responded. "Just keep her safe – and yourself as well." Marina departed, feeling like it would be the last time they'd meet.

Kellen stood next to Mike and remarked, "I'm speechless. Where the hell did you come up with a plan like this?"

Mike pointed to Margot. "It's all her." Margot smiled for the first time in a while and looked away shyly.

Kellen shook his head at them and quipped, "You two need to get laid. Who thinks of this kind of stuff at night?" Margot blushed, remembering that she kept hearing that.

"Who says it was at night?" kidded Mike.

"Well, congratulations. I'm still amazed."

Mike suggested they collect Borath's body so he can get back to the ship before Tisch threw a fit again. Kellen chuckled, knowing that Tisch was a control freak when it came to Mike.

Mike piloted the shuttle while Margot rested in the copilot's seat. Margot hadn't spoken much since the assault but now was more quiet than usual. He asked her how she felt and what she was thinking but she just shrugged her shoulders and stared ahead. Mike suspected it had something to do with Borath's frozen corpse on board the shuttle. Even he wondered if it was a good idea. There was no reason for it, just a hunch that the cyborg's technology might be leverage for something useful.

The shuttle docked in the cargo bay of the *Blue Eagle*. Wilmer and Tisch waited anxiously to hear about Mike's meeting. Mike helped Margot off the shuttle and into her wheelchair. Margot was drained of strength and needed rest. They walked with Mike as he pushed Margot back to their cabin. Mike was reluctant to share details of the meeting and requested that they just focus on Archimedes-9 and what needed to be done.

Tisch grew more concerned as Mike now seemed as distant as Margot from them. Mike was usually predictable but now she feared that he suffered depression like Margot. When Margot was settled in her cabin, Tisch stayed with her until she was asleep. Mike asked Wilmer to join him in the galley to discuss an idea. Wilmer was glad that Mike asked him for his advice on something. They hadn't spent time together in a while and he missed their friendship.

Mike revealed that he had Borath's frozen body in a cryogenic chamber on board the shuttle. Wilmer was stunned, wondering what Mike could possibly have in mind. Wilmer wondered aloud, "Don't you find it strange that Archimedes-9 had advanced equipment for grafting and for bone, tissue and organ healing? After all, Archimedes-9 is a distant facility out of the mainstream of trade."

"The answer is at a medical facility on Sargassa in the Nigus star system," answered Mike. "Can you find out how to get there?"

Wilmer thought about it for a moment and then questioned if Mike believed the manufacturer had other capabilities. Mike explained that

Margot's issue was mental and couldn't be repaired with the equipment used to heal him after he was exposed to space in a damaged environmental suit. While the idea had merit, Wilmer confessed that it was likely a long shot. Mike asked him to keep it between them in case they need to make a side trip before the Scrat meeting. Mike impressed upon him the urgency for Margot and how he feared for her life.

Tisch entered and pressed Mike for any ideas to help Margot. Mike mentioned the equipment on Archimedes-9 but nothing more. Tisch emphasized that she was there to help both of them if they needed anything. Wilmer took three beers out of the cooler and set them down.

"Things are going to get very complicated before we get out of this," Mike remarked.

"I guess you got your wish, Mike," complained Tisch. "We're in the middle of this war now."

Mike sipped from his beer and confessed, "Yeah, but I'm tired of fighting. I can't wait to get out of this and go back to what we were meant to do."

"And that is...?" questioned Tisch, curious.

"Setting up new trade routes. Going to new places and moving cargo."

Wilmer nearly choked on his beer over Mike's comment. Tisch stared at him in disbelief. "Are you serious? The Great Warrior Mike Colby wants to retire from war?"

"I do," he replied solemnly. "I realize I can't fix everyone's problems and I should stop trying."

Tisch moved behind him and hugged him. "I'm proud of you." She finished her beer and tossed it in the container. Pausing at the hatch, she asked, "How much of this has to do with Margot?"

Mike rubbed his eyes painfully and then opened up to them. "Margot would follow me into hell to battle the devil himself. She won't want to do it but she will for me. I would do this for her."

Pleased by his response, she left them. Wilmer reached across the table and took Mike's arm. "You know I have followed you into hell already and we made it back," Wilmer reminded him. "I'm your partner and your best friend. Margot is important to you but don't forget about your other friends." Wilmer finished his beer and tossed the bottle into the container. "Let me know whatever you need me to do and I'll be there."

"I might take you up on that very shortly," Mike joked.

"I suspected as much," quipped Wilmer and he left the galley.

Mike thought about the upcoming mission and regretted taking it this far. He realized that he should have let the alliance run the war instead of placing himself and his friends in the middle of it. When he finished his beer, he visited the bridge and spent time with the crew. He thanked them for their concerns and promised them that they would soon be out of the war business and go back to being boring space truckers like the family they used to be. He humbly asked them to bear with him through this next mission and then he was done with Kronos and the alliance. Everyone looked relieved after seeing what Borath did to him and Margot. He announced that Tisch was aware of his intentions and welcomed them. Tisch nodded to them, affirming Mike's remarks. They embraced him, one at a time, and pledged their loyalty to him as well as Tisch. She wiped a tear from her eye as she realized how much they all matured as a result of Mike's ambitions and were, as Mike said, a family.

Mike returned to the cabin where Margot slept. She was restless and moaned several times. He admired her for her courage and still hurt inside for not protecting her. Margot opened her eyes in a panic and gasped. "I'm here, Margot," he said softly and sat on the edge of the bed.

Margot burst into tears. "It's the same nightmare every time, Mike. I can't stop it!"

"I have an idea that might help but you have to hang in there for a little while."

"Is there a chance it will stop the nightmares?" she asked, hopeful.

"It could. There's a lot of ifs to it but I am optimistic." He then related what he told the others about his intentions. Margot was relieved and took his hands in hers. She fell back to sleep, exhausted.

Tisch met with Mike and Wilmer in the galley at his request. He revealed that he wanted to meet with the manufacturer of the medical equipment and would need a few days to do so. As a result, he asked Tisch to allow them to transport ahead to Archimedes-9 so he can make contact with them. Tisch questioned him about the viability of his plan and soon realized it was a long shot. Knowing it might be the last chance to save Margot, she agreed.

Wilmer programmed the teleport module in the shuttle to transport both ships ahead to Archimedes-9. Tisch briefed the crew and instructed Shannon to notify the transport supervisor on Archimedes-9 when they arrive for a location. Creeg entered the flight deck, fresh from his long sleep. Mike informed him of their plans and what effect it had on their meeting with the Scrat. Creeg was agreeable and supported them in helping their friend.

The *Blue Eagle* arrived on Archimedes-9 well ahead of schedule. Rebecca was on hand to greet them, but was concerned that they exposed the teleport technology in doing so. Mike informed her that Margot's health was more important than the Scrat meeting. Tisch suggested to Mike that he back off until they established their plan of action. Rebecca informed them that she spoke with Marina and was aware that there might be some – wrinkles.

Creeg exited the ship and was introduced to Rebecca. She was excited to meet him in person and expressed her hope that they succeed in their endeavor against Kronos. She also mentioned that she wanted peace with the Scrat and would work with them in any way to achieve that. Creeg appreciated her interest in their future.

Rebecca suggested that they move their discussion to a more secure area alone. Tisch was surprised why they were excluded and questioned her. Rebecca instructed her to take care of Margot first. "Mike will know what needs to be done," she said confidently and then left with Creeg.

"Well, I guess our mission just got Shanghaied," complained Tisch.

"I'm good with it," remarked Mike pleasantly. "Wilmer will have coordinates for our destination shortly." Tisch stared at him, knowing that he had something up his sleeve all along. Mike placed his hand on her shoulder and explained that Rebecca's reaction was the final piece of the plan.

"So, what do we do now?" Tisch questioned. "It seems that you are in charge, once more."

"It'll be the last time, I promise you," he said, seemingly relieved. Tisch noticed and was happy to bring this to an end – a happy end.

They boarded the *Blue Eagle* and met with Wilmer on the bridge. Wilmer and Shannon identified the location of Sargassa on the outer edge of the Nigus system. Mike recommended that they teleport since they had no idea what they would encounter along the way and their time was limited. Again, Tisch was supportive and agreed. Mike hugged her in an awkward moment of appreciation and departed the bridge.

Wilmer worked with Tisch to coordinate their arrival on Sargassa. They circled the planet, unsure of what to look for. Mike and Margot joined them in determining a place to land. They scanned a snow-covered surface for hours before spotting an abandoned facility with a landing pad on the roof. Its communications equipment on top of the facility appeared damaged. They agreed that it was the best place to start from. Zenith landed the *Blue Eagle* on the landing pad and shut down the engines.

"It looks abandoned," Tisch remarked as they watched the monitor.

"I'll go out and look around," Mike commented and then grumbled, "This might have been a waste of time." Margot insisted on joining him, while Wilmer offered to inspect the communications equipment on the roof in case they needed it.

Mike and Margot entered the control center and were disappointed. Other than blown-out windows and snow-covered controls, there was nothing unusual to note. They forced open a manual door that led to a long hallway. With the door closed, it was significantly warmer, arousing Mike's curiosity. The two of them reached an elevator and a stairwell at the end of the hall. The elevator had no power so they opened the door and took the stairwell down.

The temperature was much higher and Mike grew more interested in where the heat was generated from. Margot urged Mike not to get his hopes up and stated that she had no expectations for this visit. Mike stopped and pressed her against the wall. He kissed her and held her tight. "What's that for?" she asked, surprised by his affection.

"You mean so much to me," he replied. "I can't live without you." She appreciated his kind words, but knew they meant nothing when it came to her future. There was no way she would survive with the nightmares, even sedated.

When they reached the bottom of the stairs, both were sweating profusely. "Damn, I'm out of shape," complained Mike.

"I don't think this facility is abandoned after all," commented Margot. "Someone's operating out of here."

They paused at the door and glanced at each other. Mike pushed the crash bar and pushed the door open. Before he could enter, a tall alien woman with a greenish tint to her raised cheeks intercepted them and stood face to face with him. "You are trespassing on my facility," she warned. Mike and Margot were both taken aback by her presence, not expecting to encounter anyone.

"We're looking for Dr. Lowell," Mike informed her. "Can you help us?"

The woman stared them down for several seconds and then countered, "What do you want with her?"

Mike explained their situation and that Marina suggested that she might be able to help them. He also mentioned that her expertise in developing the equipment on Archimedes-9 was used to save him. That convinced him that she was an expert in healing.

The woman stepped back and invited them in. She introduced herself as Dr. Sima Lowell and asked why anyone took an interest in her facility now, after abandoning her for the last three years. Mike was curious and asked her to explain further. She revealed that her planet suffered a cataclysmic event when a meteor struck it and sent them into a short ice age. No one came to rescue them or offer assistance. Now that the ice receded, she had guests once more.

Mike apologized for their neglect and postulated that the war may have been responsible for that. Unaware of Kronos' aggressions in the area, Sima questioned Mike on what she missed over the last three years with the communications equipment being out of service.

Margot grew impatient and interceded with questions about Sima's work. Sensing that she was the one who needed help, she discussed Margot's reason for coming. After much discussion, she surmised that the problem was treatable but her services would not be cheap.

Mike questioned why that was an issue. Sima explained that she had two remaining fuel rods to power her generator, enough to last another month. After that, she would likely die from the cold. Margot was curious about her work and wanted to know why she didn't flee the planet for a safer location. Sima explained how she gathered much of the wildlife into captivity and attempted to maintain them in cryostasis until the planet returned to its once lush state. They were amazed at her commitment to her 'pets' and was willing to die with them.

Sima then asked what Mike had to trade in return for her services to help Margot. Unsure of what had value to her, he offered to help in whatever way he could, but she would have to tell him what she needed. Mike suggested supplies and materials to restore her control room. He also mentioned that he could regenerate the fuel rods for her generator if that helped. She grew interested over the possibility of replenishing the rods and then questioned the *Blue Eagle's* role in space travel. Margot, feeling left out, took the lead in the discussion and explained that they were space truckers and doing reconnaissance to establish long-distance shipping from Taurus and/or Archimedes-9 to other parts of the galaxy.

Sima then inquired as to what happened to Margot that left her with horrific nightmares on a regular basis. Margot related the story of the cyborg called Borath and how he nearly killed them.

Sima informed them that several ships entered the area a while ago and one landed at her facility. The men were mercenaries and took her technicians prisoner. Their leader, a business man named Klingman had a proposition for her. If she could restore his brother's missing limbs and make him whole, he would return her people to her.

Mike and Margot were stunned when they heard Klingman's name. Sima then revealed that the equipment wasn't ready, but he insisted, thinking she had lied to him. The brother's limbs were regenerated but looked more like fins and had no fingers or toes. Livid, he destroyed much of her facility and radio equipment, leaving her stranded with no way to get help.

"But the equipment on Archimedes-9 worked well," he reminded her. "What happened?"

Sima chuckled at him. "I knew they wouldn't return my technicians to me. I also suspected they would kill me once they got what they wanted. I used an original prototype that I knew was defective. Imagine what dinner is like for that family." The three of them laughed. "So, why would you fight a cyborg in the first place?" Sima asked. "That seems pretty foolish."

Mike explained that they weren't aware he was a cyborg until much later. Sima was impressed that a cyborg could be human enough as to fool everyone like that. She surprised them and asked, "Can you get me his corpse?"

Margot was shocked by her request and wondered if Mike already knew something that convinced him to obtain Borath's corpse. Mike inquired innocently, "Why would you want that?"

Sima related how she placed her husband in cryostasis when his organs began failing. Without a donor or stem cells, death was inevitable. She pointed out that a woman can get really lonely in a place like that.

Mike glanced at Margot and she nodded back. She understood now what Mike's intentions were. Mike inquired if the corpse of Borath would be sufficient for her services to help Margot. Sima agreed that it was acceptable but she wanted assurance that she wouldn't be forgotten again. She needed supplies and she had the new medical equipment she manufactured that was never picked up for trade.

Mike offered to take her to inspect the state of Borath's corpse. Sima promised that, if the corpse was salvageable, she would do an immediate analysis of Margot's brain and determine the course of action. Mike was uneasy about it but Margot promptly agreed to it.

Sima then mentioned that she performed the same procedure on Klingman's amputee brother for his nightmares that she would use on Margot. Mike and Margot glanced at each other uneasily until Sima informed them that it was successful. She joked that the man now had the full capability to know how messed up he was. "What a punishment?" she kidded. After she turned on the power for the elevator, the three of them left the lower level for the *Blue Eagle*.

On board the *Blue Eagle*, Tisch and the crew were anxious to meet Sima and were surprised to see that, even though she looked human, her skin tone and facial structure indicated she was of an alien race. Tisch glanced at Mike as they passed her on the way to the cargo bay. He nodded that everything was okay. She noticed that Margot was more upbeat than usual and was encouraged.

On board the shuttle, Sima was impressed that Borath's corpse was in good condition in its state of cryostasis. Her eyes were wide with joy as she circled the coffin-like chamber and ran her fingers across it. Mike and Margot were uneasy, watching her examine the body through the special glass cover. "Well?" Mike inquired. "Do we have a deal?"

Sima stood in front of Mike and grinned. "Oh, yes, we have a deal. This specimen is perfect."

"When do we start?" asked Margot anxiously.

"Right now, if you like," answered Sima. "My other requests regarding trade are minor compared to this and can be discussed later."

The three of them exited the shuttle and traversed the ship to the bridge. Mike asked Tisch to have the crew move the cryochamber off the ship and into the abandoned control room. Everyone helped to move Borath's body from the shuttle and then off the ship. From there, Mike and Wilmer pushed it into the facility and onto the elevator.

Once the cryochamber was stored in the lower level, Sima was ready to begin. She led Margot into a glass booth on the lower level, ventilated by small fans and HEPA filters. Margot lay on a table and waited anxiously. Mike sat in a chair, tense over the possibility that things could get significantly worse. After giving Margot a sedative through an IV solution, Sima maneuvered a large machine, resembling an X-ray machine over her head. The machine hummed for several minutes.

Sima explained to Mike that there are many pulse signals in the neural network that carry memories. When the memories are accessed, they are reenergized by the network. When the memories are forgotten over time, the network ignores them and the pulses in that region weaken. In Margot's case, there is likely damage to that part of the network from the moment in time that her nightmare originated. As a result, the pulse signal generated from her head trauma is caught in one of the legs. Bouncing like a ping-pong ball, the memory is re-energized over and over as the network thinks it is being accessed. When the machine stopped, Sima maneuvered it away from the table and studied the image on the machine's display. "There is minor scar tissue that's pressuring a portion of the brain," she explained to them. "It's one of the better areas for a procedure like this to be performed."

"What are the risks?" Mike asked, uneasy about this procedure.

"For this region of the brain, possible loss of sensation in some parts of the body and possible loss of some memory. I'll be honest with you. It is a complex procedure but one I am comfortable with."

Mike looked to Margot for her thoughts. She nodded to him and consented for Sima to proceed. Sima suggested Mike find something to do as it would be a while before Margot awakens and they can verify if the procedure was a success. Mike waited for Margot to go under from the sedative in the plastic bag, feeding her arm intravenously. He informed Sima that he would take the spent fuel cells to the *Blue Eagle* and begin their regeneration.

From the abandoned control room, Jonas helped Mike carry the fuel cells into the *Blue Eagle* and install them inside the regenerator. He questioned Mike about Margot's condition and their relationship. Mike related how brave she was and adept at holding her own in critical situations. He also mentioned that he no longer wanted to put her at risk. The two of them had done more than enough to help the alliance and it was time to walk away. Jonas, optimistic but not adventurous like his sister, was relieved to hear that from Mike.

Wilmer joined them and announced that the communications system was repaired and Sima would be able to transmit and receive messages again. Mike thanked both men for their help and suggested they return to the ship.

Tisch stood alone on the roof of the building and stared out at the white mountains. Everything looked so peaceful considering the planet suffered a catastrophic event when a large meteorite crashed into it several years back. While staring at the clouds over the peaks, she thought about her father and what he would think about how far she came with the *Blue Eagle*. A chilly breeze blew and convinced her to end her quiet meditation. When she boarded the ship, she found everyone gathered around Shannon's station. Curious, she approached and drew their attention. "What's going on?" she asked.

Shannon pointed out that there were seventeen colonies in the star system. Mike commented that it might be fun to explore new opportunities on those colonies when they finished with Rebecca and Creeg. Tisch liked the idea and, barring any new orders, agreed they should pursue them.

Evening approached and Mike grew antsy. Jonas and the women hung out in the galley, anxiously awaiting news of Margot's procedure. Jonas and Zenith had developed a relationship and Shannon enjoyed teasing them about it. Tisch and Wilmer remained on the bridge, searching for additional information on the Nigus star system. Unfortunately, there was little to be found. Mike informed them that he was going into the facility to check on Sima's progress.

When Mike arrived on the lower level, he heard voices and became excited. He hurried into the lab where he found Margot sitting upright. Sima questioned her and tested her reflexes. Mike approached anxiously and stood by Margot. It was then that his heart broke. "Who are you?" Margot asked pleasantly.

Sima explained that the procedure was successful and the nightmares should be gone. Her memory loss may have been expanded but there was no way to know for sure if it was temporary. Until the inflammation went down and her brain activity returned to normal, they could only wait. Mike sat next to Margot and reminded her who he was. He explained what happened to her and how he brought her there to heal.

Margot felt the stitches in her face and panicked. "Who did this to me?" she cried. Mike told her that there was an accident and it would heal.

Sima revealed that she had skin grafting machines as well as regenerating units that never shipped, just like those on Archimedes-9. She offered to place Margot in the grafting unit and heal her face. Mike convinced Margot that it was a good idea and he knew from experience that it worked. The process didn't take long and, when it was finished, Margot's face was healed.

Mike thanked Sima and invited her to dine with them on board the *Blue Eagle*. He feared that Margot might choose to stay at the facility if she didn't recall anyone on the ship and hoped that Sima could help with coaxing her memory back. The three of them left the lab and returned to the ship.

The crew assembled in the galley and the women prepared a decent dinner for their guest. After discussing the initial results of Margot's procedure, everyone but Mike was relieved. Zenith and Shannon were anxious to know about Sima's world before the meteor struck and the animals she sheltered. Tisch questioned where all these animals were kept. Sima explained that there were many more levels to the facility and it spread much further than was visible from the surface. With much of the facility under ice, she had sealed off many of the compartments to save energy and maintain adequate heat only where needed. She invited the women to help her re-animate and release the animals in the morning. She felt that the temperatures had moderated enough for them to have a chance to survive on their own. Mike asked Tisch to consider her offer so that they would have more time to evaluate Margot's progress. Agreeable, Tisch was eager to see some of the animals and was curious enough to join the women for the release.

When dinner was finished, Mike and Margot escorted Sima back to her lab. She cautioned Mike to be on the alert for a spacecraft that flew by every few days. She suspected that they belonged to Klingman's group. Curious, Mike suggested to Margot that they take a short trip in the shuttle in the morning that might stimulate her memory. Bored, she was more than happy to go for a trip alone with her handsome 'stranger'.

When the women left to release the animals, only Wilmer remained on board with Mike and Margot. Mike invited him to join them in further discussion, much to Margot's disappointment. She had hoped for some private time with Mike to talk about what their relationship was. Wilmer was reluctant at first, but Mike mentioned the craft that took Sima's technicians. He felt it would be good to have Wilmer's expertise with them to operate the cloaking mechanism and the teleport module, if needed. Mike didn't want to alarm Tisch but there was no harm in doing a quick scan of the sector.

The three of them boarded the shuttle and prepared to depart. Wilmer activated the teleport module and transported them to an area between Sargassa and another planet closer to the center of the star system. Mike performed a scan of the area while Wilmer navigated the shuttle. Margot rubbed Mike's shoulders and playfully kissed his neck. She soon grew frustrated as Mike ignored her advances. Mike took her to the rear of the shuttle to voice his concerns about her behavior and why he couldn't be affectionate with her. He felt as though he would be taking advantage of her when she wasn't herself. "Maybe I am," she kidded, "and you just never noticed."

Mike considered that she had a point and embraced her. Just when they kissed, Wilmer interrupted. "Hey, Mike! You might want to see this - NOW!"

Mike groaned and led Margot by the hand to the front of the shuttle. Wilmer pointed to the monitor and looked up at Mike. Forty ships appeared suddenly and were leaving in a hurry.

"What the hell is that all about?" Margot asked uneasily.

"That's a lot of ships heading in one direction," Wilmer remarked, realizing this was a big deal.

"Can you get us closer to the source of those ships in cloaked mode?" Mike requested.

Wilmer hurried to the panel with the teleport module and inserted a new set of coordinates. He returned to his seat with Mike in the copilot's seat. Ahead of them was a huge space station with the Kronos symbol on the front sensor surface. "Holy shit!" exclaimed Mike. "We just found base number three! Get us out of here fast!"

Wilmer reset the teleport module and they returned to the cargo bay of the *Blue Eagle*. When they exited, Tisch was waiting, arms folded and foot tapping.

"I can explain," blurted Mike, "but right now we need to get back to Archimedes-9! I'll explain on the way."

"This had better be good," warned Tisch.

Mike rushed out to find Sima. When he found her, she was in the abandoned control room assessing the damage to the facility's control system. She was pleased with the release of the creatures back into the environment and was anxious to speak with Mike. He interrupted her and urged her to come with them for her own safety. Sensing the urgency, she immediately followed him to the *Blue Eagle*.

Wilmer programed the teleport module to move both the shuttle and the ship back to Archimedes-9. Tisch waited patiently until Mike explained what they found and, thanks to Sima mentioning Klingman's visit, why they searched the sector. Tisch was flustered as they were once again back in the middle of the war. She understood the importance of it but hated that Mike always discovered these things. When they appeared outside the station, Zenith contacted the transport supervisor for a docking location. She then requested that Rebecca meet them at the personnel hatch for an urgent matter.

"Margot, you really have to find a way to keep him occupied," Tisch teased.

"I tried," she said disappointedly. "He just keeps on going." Margot then revealed that she knew they had a connection and that Tisch was important to her. She couldn't remember why but knew there was something meaningful between them. Tisch suggested they discuss it in private sometime and perhaps it would help her regain her lost memories.

Mike rushed through the personnel hatch and met Rebecca and Creeg. Behind them stood a decorated female officer, General Lennox. Tisch, Wilmer and Margot joined them. When Mike informed Rebecca that they found the third Kronos base, Rebecca stared at him in disbelief. "There's more," he uttered urgently. He explained how they saw over forty ships leave the base in a hurry, headed in one direction.

Rebecca pondered aloud, "I wonder if the Scrat started their attack. We need to leave now before it's too late." Creeg was silent but he understood what was happening. General Lennox left, after only observing them.

Mike, Margot, Rebecca, Wilmer and Creeg boarded the ship and hurried to the shuttle. Wilmer programmed the teleport module for their previous location on the Scrat world. Mike briefed Creeg on what they discovered and what it could mean if the Scrat were ambushed. Rebecca informed them that General Lennox arranged for a portal to be created near the second Kronos base. She already had twenty Federation cruisers on standby in case of something like this. Creeg was grateful for their concern for his people.

The shuttle appeared near the Scrat worlds and landed in the same area as before. When they docked, Mike exited and was shocked to see two wrecked salvage ships near the original Kronos wrecks. Mike put his hands on his head and paced rabidly. "This is really bad!" he blurted. "We have to find Gendry fast."

Mike hurried to the tunnel and shouted for Gendry. Margot followed with Wilmer and Rebecca close behind. Tybus appeared with five Scrat soldiers. Paying no mind to Creeg, he threw a punch at Mike and staggered him. Margot, red-faced, threw a left-handed punch and struck him under the jawbone joint. He staggered backwards and fell to the ground. "I wonder where you learned that from," Tybus remarked sarcastically.

Margot stared down the fallen Scrat, who was stunned by her quick reaction. Rebecca and Wilmer glanced at each other, stunned by what they just saw. Creeg stepped forward and ordered the men to take them to Gendry immediately. They traversed the tunnel to a cavern where the Scrat had constructed their underground base. Two of the Scrat remained behind to usher Tybus after them.

Mike instructed the others to let him and Creeg do the talking for now. Rebecca was confident that she'd know when to step in. Wilmer was content to be a bystander and let them handle the discussions. Margot stared at Mike until he acknowledged her with a kiss on the cheek. "You're in this, too, Honey," he assured her. "I'm not forgetting you."

Gendry approached and was elated to see Creeg. The two embraced and placed their foreheads against each other. They exchanged all the pertinent thoughts and information without saying a word in Scrat or otherwise. Everyone waited anxiously, wondering what they were doing. After several moments, Creeg informed Mike's group that Tybus' team shot down the salvage ships. He informed Gendry that now Kronos knew there was still a Scrat military force present here and Kronos dispatched a second fleet to finish them.

Mike confirmed with Rebecca that the Federation ships were waiting at the portal and watching. He then recommended that the Scrat send ten ships to Kronos' base and lure their ships out. Once the Federation sees their numbers, then they should send a second wave, just enough to handle them. The Federation ships will also engage to help keep the battle short. When the reinforcements appear for Kronos, then the remainder of the Scrat fleet should emerge from hiding and join the attack from behind – a surprise attack. Creeg and Gendry understood and were supportive of the plan.

Creeg instructed Gendry that he wasn't there to take back his command but only support him. Creeg then praised him for doing an exceptional job of protecting their resources after the attack. Gendry promised to punish Tybus when the time was right for jeopardizing everything they fought to protect. Mike then suggested that they leave the area so they can watch for any additional forces that Kronos might summon to the battle. Creeg understood and stayed with Mike's crew. Gendry assured Mike that he would have his cooperation in the future and thanked him for honoring his promise. Mike thanked him for his patience and wished them well in their attack. Mike's group then departed the premises.

On board the shuttle, Rebecca questioned Creeg why he chose to stay with them versus joining his forces. Creeg explained that he felt that he didn't belong there anymore, but he didn't fit in with the humans on Taurus either. He hoped to be of value by monitoring Kronos from afar with Mike.

Sima emerged from the small cabin in the rear of the shuttle, having just awoken. "What's all the commotion?" she asked, while rubbing her eyes.

Mike forgot that she was still on board. She took notice of Creeg and seemed to be attracted to him. Ironically, Creeg appeared interested in her as well. They moved to the rear of the shuttle and eagerly spoke to each other. Mike and Wilmer stared in disbelief. Sima glanced back and commented, "Pheromones." She then resumed her conversation with Creeg.

Mike muttered, "What the...? Who'd have thought."

Rebecca transmitted several messages to one of her sources, likely Marina, and then informed Mike that they can return to Archimedes-9. The Federation would provide backup and reinforcements for the Scrat. Mike shrugged his shoulders and sighed, knowing they were back on the bench while the war was being fought.

When they reached Archimedes-9, Mike left the ship alone and went to the nearest pub. After two shots of whiskey, he took a mug of ale with him to a table in the back corner. Sitting alone, he pondered what the future held for him. Here was his opportunity to leave the *Blue Eagle* if he chose. It was also his opportunity to settle into something more relaxed with a crew that was more like family every day. He had concerns about Margot and her memory loss. Then he recalled the strange interaction between Sima and Creeg. His world was changing at the speed of light and he had no control of it.

Margot entered the pub and scanned the customers until she spotted Mike in the back. She sighed, disappointed that he chose to be alone, and approached him. Mike was surprised when she sat down next to him. “Okay,” she started sarcastically. “What gives?”

Mike finally looked up and acknowledged her presence. “Everything and nothing,” he responded. “I don’t know what to do.”

“You want to break up? Would that make you happy?” she inquired, her frustration with him becoming more evident.

Mike confessed that there were many issues on his mind and he missed having her there to help him. It was still Margot to him but their connection was gone. Margot gestured for the waiter and ordered four whiskey shots and a pitcher of ale. “I can tell this is going to get complicated,” she remarked cynically.

Mike admitted that he feared letting her go and then her memory should come back. That would be the ultimate betrayal. He also felt that it wasn’t fair to expect her to stay with him if he couldn’t love her like before. “Wow,” blurted Margot. The waiter served their drinks and left them. Margot did two shots and sipped her ale. “That was pretty deep.”

“What should I do?’ he asked. “I’m lost.”

Margot leaned back in her chair and smiled at him. “Don’t worry about it,” she suggested. “Think about it.”

Tisch and Rebecca entered the pub with a little girl and joined them. "And who is this precious little girl?" asked Margot playfully. She reached down and lifted the little girl onto her lap. The girl giggled and poked at Margot.

"That is my daughter Aries, after the goddess of war," quipped Rebecca proudly. "She's going to be a battler like her mother." Mike was impressed, never suspecting Rebecca as the maternal type.

"I should have known you'd be here," Tisch chided Mike. "You don't drink with the commoners anymore?"

Mike looked down, embarrassed. He realized that the perception he created among the others recently was distant. Margot commented that Mike was going through an early male menopause and misplaced his spine.

"What the hell, Margot?" he uttered. "Where did that come from?"

Rebecca related to Tisch how Margot defended Mike and laid out a nuisance Scrat with a left hook. Tisch was impressed "You did that again?"

Margot smiled with a sheepish expression. Rebecca was impressed and questioned how she was able to take down a bigger opponent twice with one punch. Margot pointed to Mike and revealed how she learned the Scrat weak spot from watching him. "You learn quick," commented Rebecca.

Tisch suddenly realized that Margot's memory seemed to be back, at least somewhat. As a test, she mentioned how she related their story to Creeg and Dr. Lowell about how Margot rescued Mike in the bay in an environmental suit. Margot giggled and remarked, "This big oaf was worth saving." Mike still didn't catch on.

Tisch informed Mike that General Lennox and her people were installing portals in strategic locations to help them with their long-distance travels and reconnaissance. Rebecca added that Mike had a knack for seeing things that others didn't and felt that he would help monitor their sectors in the event Kronos returns. She then invited the crew to join her on Archimedes-9 whenever they wished. "Oh, and an update for you," she added eagerly. "The first part of the attack on Kronos was a success. The Scrat forces are now waiting to ambush the Kronos reinforcements."

"That's great!" exclaimed Mike. "What about Kronos base number three?"

"The Federation has taken it over. Kronos didn't have much to defend it with and, I'm sure, never expected it would be discovered. Thanks to you and your friends, we now have them at a disadvantage." Mike cautioned her that Kronos was still dangerous and not likely to go away easily. Rebecca thanked him once more and left with her daughter.

Tisch teased Mike playfully and inquired, "What now, your Highness? You've been recognized for your infinite wisdom."

Mike groaned and finished his ale. "I really need something bad and it ain't here." He barged out of the pub.

Tisch eyed Margot and suggested it was time for her to step up. Margot grinned and countered innocently, "What, pray tell, do you mean?"

"We have a connection, remember?" Tisch reminded her. "I know what's going on here." Instinctively, the two women high-fived and tapped glasses in a toast. Each did a shot of the remaining two whiskeys. "Maybe it's time to hit the high note with Mike," Margot kidded. "He's suffered enough."

"Please," begged Tisch. "For all our sakes, do something with him before he comes up with another crazy idea."

Margot replied, "I got this... for the team." The two women burst into laughter and left the pub.

Mike laid in bed on board the *Blue Eagle*. Frustrated, he considered taking the shuttle to investigate the third Kronos base, or what was left of it. Margot entered and stood over him. "It's time to put up or get out," she teased and removed her shirt.

Mike repeated that he won't do this until her memory returns. Margot was determined that she wouldn't take no for an answer. She undressed and slid under the covers, insisting that he join her. Mike was so frustrated with her until she coaxed him into it. Later, the two were exhausted and lay next to each other. "So, where do we go from here?" Margot asked.

"I hope you're happy," he complained. "You got what you wanted from me."

Margot teased him about how smart he was but such an idiot when it came to love. She asked why he didn't suspect anything when she decked Tybus during their meeting with the Scrat. Mike thought about it but, humbled, said nothing. She mentioned that she dropped numerous hints in their conversations and he never caught on.

"Are you telling me you've had your memory back for a while now?" he asked.

Margot nodded with a seductive grin. She revealed that it came back gradually and seems normal now. Mike was overwhelmed and embarrassed that he didn't catch on. The two of them burst into laughter and embraced once more. Mike was ecstatic to have her memory issue behind them.

Later in the evening, everyone gathered in the galley for a meeting with Mike and Margot arriving last as usual. Tisch stared at Margot, awaiting some kind of hint from her about Mike. Margot announced that everyone can relax. She's made sure that Mike would have no new ideas for a while. Knowing that she finally seduced him and took the wind out of his sails, everyone cheered.

"Jeez!" complained Mike. "Is everyone in on this?"

"You big dummy," teased Margot. "Of course, they were."

Margot requested time for a quick visit with the doctor to see what could be done about lingering soreness in her ribs and then departed. Tisch considered a mini-vacation for the crew on Archimedes-9 until Mike,

Margot and Wilmer returned from Taurus with Creeg and his command ship. Shannon volunteered to join the men while Zenith and Jonas were happy to have quality time off the clock on Archimedes-9.

"What about you?" Mike asked Tisch, concerned that she would be alone.

"I plan on spending some time with Rebecca and learning about how they execute their supply runs out here and where the Federation could help with portals."

Mike suggested that they focus their resources on the Nigus star system and see what new business they can find. Tisch reminded him that they needed to return Sima to her facility first. Margot was already gone when he turned to seek her thoughts on their plan. Tisch took the opportunity to kid Mike about rounding up his children. He groaned and questioned where Creeg and Sima were. Tisch just smiled as it was his problem.

Mike, Wilmer and Shannon went to the shuttle where they found Creeg and Sima in a serious discussion inside. Creeg informed Mike that, once they return his ship and crew to the Scrat world, he would join Sima at her facility on Sargassa and stay with her. Mike was surprised, but agreed to support his friend.

Mike and Sima took advantage of the time on the *Blue Eagle* to discuss ways that they could help restore her facility through trade and the sale of her medical equipment. He was stunned to learn that she had twenty of the skin graft machines and fifteen of the regen machines as well to be loaded on the *Blue Eagle*. Mike now understood why Archimedes-9 had the only machines in the galaxy. The equipment never made it off Sargassa when the Federation abandoned her. He then explained to her how they planned to visit the other colonies and possibly set up a trade network between them.

Margot entered the galley and embraced Mike with a hug and a kiss. "Wow! What was that for?" he asked. Margot explained that the regen machine completed the healing that started after the surgery to her lungs. Now she was pain-free. Mike placed his arm around her and kissed her cheek.

When the *Blue Eagle* arrived on Sargassa, Sima announced that she was pleased with the results of their discussions on Archimedes-9. The crew swapped cargo, delivering the supplies that Sima needed and then loaded additional equipment she prepared for trade. Creeg embraced Sima and assured her that he would return soon to help her manage the facility. With the crew and Creeg anxious to continue their journey back to Taurus, the *Blue Eagle* departed Sargassa.

Mike boarded the shuttle with Margot, Wilmer, and Shannon. Margot initiated startup for the shuttle, while Mike contacted Zenith and requested she open the cargo bay doors. Once fully opened, the shuttle departed the cargo bay and glided away from the *Blue Eagle*. Tisch wished them a safe trip and affirmed that she'd see them on Archimedes-9 when they returned from Taurus. Mike echoed her wishes and ended the transmission.

CHAPTER 8

PAY BACK

Julian waited patiently in the executive meeting room with a cold beer in hand. He wore an expensive, blue tunic with gold trim and leather sandals. Clean shaven and bald with a thick mustache, he enjoyed his new role and the perks that came with it.

Sara entered and informed him that the Empire armada, forty ships in all, just departed its headquarters. She mentioned that Korick's men were preparing to take over the base as soon as the armada exited the sector.

Gemini arrived and announced that the Scrat were scrambling their fighters. "I assume you got word that they're coming," she remarked.

"Just got word," Sara responded. "The Scrat command ship should be pulling out shortly."

"How does it look for us?" Gemini asked, feeling nervous.

"It's going to be dirty," Sara confessed. "We're evenly matched."

Gemini cussed and wished aloud that Mike was there. Julian urged her to have faith. "Do you think Mike would really leave us hung out to dry, knowing that an attack was imminent?"

Gemini grew irritated and complained, "Well I don't see the cavalry coming over the hill to help us."

Sara voiced her concerns about traitors on site that could be a problem, especially if they know the armada is on the way. If there was to be another insurrection by traitors, now was the time.

Twenty security sentinels betrayed Captain Tieg and took over the eighth floor. They breached the transport control center and, at gunpoint, forced the supervisor to close any open gates and then disable all the gates. When Sara stepped off the elevator, she was met with gunfire and struck several times. She desperately reached for the panel and pressed the button for the elevator doors. They opened immediately and she was able to crawl inside. With multiple wounds, she weakened and fell to her knees. A few moments later, the door slid open and she crawled into the corridor. Barely coherent, she contacted Gemini for help and then was unconscious from blood loss.

Gemini and Julian rushed to her aid, horrified by the turn of events. Julian warned Gemini that Sara went to the eighth floor to meet with the transport supervisor to ensure the Scrat fighters were released from their bays. Julian took Sara's transmitter and alerted Captain Tieg. Gemini contacted the med-techs and summoned them for help.

Captain Tieg and twenty men arrived from opposite ends of the floor and fired at the mercenaries. The mercenaries laid flat on the ground and fired in both directions. The shootout with Captain Tieg's men left many casualties on both sides. Captain Tieg was aware of the importance of those fighters being released from their bays and fought furiously. His rage fueled his bravery as he hated having traitors once again among his men.

The leader of the traitors. Sergeant Schiff, shouted at Captain Tieg to retreat or he would blow a hole in the hull of the station if they didn't back down. Captain Tieg attempted to negotiate and asked what Antwan was paying them. Schiff mockingly stated that it was a lot more than they'd ever see working for Taurus security. Tieg informed him that Antwan was taken into custody by the alliance so they could forget about payment. The mercenaries laughed at him, expecting this was a ploy to lure them out.

Captain Tieg lost his patience with them and mocked, "The only thing worse than dying a traitor is to die a poor one. You losers picked the wrong side." Schiff scoffed at his threats.

Captain Tieg reminded them of the penalty for treason and offered them one last chance to surrender. Six of the men had second thoughts and surrendered. Schiff shot them in the back before they could reach Tieg's men. Tieg thought to himself, *That's six less to worry about.* The shooting continued but Schiff's men took shelter in both the transport control center and an adjacent office down the hall.

The med-techs took Sara to the hospital level and began emergency treatment. Captain Tieg called to them over the transmitter and requested an update when available. He requested the med-tech use her transmitter to contact her people for support on level eight.

Down at the main level, the GSS agents fought mercenaries from one of the freighters that docked earlier in the day. The agents had the same problem while being pressed for time. The mercenaries were embedded and only interested in preventing the Scrat fighters from exiting the bays.

Julian paced the floor and wondered what Mike would do in that situation. Gemini shouted at him, fearing she was about to lose everything. Then Julian recalled what Mike told him about Archimedes-9 and how he accessed the bay through the maintenance hatch overhead. He contacted maintenance and instructed them to open the outer bay doors on the selected bays using the mechanical override from the catwalks. Gemini realized what he figured out and regained her composure. She poured bourbon into two glasses and set one in front of him. "You earned this," she said somberly. "Don't get used to it, though. I never served a drink to anyone before." Julian realized this was a rare moment and he was proud that he proved his worth.

Empire's armada of forty ships arrived near Taurus and positioned themselves for attack. Their leader contacted Gemini and offered her one chance to surrender. Twenty of Captain Tieg's cruisers arrived as well as fifteen of Gemini's armed freighters. to defend Taurus. The Scrat command ship appeared from another direction and aligned with them in a defensive formation.

The Empire armada opened fire first with Taurus' defenders returning fire. Gemini's freighters took heavy damage early with several dropping out of the battle. Two of Captain Tieg's cruisers were crippled and useless. Then, one by one, five of the bay doors opened slowly and the Scrat fighters darted out. They swarmed on the Empire freighters and forced them to break formation, thus reducing their ability to fire on Taurus' ships. Both sides incurred significant casualties but neither would stand down.

A variety of armed vessels totaling thirty-five from the pirate haven approached Empire's armada from behind and unloaded a barrage of cannon fire at them. Once Empire's ships realized they were overmatched, they attempted to flee. The pirate vessels pursued and destroyed them. The pirate vessels did a victory lap near Taurus and departed for their new home at Empire's former base.

When Korick received word from his friends that they were successful, he contacted Julian and informed him of their new lodging. He apologized for their losses and for his ships not arriving sooner. Julian was thankful just the same for their support and promised them that they would not be harassed by any of their people. He did request that they meet to discuss the potential for some honest business in the near future. Korick would only agree if Julian paid for the drinks. The two laughed and planned their meeting.

Gemini and Julian waited outside the recovery room. Gemini admitted that she normally would be celebrating their victory but was more concerned with her sister's well-being right now. She related to Julian that they were never really close and the only time she saw Sara was to ask for a favor. Now she regretted it and vowed to treat her better if she made it out of surgery. She confessed that she could really use Dax's support but he was away on a special project for her. Julian, despite his better judgment, placed his arm around her and comforted her.

A few moments later, the doctor entered the waiting area and informed them that Sara was going to make it, but her fighting days were likely over. He advised them that her heart was in a weakened state despite all they could do for her and she suffered a concussion that may have scarred her brain. The best advice he could offer was for her to take a desk job. Gemini was anxious to see her but she was asleep and likely would be for a while. Julian suggested that perhaps she could join them in coordinating their operations with Tieg and GSS. Gemini doubted she would accept such an offer but thought it would help to suggest it. Then she burst into tears and hugged Julian.

Mike's shuttle arrived near Taurus and requested a location to dock. They were all appalled at the wreckage surrounding Taurus. "Looks like the battle is over," remarked Mike.

"And it looks like Taurus is still standing," added Wilmer.

The main corridor was heavily damaged from pulse fire and the med-techs assembled the corpses on a wagon attached by a tow bar to an electric cart. The wounded had already been removed from the area and the survivors who surrendered were rounded up by Captain Tieg's men and incarcerated.

Mike's group entered through the personnel hatch from the bay and were stunned by the damage. They believed that all the traitors had been filtered out after this setback. Concerned that no one was there to greet them, Mike led them up to the eleventh floor, where they encountered Captain Tieg in the corridor. He informed them of Sara's condition and the concern for her prognosis.

Captain Tieg led them to the security center on the seventh floor for a debrief. He summoned Julian to join them before beginning. Wilmer and Shannon opted to have a meal in the pub with Creeg while Mike and Margot handled the official affairs. To their surprise, Gemini showed up, looking glum.

"This is still my corporation, in case any of you forgot," she remarked, sober. "Although I hear there is much to talk about. Proceed, Julian."

Captain Tieg started with a detailed explanation of the attacks prior to the Empire armada appearing. He thanked Julian for quick thinking to get the bay doors open and release the Scrat fighters. Mike was impressed and gave him a nod of approval. Then he mentioned the surprised visit by the unknown armada that blind-sided Empire's ships and prevented more casualties. Mike and Margot glanced at each other, grinning sheepishly.

Captain Tieg mentioned that there was a rumor that pirates will be operating out of Empire's former base and wondered if Mike could elaborate. Mike explained the arrangement and then suggested that they were potential employees or contractors who could help Taurus grow. Margot interjected that more discussions were required but the new occupants of Empire's base agreed to pose no problem for Taurus or its ships. For once, Captain Tieg smiled. He was amused by the plans that Margot plotted and Mike was able to execute. He commented to Margot, "You and Mike really need to get a night life. Now it's two of you coming up with this crazy stuff."

Margot turned to Mike with a somber look and asked, "Why does everyone keep alluding to our night time activities?" Mike shrugged his shoulders innocently with nothing to say. "Well, I see we're going to have to start a new program to improve what we do at night," she remarked playfully. Everyone burst into laughter, while Mike covered his eyes, embarrassed.

Julian then inquired about the rumors he heard about their adventures elsewhere. Mike turned to Margot and suggested she tell the story. Surprised by his consideration, she related everything that happened. Mike added that she forgot to mention the Scrat officer she decked, not once but twice. Captain Tieg complained, "Great. Now we have double the trouble - a female version of Mike."

Julian grinned and quipped, "If you only knew."

Mike inquired as to how much they heard about their recent trips. Julian replied that Rebecca was in touch with Gemini and revealed just about everything.

"Gemini must be going through a lot of bourbon," Mike kidded. Julian nodded with a wide grin as Gemini rubbed her temples with a pained expression. Then Mike revealed their plans to return to the Nigus star system and investigate other opportunities for Taurus to expand. Gemini's first question reminded Mike of her selfishness and that she was still all about the business. "When will I see a return on investment?" she inquired.

Julian attempted to smooth over her intent and explained that, from a logistical standpoint, what could they expect from all these changes and how should they approach them.

Mike suggested, for starters, that they establish a good rapport with Korick and Kellen since they were now running two operations. With piracy becoming less profitable, there was a valuable resource of labor and ships to replace the losses from the battle. Gemini questioned their loyalty, but Mike countered that she should offer them the opportunity to be contractors for her or employees. Julian felt it was worth a try and would rather keep them as allies, as they did save their asses against Empire, than competitors or enemies.

Margot then revealed the support they received from the alliance in developing portals to make travel between Taurus and key points convenient. Gemini wanted to know more and pressed them for information. Mike suggested that this falls under GSS and Taurus Security's jurisdiction to determine what is safe and how to protect it. Gemini knew he was dodging the topic but backed off.

Julian was curious to know when they could meet again to discuss a new business plan. Mike promised to stay in touch and report regularly on their progress in the Nigus star system. In the meantime, he reiterated that they work the new routes to Archimedes-9 and integrate Korick's people into the plan. Julian agreed that those two things alone should keep Taurus busy for a while. Captain Tieg questioned Mike about what security issues remained that he and GSS should be concerned with. Mike chuckled and replied, "For now, only pissed off ex-employees of Empire."

Captain Tieg welcomed the change. He had enough mercenary attacks and shootouts to last a lifetime. Gemini asked if there was anything that they needed to support their work. Mike placed his hand on Margot's leg, a clue that he was going to do something stupid. "Well, since you asked, we could use about twenty cases of beer and ten cases of rum – the good stuff."

Julian covered his mouth to hide his smile. Captain Tieg shook his head in disbelief that Mike would make such a bold request, but then he grinned as well. Gemini tapped her finger on the table and stared him down. Margot kicked Mike's shin, knowing that he just angered Gemini.

"I saw what the liquor cost me the last time the *Blue Eagle* went out," she complained. "You'll get half and you'll like it."

"Damn, you drive a hard bargain, Gem!" Mike blurted, feigning disappointment. With that, they ended the meeting. Mike thanked Julian for his support and assured them that they would have more opportunities to come, possibly with new technology in the medical field. Julian complimented Margot for doing a good job in keeping Mike under control. She laughed and countered, "If that's what you consider under control, what was he like before?"

Julian smiled and walked away. Margot stared at Mike and chided, "Now I see why everyone tells me to occupy you at night. You're like a child who can't sleep at night and thinks of new ways to get into trouble."

Mike placed his arms around her and kissed her. "You've got me all figured out," he teased.

Four dockworkers loaded the cases of beer and rum onto Mike's shuttle. Creeg questioned Mike about the value of spirits. Mike explained the necessity of mind numbness when dealing with Gemini and Tisch. Creeg made an odd noise which equated to a Scrat laugh. "You are a strange human," Creeg jested. Margot complimented Creeg on his wisdom, much to Mike's chagrin. Creeg instructed Mike to move the shuttle into the Scrat command ship's transport bay and he would make final preparations to depart. Their plan was to use the module to transport the Scrat ship with the shuttle back to the Scrat worlds.

Wilmer and Shannon finally boarded the shuttle. "I hope you weren't going to leave without us," Wilmer commented cynically.

"I forgot all about you two," Mike countered playfully.

Shannon revealed that they went to see Sara. She apologized for the delay but Mike was more than understanding. Shannon informed them that Sara was still unconscious and would likely be so for a little while. Mike assured them that they'd keep in touch over the status of her condition.

Wilmer and Shannon stared at all the cases of beer and rum. "What the hell did you do?" Wilmer inquired, concerned. "Gemini's going to kill you!"

Margot assured him that it was all good and Mike's negotiating tactics, once again, worked well. She frowned at Mike briefly and then remarked, "I wonder who's going to drink all that."

"It won't go to waste," he promised her. "Now, let's get out of here before Gemini changes her mind."

CHAPTER 9

NEW HORIZONS

Creeg confirmed that his ship was secure for transport. Wilmer programmed the teleport module in the shuttle to send both ships to the Nebula Galaxy. He initiated the teleport module and then they waited. Mike stared at the monitor and became uneasy. Wilmer got down on his knees in front of the open panel and studied the teleport module for a moment. Suddenly, he looked ill. "Uh, Mike. I think we have a problem," he muttered.

Mike replied somberly, "Yeah, this doesn't look like the Nebula Galaxy."

Wilmer rushed to the copilot's seat and operated the computer. Margot and Shannon watched over his shoulder, concerned about their situation until he ordered them to back off. Creeg left the shuttle to meet with his officers. Mike and Wilmer glanced at each other, hoping they didn't create a problem for the Scrat.

After doing multiple calculations and altering coordinates, Wilmer determined that they were somewhere between Archimedes-9 and the Nebula Galaxy. Margot commented to Shannon, "We could be stuck in this shuttle for a long time." Shannon nodded disappointedly. "And with these guys, that could be painful." Again, Shannon nodded while frowning.

Mike and Wilmer discussed what happened to the teleport module and if it could be repaired. Wilmer suspected that the module was fine but the coil overheated and lost power.

Creeg returned and informed them that the command ship could make the trip home from there in a reasonable amount of time. He reminded them that he was returning to Sargassa to work with Sima. Then he mentioned, "Not to pressure you both, but I would like to get back to Sima before she is old and decrepit."

Mike and Wilmer became nervous but then Creeg made another of his odd noises and told them he was kidding. He informed them that his people did their own calculations and determined that the shuttle could make it to Archimedes-9 in a reasonable time as well, but only if the fuel held out. This wasn't an issue for them and they weren't anxious to reveal the details of the fuel regeneration system they received with their upgrade.

They agreed that it was their only option at this point so Creeg instructed his lead officer to open the bay for their departure. Mike apologized for the setback but Creeg understood that this was beyond their control. Soon, they were underway on their own, while the Scrat ship continued toward the Nebula Galaxy. Shannon and Margot took over and piloted the shuttle, while Mike and Wilmer attempted to repair the damaged coil.

After hours of troubleshooting, they discovered the damaged component on the coil. Wilmer became frustrated with the system and paced back and forth, hoping for a solution. Mike inquired if they could cannibalize any parts off the cloaking system, even if was just enough to get them to Archimedes-9. Wilmer's eyes widened and he anxiously opened the other panel where the cloaking system was located. After browsing over the components, he removed one and swapped it with the defective one on the coil. "It's a bit undersized," cautioned Wilmer, "but it should get us back to Archimedes-9."

Shannon and Margot high-fived. Margot commented, "I knew there was a reason we keep them around." Mike and Wilmer frowned over the ribbing.

Wilmer powered up the teleport module and watched nervously until the green ready light appeared. He glanced at Mike and asked, "Do you feel lucky?" Impatiently, Mike urged him to activate it and get them out of there.

With the module temporarily repaired, they teleported inside the cargo bay of the *Blue Eagle* on Archimedes-9 and exited the shuttle. Mike was disappointed that the module wasn't likely to last and considered if they could repair it somehow. Wilmer advised him that they should restore the cloaking system and forget the teleport module. Mike hated to do it but he knew Wilmer was right.

Tisch and her crew entered the cargo bay, eager to hear what trouble Mike got into now. Margot assured her that it was nothing out of the ordinary, leading to much laughter. Tisch suggested that they move their meeting to the third-level pub in the station in the event Rebecca chose to join them. Creeg elected to remain on the shuttle and rest.

In the pub, Rebecca already waited for them at a table with pitchers of ale and whiskey shots. Mike was overjoyed and offered to hug her for her hospitality. Rebecca politely declined. "I'm afraid some of your luck will rub off on me, Mr. Colby," she added stoically. "I do have a daughter to protect."

Everyone enjoyed seeing Mike take flak for his ambitious nature. Mike said nothing but was annoyed with the constant ribbing. Rebecca inquired as to how productive their recent trip was. Mike was content to let Margot and Wilmer tell the story of their adventures while he imbibed on the drinks. She was pleased to hear that Empire was defeated and lost their base. Reluctantly, she praised Mike for a brilliant idea with the clientele at the pirate haven.

After a brief hesitation, she inquired, "Is the teleport module really shot or is this like the cloaking system that you don't have on the shuttle?" Wilmer assured her that it was inoperative, although, he didn't rule out finding a way to repair it.

Rebecca was interested in where they planned to go next and if she would see them again. She expressed her pleasure in the time spent with them. Tisch felt that Archimedes-9 was best suited to be the hub in the sector so she hoped to coordinate all trade through it. Rebecca was pleased and offered any support that they required – except for spirits. Mike looked heartbroken and then she mentioned that she heard a rumor that half of the *Blue Eagle's* expenses were beer and rum. Mike looked appalled and asked hurtfully, "Who started that rumor? I'm mortified!"

Everyone stared at him in disbelief, knowing he managed to obtain quite a supply of liquor. Mike blushed and stated that it helped him think. Margot shook her head and promised to limit his thinking. Everyone cheered and did a shot of whiskey to encourage her.

Rebecca stood and excused herself for the night. Tisch promised her that she'd stay in touch and the two women embraced in a friendly hug. Rebecca waved to them and departed the pub. Tisch returned to the table and gave Mike a serious look. "What's wrong?" he asked.

"Were you serious about being tired of the fighting and risk-taking?"

"I was. I still am. After what happened with Borath, I've had enough."

Margot rolled her eyes and chided, "We'll see how long that lasts."

Tisch reminded her that it is her responsibility to occupy him at night to prevent more zany ideas. Margot groaned at the responsibility and did two shots. They ended the evening and returned to the *Blue Eagle*.

When Mike and Margot entered their cabin, Mike gently pressed her against the wall and kissed her. Margot crooned and savored his kisses. She suggested they move to the bed but was stunned by Mike's next comment. "I have some ideas I'd like to run by you before we go to bed," he whispered.

Margot pushed him away and glared at him. "No ideas!" she exclaimed. "Just get into bed and forget about them." Mike reluctantly obeyed.

Zenith prepared breakfast in the galley for the crew. She enjoyed cooking and was happy to be the crew's cook as well as the ship's pilot. Their trip to Sargassa through the portal was a short one, taking a few days and everyone was excited to see what lay beyond that. Mike and Margot arrived and sat by themselves at a table. Tisch wasted no time in annoying Mike with a witty comment. "So, what great ideas do you have to bestow on us today, oh wise one?" she asked playfully.

Mike covered his face and wondered if he should have stayed in bed. Margot took the initiative and replied, "Mike has no ideas today. Right, Mike?"

Mike complained, "I had a few things I wanted to discuss but, for the life of me, I can't remember what they were."

Everyone cheered and congratulated Margot for her success. Zenith, not known for her subtlety remarked, "That must have been one heck of a night of great sex if Mike can't remember what he was thinking."

Mike frowned at her and sighed. Tisch shook her head at Zenith, indicating discretion. Zenith then praised Margot for being her idol. Margot blushed and then commented, "Sometimes a girl's got to do what a girl's got to do."

Tisch, Shannon and Zenith replied in unison, "Amen, sister."

Mike shook his head in disbelief. "How about a little help here, Jonas?" he asked. "After all, she is your sister."

Jonas was surprised to be included in the discussion and was embarrassed. "Don't ask me for help," he replied giddily. "I didn't sleep with her." Everyone got a laugh from their banter. Mike covered his eyes, humiliated that everyone took an interest in their night time activities.

Tisch announced that they would arrive at Sima's facility soon and there was a lot to do. She requested that Mike and Margot assist the others in offloading cargo. Mike feigned surprise and inquired, "Cargo? What cargo?" He hoped to avoid being involved in the cargo transfer for other options.

Tisch explained that, while he was racing around the galaxy, she conducted the business they were supposed involved in. Mike realized he missed quite a bit when they were away in the shuttle and relented that he should help.

Zenith landed the *Blue Eagle* on the pad outside the abandoned control room. Creeg was anxious to see Sima again and hurried off the ship to find her. The crew promptly set to unloading four containers of supplies for Sima onto the pad area. Tisch expected that, with their help, they'll be there a day or two to help store the supplies after off-loading.

When the containers were staged on the ground, Mike became concerned that they hadn't seen any sign of Creeg or Sima yet. Margot thought it strange as well and suggested they check Sima's lab in the lower level. Tisch shook her head, knowing that the two of them couldn't mind their business and suspected their new friends were having alien sex or some other ritual she was unfamiliar with. Tired of their antics, she gestured for them to go while she joined the crew in the galley for a break.

Mike noticed that the service elevator was powered up and took advantage of it. Neither he nor Margot looked forward to the warm humid air and using the elevator instead of the stairs was a blessing. When the elevator stopped at the bottom level, the door opened. The sound of clanging metal and groans alerted them that something was wrong. They rushed to the source of the sounds coming from Sima's lab and were horrified to see Borath fighting Creeg. Sima was pinned against the wall with a conduit piercing her shoulder. She struggled to get free but to no avail.

"You've got to be kidding me!" Mike exclaimed.

Margot seemed undaunted by Borath's presence and instinctively grabbed another piece of conduit. Sima shouted, "The left side is cyborg! His right half is vulnerable!"

Creeg was relentless, striking Borath repeatedly while staying beyond his reach. Margot rammed her conduit into the back of Borath's right knee and forced him to the ground. Despite repeated shots to his head, Borath got up and fought back.

Mike picked up a steel plate from the construction supplies and cautiously approached, looking for a kill shot. When Borath grabbed Margot's conduit and held it, Creeg leaped on his back and choked him from behind. Mike rammed the plate into Borath's right knee and forced him to the floor once more. Creeg nodded to Mike and released his hold on Borath. Mike jumped onto the table and leaped at Borath. He drove the plate into Borath's skull with a sickening thud. Borath froze with a blank look in his eyes. Taking advantage of the lapse, Mike rammed the plate into Borath's neck and partially severed the head. Creeg gestured for the plate and Mike tossed it to him. He swung the plate sideways and decapitated the head completely. Borath's corpse fell to the ground.

Creeg rushed to Sima and removed the conduit that pinned her to the wall. They embraced while Mike and Margot stared at Borath's body, horrified. They glanced at each other, wondering how Borath was there and still alive. Sima instructed them to take the corpse and the head to the furnace several doors down from her lab. "We have to melt that bastard," she uttered. "He can't be allowed to regenerate."

Stunned by her words about regeneration, Mike and Creeg dragged the heavy corpse to the furnace room. Margot accompanied them, carrying the head. After several attempts, they figured out how to start the furnace and then disposed of Borath for the last time. When they returned, Sima instructed them on how to treat her injury and then operate the regen machine. Mike was eager for an explanation about Borath's regeneration but knew this wasn't the time.

When Sima was healed by the regen machine, she escorted them back to the elevator. “The cyborg is more than just a cyborg,” she revealed. “I thought I could combine it with my husband’s body and awaken him from cryostasis.”

“So, what went wrong?” questioned Margot.

“The cyborg controls a flow of xenobots that used my husband’s flesh for power to regenerate and replicate itself. They basically recreated Borath from my husband. The cyborg *is* Borath.”

“So why burn him?” asked Mike. “Isn’t he dead?” Sima then explained that Borath was no longer flesh, but a body of tiny, living robotic organisms. Margot wiped beads of sweat from her forehead. She wasn’t worried about nightmares this time as now she was sure Borath was gone forever.

They stepped off the elevator and exited the facility. Tisch noticed the bandages on Sima’s shoulder and questioned her out of concern. Margot responded for her that there was a minor mishap but everything was handled. Sima appreciated her concern and assured her that she was fine. Tisch thought it strange, but said no more about it.

Wilmer and Shannon opened the cargo containers for Sima to inspect. She looked surprised and mentioned that she didn’t request all the building materials. Mike suggested she speak to Tisch about it. Creeg and Mike opened the doors to the other four containers, while Margot summoned Tisch. Sima was ecstatic with the fuel cells, staples, construction materials and electrical equipment. When Margot escorted Tisch from the ship, Sima approached her and explained humbly, “I appreciate this but I can’t pay for all of it.”

“Rebecca sent this on the house,” Tisch replied. “She apologizes for the Federation not sending a rescue ship here after the meteorite struck.”

Sima hugged her first and then the others. “Once the facility is up and running, I’ll have much to trade that will benefit everyone!” she exclaimed. “This is wonderful!”

Creeg finally spoke. "And I'll be here to help make that happen." He embraced Sima and placed his forehead against hers. She smiled at him as the two exchanged thoughts.

Tisch suggested that they unload the containers in the morning so they can reload them and depart by early afternoon. Sima instructed them to use the service elevator and place everything on the second level down. She took Creeg by his arm and escorted him inside. "We'll see you in the morning," she announced to them.

"All right, you two, back to the ship," Tisch commanded Mike and Margot. "We have work to do."

Mike grumbled, "Taskmaster." Tisch and Margot giggled at each other, knowing Mike hated taking orders from anyone.

The three of them entered the galley, joining the others for dinner. Tisch proposed a toast for the first boring task in a long time and credited Margot for that. Mike shook his head as everyone cheered. "Something I should know about?" Tisch inquired.

Mike was about to speak but Margot kicked his shin. "Nothing worth talking about," she commented. Tisch suspected something happened but no news was good news, as far as she was concerned. Zenith announced that she and Shannon completed a map of the Nigus star system and, after several pointed scans, were able to identify where they were likely to find the colonies. Wilmer informed them that Jonas' training went well and he was competent to work on several of the ship's systems including the onloader. Jonas affirmed that he was comfortable with them and complimented Wilmer for his tutelage.

Mike and Margot sat quietly and enjoyed the calm atmosphere with no drama. Tisch pressed Mike to reveal what happened inside Sima's facility. She admitted that the suspense was killing her. Zenith prodded Mike, insinuating that he was getting too old for action and thus, nothing to report. Margot assured her that wasn't a problem. Everyone laughed while Mike, once again, was the butt of their humor. Feeling the need for redemption, he revealed the return of Borath and Sima's attempt to reinvent her husband.

Tisch grew concerned and questioned Margot about how she felt about it. "I'm okay," she said confidently. "We teamed up with Creeg and did what needed to be done. I actually feel vindicated."

Jonas quipped, "That's why I stay near the ship. I can't get into any trouble here." Zenith poked him and teased him about being a wuss. He responded playfully, "I think you like wuss." She kissed him passionately and responded, "So we know who wears the pants here and who removes them." Jonas smiled and kissed her back in response.

Mike mentioned that he wanted to make contact with the Federation representatives on the former Kronos base to get an update on the war with Kronos. Tisch was fine with it so long as he didn't drag them into any more dangerous situations. He assured her that it wouldn't be the case.

Wilmer suggested that Zenith and Jonas join Mike for a change of pace. Tisch was confident that she could handle things on the planet Tandenar with just Wilmer and Shannon to accompany her, so she agreed to their plan. Mike took his group to the shuttle and departed the ship.

Tandenar was a heavily forested planet with many mountains, lakes and several oceans. There were numerous locations with basic dwellings, clearly organized into communities. Zenith identified an outpost and landed in a nearby clearing. Several men and women approached, curious to meet their visitors. The people dressed in simple clothes and were very friendly. When Tisch requested a meeting with their leader, one of the women pointed to a castle built into the side of a mountain.

Another man named Kai, indicated that he would take them there. He led them to an adobe garage where he kept an electric cart, built for four. They climbed in and he drove them to the base of the castle. Kai brought them to an open-air elevator with a well-made pulley system, using counterweights and cables of hemp coated with a resin.

Zenith commented, "This is like a cross between Medieval and Steampunk culture." Impressed, Tisch and Jonas agreed with her.

Tisch questioned Kai about their interaction with other villages. They boarded the elevator with him and ascended to the top of the mountain. She was surprised to hear that there were hostile groups on the planet that felt they were superior to everyone else, making interaction limited to a few. When they stepped off, they were met by a brigade of guards who questioned their presence. One of the men relayed the information to his superior.

After a brief delay, they were permitted to access another elevator. From there, they descended four floors to the interior of the mountain. Kai led them from the elevator down a long corridor to a chamber at the end. He used retinal identification to gain access and stepped back as the door slid open. Tisch led her team forward to an ornate chamber.

The leader, an emirate named Cabistero, greeted them, dressed in regal garb. Tisch expressed their unawareness of the local customs and requested his forgiveness for any disrespect they might display. When she revealed the purpose for their visit, Cabistero was pleased and agreed to afford them adequate time to discuss their intentions. Tisch gave her adlib presentation for their visit and how they hoped to build regular trade routes to each of the colonies. Then Cabistero grew somber and explained that they had established a good trading partner with Kronos but at a price. Their ships would visit regularly to trade supplies for food. He then inquired if Tish's crew was behind the demise of Kronos' forces and if his people were in danger as a result of it.

Zenith grew edgy as she sensed they might be in trouble. Tisch maintained her composure and, while admitting to not being involved in any of the activities against Kronos, she revealed that she did have information about what transpired. Cabistero was eager to hear more about

Kronos and the changes that would affect his colony. Zenith was relieved and felt a renewed trust in Tisch to handle such matters without Mike.

Tisch inquired about the other colonies and what he knew of them. Cabistero revealed that the colonies rarely interacted and trade among them was nonexistent. Tisch questioned if this could change. While he supported it, he was not optimistic due to the difference in cultures and defensive natures of the other colonies. They were surprised when he revealed that ships were a luxury and rare so interstellar travel was very limited. That's why Kronos was such a valuable trade partner.

Tisch was anxious to learn more about the culture on Tandenar. Afterwards, they were provided luxurious accommodations for the night.

CHAPTER 10

THE KRONOS DATABASE

Mike piloted the shuttle toward the docking bay of the Kronos base. The bay gates automatically opened as they approached. Inside, three cruisers belonging to the Federation were docked along with two Kronos shuttles. Mike grew suspicious when no one contacted them about their approach or their entry into the bay. Margot suggested that Kronos left some sort of defense mechanism to prevent their enemies from accessing the facility in a situation like this and the Federation's personnel had been neutralized. Mike considered her words and wondered if their troops were ever in control of the base at all. Perhaps they weren't even alive.

Mike retrieved a box with two fiber-optic inputs and a digital output from a locker in the rear of the shuttle. He handed it to Zenith with instructions for her and Jonas to access the database in the control room and download everything. Jonas questioned what they were looking for and how much to take off of the database. Mike's answer was short. "Everything."

Zenith opened the box cover and found five portable drives, installed in internal ports. She stared at Mike and questioned whether he had planned this for some time. He reminded her that opportunity only knocks once and he wasn't about to miss this. She was sure they could get most, if not all, of the information from the database. Then Jonas asked the question no one wanted to hear. "Will we be in danger while we do this?"

Mike promised them that he won't let any harm come to them. Zenith then assured Jonas that they would be fine. Margot distributed pulse pistols to each of them. She instructed Zenith and Jonas how to use them if needed. Jonas was uncomfortable that pistols were needed at all, but accepted the weapon just in case. Zenith was excited at the opportunity to get involved in one of Mike's big adventures. Mike reminded them to be vigilant as they don't know the status of the Federation personnel or the condition of the base for human survival.

When the bay gates closed and sealed for containment, oxygen filled the bay and allowed for them to exit the shuttle. Mike led them across the dock to the access hatch and then through an airlock hatch. Once on the other side, they were inside the base's environmentally controlled zones and proceeded to the control room. Based on the design of the exterior of the base, Mike assumed the most logical location for the control room and, using his instincts, found it with relative ease.

Margot teased, "You been here before?"

Mike chuckled to himself and then responded, "It's similar to the Scrat command ship. Piece of cake."

"But where is everybody?" questioned Zenith. "We should have seen bodies at least."

Mike pressed the entry pad for the control room door to slide open. When they entered, they were amazed at the size of it. With a plethora of control consoles and a second-tier along the circular perimeter, which housed the ship's logic controllers and computer relays, Zenith and Jonas were lost. Mike pointed to the second-floor tier and directed them to search there for access to the database. Meanwhile, he and Margot checked all of the monitors on the control consoles for any sign of the missing troops.

Morning came and Tisch met Wilmer in the hall outside their rooms. She mentioned how good it felt to do business like she always hoped and to do it without drama. Wilmer warned her to be wary and that all may not be what it seems. Disappointed by his approach to their paradise, she realized that he was right. Shannon joined them and the three descended the stairs to the ornate hall. Two guards greeted them and led them outside to a veranda overlooking the valley. Cabistero sat at a table and enjoyed a glass of fruit juice. He gestured for them to join him.

Tisch greeted him and thanked him for his hospitality. She announced that they would depart shortly to meet with the leaders of the other colonies to establish trade routes between them. It was then that her dream came crashing down. Four men in dark uniforms entered and stood by them. Cabistero informed her that the men had questions for them and would validate her crew's legitimacy for him. Wilmer clenched his fist, suspecting a trap, but Tisch gestured for him to remain calm.

Cabistero instructed the men to sit with him, while the servants served them breakfast. Another stranger joined them and took a seat as well. It became apparent that he was in charge of the other four men when he nodded for them to back away from the group. The man introduced himself as Lazaro, a security officer with Kronos. Shannon kicked Wilmer in the shin, knowing this was bad news. He held her hand for assurance.

Lazaro questioned Tisch about her motives for coming there and who was in charge of her operation. She mentioned that she was an independent and only sought business in an area that required it. Then Tisch commented that she wasn't aware that Kronos operated in that sector. She inquired if her ship's presence was a problem for them.

Lazaro replied, "That remains to be seen." He questioned her about her affiliation with the Federation and who provided protection for them from pirates. She denied knowing anyone in the Federation and commented that they traveled alone. She admitted that they wound up there when a war broke out between competing corporations and they needed a safe place to execute trade.

"Would your ship happen to be the *Blue Eagle*?" he inquired, curious. "I've heard many rumors about its capability to travel long distances."

Tisch giggled and replied, "I've heard the rumors as well. The *Blue Eagle* is an old freighter that was modified, if you believe the stories."

"Your ship does appear to be an odd design," he commented.

Wilmer interjected and explained, "Our ship is a medium-range hauler and we're hoping to establish the connections for long-range hauling prior to the Federation setting up their portals to overcome the obstacles posed by long distances."

"So, the Federation has aspirations of placing portals in our region," he commented, concerned.

"We don't know for sure what their intentions are," Tisch responded. "I see that as an expensive project for them to assume, but I'm sure someone else will develop portals if they don't."

Lazaro informed Cabistero that he was comfortable with him conducting business with Tisch – for now. Tisch asked what he meant by that.

"Someone discovered our base and reported it to the Federation," he explained. "We were short-handed, but managed to keep control of it."

"That's good. Isn't it?" she responded innocently.

"Yes," he answered, "but I want to know how it was discovered and who reported it."

Tisch assured him that her goal was to remain neutral in such matters but would report anything strange, if he wished. Lazaro instructed her to keep Cabistero updated on her progress and her itineraries. If she complied, all would be well. With that, he excused himself and departed with his men. Tisch questioned Cabistero if the men were based there on his planet. He pointed to the east as two cruisers took flight and vanished in the sky.

During breakfast, Tisch inquired as to what suggestions Cabistero had for them regarding the other colonies. He warned that all would be suspicious of outsiders so tread carefully. He then apologized for not giving them notice of Lazaro's visit but he was only following orders. Tisch understood and hoped to gain his trust over time. She compiled a list of items that Cabistero was willing to trade, including lumber and ore, along with the items he hoped to procure through her. They finished breakfast and were escorted to their ship by Kai.

Once on board, Tisch sent an urgent message to Mike and warned him to stay away. She mentioned that they were safe, but his presence would endanger everyone. She then turned to Wilmer and thanked him for his warning earlier. He commended her for handling the situation with tact. She admitted that she feared Mike would still return and jeopardize all of them.

Shannon then asked if they thought Kronos recaptured their base and would return there. Then Tisch realized that Mike was there with the others. Wilmer suggested they continue with their plan and let Mike adapt to what they were doing. Tisch agreed and left them on the bridge. She returned to her cabin to consider what was ahead for them.

Margot continued to check monitors while Mike went upstairs to see what progress Zenith made on the database. He was pleased to see that she was downloading on the third drive and was more than halfway through.

Jonas watched, unaware of what she was doing. He was with Special Forces a few years before Margot. Life for him was good until he was nearly killed in an explosion. With most of his unit dead and a severe head trauma, he had to endure the memories of their grief-stricken families at the funeral. Since that time, he lost his desire for combat and sought peaceful means of resolving problems. When he and Margot left the force, Marina's people recruited them. While he was a valuable backup for Margot, she grew bolder, knowing that she had to protect him.

Margot shouted for Mike from one of the consoles. He rushed down the stairs and approached. "What is it?"

Margot pointed to two of the monitors and stepped back. One of them showed prison cells on the lower level with about twenty Federation soldiers inside. The other monitor showed two Kronos cruisers heading for the base. "We've got to hurry and get out of here," he uttered, disappointed. Margot suggested they release the soldiers and let them fight it out. Mike agreed and returned to the second-floor. He instructed Zenith and Jonas to finish and return to the shuttle as soon as possible. He also warned that if the airlock was inactive, then Kronos' people were already in the bay. Zenith informed him that they just finished loading the fourth drive and already installed the fifth.

Mike and Margot rushed to the elevator and descended to the lower level. As soon as they stepped off, the prisoners shouted to them for help. Mike used pulse fire from his pulse pistol to melt the locking device on each gate until all the men were released. He warned them that their captors were returning. One of the officers, Lieutenant Bartholemew Tieg, thanked him and attempted to question him about his presence there. Mike diverted from answering the question by asking if he had a brother Jorgan on Taurus. When he acknowledged their relationship as brothers, Mike mentioned that he and Jorgan were good friends and fought many battles on Taurus against Kronos' mercenaries.

The other men searched the floor for weapons while Mike and Tieg talked. Mike informed him that they were leaving while there was still time and wished them well. Tieg returned the wishes and then organized his men for an attack on their captors. Mike and Margot hurried to the elevator and rode it to the top level. When they reached the control room, Zenith and Jonas were already gone. They hurried back toward the transport bay but found the airlock inactive.

"Damn!" muttered Mike. "They've docked already."

"What now?" asked Margot.

Mike grabbed her arm and hustled her down the hall. They checked each door until they found a supply closet unlocked. He opened the door and pushed her inside. After looking each way and seeing no one, he stepped inside and closed the door. "Looks like we're stuck here for a while," he complained.

"What about Zee and Jonas?" she asked uneasily.

"Let's hope they made it to the ship."

The sounds of footsteps in the hall followed by pulse fire filled the air. The battle in the corridor continued for over an hour before the Kronos troops were defeated. Mike heard Lieutenant Tieg speaking to his men and was relieved. He stepped out, surprising the young lieutenant. "I had hoped that you were gone by now, but I'm glad you're still here," Tieg commented.

Mike glanced at Margot, wondering what he meant. Tieg went on to explain that his technicians found that much of the database was missing with only operating files for the base's automated systems left intact. Mike swore he knew nothing about those and consented to a search to prove his claim. Tieg agreed and instructed one of the females to conduct a search of Margot, while he personally checked Mike for anything that could hold that much information. He mentioned that if Mike had already left, they would have had to pursue him under the assumption that he had the information on the database.

Margot kidded that a database like that would need a big storage device or a lot of small ones. Tieg agreed with her and admitted that Kronos likely took the information as a precaution, leaving only the files for operating the station so they could return.

Mike related to him about their interactions with General Lennox and the Scrat against Kronos. He proudly announced that he was the one who discovered the location of the base and passed it on to Lennox through Archimedes-9. Content that Mike and Margot had nothing to do with the missing database information, he allowed them to leave. Lieutenant Tieg thanked them once more and shook their hands.

Mike and Margot left them and returned to the transport bay. Mike glanced at Margot and smiled. Margot was tense and blurted, “Shit, Colby!”

They reached the shuttle and opened the hatch. Margot entered and was relieved to see Zenith and Jonas downloading the drives onto the shuttle’s computer. Mike followed and closed the hatch. He was elated to see them and high-fived his friends. Anxiously, he started the shuttle and piloted toward the bay doors. It seemed like forever for the bay to purge and the doors to open. Once they left the bay and entered open space, Mike relaxed. He set the shuttle to autopilot for Tandenar and then listened to Tisch’s message. Margot overheard it and took her seat next to Mike. “What’s going on?” she asked.

“I’m not sure, but it looks like we aren’t going to Tandenar.”

They considered their alternatives until Mike came up with a plan. He took the shuttle out of autopilot and set a course for Terran, the furthest colony from Tandenar. There they would stay until they reviewed the information from the Kronos database. The trip took close to a week and left them low on food. Zenith worked tirelessly on the information from the database. Jonas paced about, feeling useless and neglected. Meanwhile, Mike and Margot studied a scan of the planet and discovered several towns, spread far apart from each other.

“Where do we start?” questioned Margot.

“Let’s start with someplace small and in between,” he suggested, “until we know what we’re dealing with.”

Mike set the shuttle down on the side of a mountain in a small clearing, surrounded by dense forest. He instructed Zenith to continue analyzing the data and for Jonas to keep watch at the hatch. He also warned them to keep the hatch closed to avoid engaging with anyone until he returned. Zenith wasn’t thrilled with the idea and grew weary from her search.

When Mike and Margot were gone, she suggested to Jonas that they sit outside and get some fresh air. Jonas was more than happy to leave the shuttle with her. The two sat outside on a fallen tree and discussed where they hoped to be in the future. Then Jonas inquired why Zenith was searching data files for information. He suggested that a log of their communications might reveal more than all their standard operating procedures and itinerary logs. Zenith grabbed his face with her hands and kissed him. "Jonas, you are so right!" she shouted.

Zenith rushed back inside the shuttle and searched for the communications log. Once she found it, she was able to see the signatures of all correspondence with the station along with time stamps. She then transferred the signatures into the shuttle's communications console and set the system to ping each of the signatures for a location. Jonas advised her to wait but her enthusiasm got the better of her. "Don't worry, Jonas," she responded. "What could possibly go wrong?" Jonas cringed as he knew better.

CHAPTER 11

THE PACT

Mike and Margot marched through the forest towards the valley at the base of the mountain. Heat and humidity made the trek difficult. Margot complained that perhaps this wasn't the best idea and Mike reluctantly agreed. They stepped into a clearing and were immediately surrounded by strange creatures with spears. With green leathery skin, each of them crouched like monkeys. Their faces appeared almost human but with pointed ears. Grunts were the only sounds they emitted and seemed to communicate that way. Mike was surprised that they exhibited signs of intelligence when one of them pointed to their pistols and held his hands out for them. After they handed the pistols over, the creatures prodded them along a rocky path.

"Got any more bright ideas?" Margot chided. Mike gritted his teeth and said nothing.

After what seemed like hours, they reached a narrow cave that ascended in a spiral design. When they emerged into daylight, they found themselves on a plateau jutting out in the opposite side of the mountain from where they landed.

Ahead of them were numerous buildings, painted in camouflage and surrounded by lots of shrubbery. Atop each of them was a turret with twin cannons and a laser scope for targeting. A single building stood out with ornate double-doors and stained-glass windows. One of the creatures approached the doors and rapped three times with its spear. The door opened and a young woman stepped out. She gestured with her hand for Mike and Margot to enter.

Inside the building was a lobby with a desk and several electronic devices. One appeared to be for communication, another for monitoring approaching spacecraft and several others for surveillance around the colony. Two doors were located behind the desk on either side. Mike and Margot were instructed to sit on a bench to the left of the doors and wait. The woman, named Alanna, stood off to the side of the doors.

Mike waited patiently while Margot fidgeted. Mike placed his hand on her thigh and rubbed it affectionately. She smiled and calmed herself. Mike had a way of exuding confidence even in the most dire of circumstances – one of the qualities she loved about him. The left door opened, drawing their attention. A tall, bearded man with dark skin and a shaved head entered the room and stared at them, taking note of every detail about them. Mike and Margot immediately stood up and waited for the man to speak.

The prolonged silence became uncomfortable, so Mike opened with introductions. The man was unimpressed and gestured for them to sit. He announced himself only as Jackson. "Did Lazaro send you to harass me again?" he inquired.

Mike and Margot were befuddled by his question. "Who is Lazaro?" questioned Mike.

Jackson approached them and placed his hands behind his back. "If Lazaro didn't send you, then who did?" he asked in a gruff voice. "I'm sure Kronos has something to do with this."

Mike calmly explained that he was there on behalf of Tisch to evaluate the potential for trade routes among the colonies. Jackson burst into laughter at the idea. Mike grew irritated with the man and pressed him to explain himself. Jackson whispered to the woman and she left them. He took a seat behind the desk and leaned forward. “How did you get past Lazaro’s ships?” he inquired curiously.

Mike explained the situation with Kronos’ base and their control of the region. He was surprised to learn from Jackson that Kronos’ troops under Lazaro not only controlled trade, but taxed it as well. As a result, all the colonies limited their trading and became reclusive. Tandenar was the only colony to retain their relationship with Kronos and, as a result, its ships were the only ones that transported cargo. Its leader, Cabistero, was a puppet of theirs and untrustworthy. Both Mike and Margot tried to assure Jackson that the problem was dealt with and that the Federation controlled the base now.

“The Federation is no better than Kronos!” he barked at them. “They dumped groups of us on each of the planets in the Nigus star system to set up colonies and expand. Then they forgot about us; no food supplies, no medical supplies, and no construction materials. How thoughtful of them.”

Mike admitted that he knew nothing about this and considered that it happened as a result of the war with Kronos. Alanna returned with glasses of tea and set them on the desk. Jackson pointed and offered the teas to Mike and Margot. Thirsty from the hike, they graciously accepted. Mike then challenged Jackson with a question that caught him by surprise. “What would it take to restore the trade among the colonies?” Jackson stared at him for a moment, wondering if he should take him seriously or not.

Margot interjected and reminded him that Kronos is no longer in control of the skies over the colonies anymore. He folded his arms and leaned back in his chair, considering the changing circumstances. “What assurance do I have that you can protect our ships?” he countered. “None of the colonies can afford to lose the few ships that we have left.”

“What do you use them for now?” Mike asked, curious.

Jackson explained that all ships in the colonies have been mothballed, to be used for emergency evacuation only. Mike suggested that the *Blue Eagle* could run the trade routes for a period of time until the colonies were comfortable. Then they would take over.

"So, what do you get out of this?" Jackson inquired, expecting tariffs or fees of some sort.

Mike chuckled at him and replied, "Now we're getting somewhere." He then revealed that the *Blue Eagle* was primarily for long-distance hauling and would link the colonies to Archimedes-9 where they could trade for a wider range of products that weren't available to them now, such as medical devices, technological equipment and tourism.

Jackson was intrigued by the offer and suggested he could summon the leaders to discuss Mike's offer; however, he cautioned that Cabistero would likely be a problem as his relationship was quite profitable under Kronos. Mike admitted that Cabistero would make a lot less under the new system and if he declined to be a part of the group, he would make nothing at all.

Jackson laughed as he enjoyed the idea of humbling Cabistero. He then added that an act of good will by Mike, such as transporting the trade leaders to Terran for the meeting and then returning them home, would go a long way towards reassuring them that it was safe to resume trade again.

"Consider it done," announced Mike, proud of their progress. He and Margot both stood and shook hands with Jackson.

Jackson invited them to stay as guests while he made the arrangements for the meeting. He introduced Alanna as his daughter and instructed her to show them around the facility. They thanked him again and were escorted by Alanna from the building.

As they walked along with Alanna, Margot inquired about the creatures that brought them up to the facility. She explained that there were numerous primitive tribes on the planet and that they were friendly. When the colony was started, they had difficulty finding food and shelter.

The tribes were eager to help and since that time, they have looked out for each other.

Alanna took them to another camouflaged building. Inside was a recreation room with a pool table and several games. She commented that these were the few luxuries they brought from their world years ago. They followed her up a stairwell to the second floor, where ten apartment units were located. At the end of the hall, Alanna paused and opened the door for them. "I think you'll find the view from the balcony very pleasing," she said. "I'll come by for you in a little while for dinner." They thanked her and she departed.

The apartment had a compliment of furniture made from bamboo: a square table in the middle of the living room, surrounded by four chairs; a single bed in the second room with a bureau and chest. Two doors made of bamboo and palm leaves led onto a balcony with a view down to the valley. A bamboo railing prevented an inadvertent fall from occurring.

Margot eagerly explored the balcony and was impressed. She summoned Mike to join her and took his arm in hers. "Reminds me of a honeymoon suite on a Polynesian island on Earth," she mentioned coyly.

"You've been to Earth?" he asked, wondering how and when.

"Once. A long time ago. It was beautiful until war broke out. I was one of the security detail sent to negotiate a truce between the warring factions, but we failed." Margot grew saddened by the memory.

"We can't win them all," Mike commented. He embraced her affectionately and then kissed her. "A honeymoon suite, huh?" he remarked. Margot smiled and followed him to the bed.

Tisch, Shannon and Wilmer manned their stations on the bridge of the *Blue Eagle* in silence. Each wondered what to do about Mike and Margot. When the transmitter pinged for an incoming signal, Tisch and

Wilmer stood by eagerly as Shannon acknowledged it. The trade leader for Cirrus requested a pickup for a meeting on Terran. The three of them stared at each other, wondering what brought this on. Shannon requested coordinates and as soon as they were received, she piloted the *Blue Eagle* toward the source.

Tisch wondered if Cabistero had stepped up to help them or if they were being lured into a trap. Wilmer reminded her that they intended to meet with the various leaders of the colonies anyway, so they'd have faced the same risks.

"Damn, I wish Mike was here," grumbled Tisch.

Shannon informed them that they weren't far from the Cirran colony. Shortly after, they received another message. This one came from Cabistero himself. He instructed them to pick up each of the colonies' leaders for a meeting on Terran and keep him informed of what they were up to. Tisch responded with a request as to why he wasn't attending. He informed her that he was concerned for his safety and that they might attempt to trap him. She wondered why they'd go through all the trouble after so long. Shannon sent a follow up, confirming his instructions.

Wilmer and Shannon waited anxiously for further instructions, but none came. Tisch excused herself and left the bridge. Wilmer surmised that Tisch wasn't happy with the risk she was assuming without Mike for backup. Shannon recommended that they arm themselves and be prepared for anything. They proceeded to the first colony for the for the initial pickup.

When they arrived, they were given docking instructions to a camouflaged port. Tisch returned to the bridge and instructed them to stay inside the ship and prepare for immediate flight if anything went wrong. Wilmer suggested going with her but she rejected his offer.

Tisch exited the ship through the open personnel hatch and was greeted by two men. Both appeared to be of Indian descent and stood with their arms folded. Neither appeared armed. The first man introduced himself as Gundor and his partner as Filson. He informed her that they were ready to depart as soon as she was. Tisch stepped back and invited them to board.

Once the hatch was sealed, Gundor gave her coordinates to the next pickup location. Shannon programmed the coordinates into the navigation system, while Wilmer sat in the captain's seat. Tisch stood in front of the men and contemplated where to begin questioning them.

Fortunately, Gundor broke the silence and congratulated her on the plan to unite the colonies into a trading confederation. Tisch nodded, unsure of what he referred to. Filson then commented how surprised they were to hear from Jackson on Terran. Gundor added that Tisch's man Mike must have done a heck of a job convincing Jackson to participate in this.

Now curious, Tisch inquired what they knew of Mike's visit to Terran. Gundor related everything he heard from Jackson about how they handled the Kronos' ships and her plan for establishing trade among the colonies and with Archimedes-9. Tisch was pleased, knowing that only Mike could reference Archimedes-9.

Concerned for Mike, Wilmer questioned the men if Mike was going to participate in the meeting on Terran. They affirmed that he would be there as well.

Zenith and Jonas sat outside the shuttle on a log. Jonas mentioned that he wasn't really happy with the work they were involved in. Zenith was surprised and wondered if this was leading up to the end of their relationship. He explained to her that he preferred to do detective work rather than deal with the day-to-day problems of being a space trucker. Now Zenith was disappointed. She knew what was coming next and feared how she would respond.

"When we get back, I'd like to speak with a GSS rep about doing investigative work for them in the field. If they have employment for me, would you join me?"

And there it was. Zenith was crushed, knowing that he was leaving, with or without her. She explained that the crew was her family and the *Blue Eagle* was her home. Then she added that she had hoped that Jonas would be part of that family and make a life with her. He held her hands in his and promised that he would always be her friend if he left. She became teary-eyed and lowered her head.

Several branches snapped and startled them. Six of the creatures emerged from the trees and surrounded them. They both realized that they had orders to stay inside and keep the hatch closed but now they were vulnerable. Zenith attempted to reach the shuttle's hatch but two of the creatures intercepted her and pointed their spears at her. Another of the creatures pointed down the path that Mike and Margot took. He grunted and nudged them with his spear. They reluctantly followed the path down the mountain.

Zenith fretted and uttered, "We can't leave the shuttle open like this. Mike will kill me!"

Jonas warned her, "Keep your mouth shut and do what they want. I'm not ready to die today." Zenith realized he was right. They had no choice but to obey their captors. During their march, Zenith queried Jonas about his determination to change careers. She reminded him that Tisch gave her a chance that no one else would. Jonas urged her to be calm and see what happens. He remarked that sometimes things just aren't meant to be. Saddened, she said nothing more.

When they reached the bottom of the mountain, Zenith stumbled, fatigued from the hike, and fell down. Jonas put his arm around her waist and supported her. The sky darkened as nightfall approached. They finally reached the narrow cave and then made the ascent up the spiral steps. Both of them were sweating from the warm, humid air as they emerged onto the plateau. Jonas noted that they should be near the end of their journey, hoping to reassure Zenith.

The creatures prodded them toward the main building where Alanna greeted them. Unsure of her purpose, they remained quiet. She led them inside the same building where Mike and Margot first arrived and directed them to sit. Jonas attempted to question her but she gestured for silence and left the room.

"I don't have a warm feeling about this, Zee," he complained.

"Mike and Margot have to be around here somewhere," she responded, hoping for their appearance. Alanna returned with iced tea for them and asked them to be patient.

"Have you seen our friends?" Zee questioned her.

Alanna smiled and assured them that their friends were fine. She departed the lobby again. Jonas commented that they were left near functioning equipment, so it was unlikely they were prisoners.

After several minutes, Jackson entered with Alanna. He inquired how they knew Mike and Margot. Once he realized they were part of Mike's crew, he instructed Alanna to take them to their accommodations. She gestured for them to follow her as she departed the building. Once outside, she revealed that she was taking them to see Mike and Margot.

They arrived on the second floor and followed Alanna down the hall. She knocked on the last door and stepped aside. The door opened and Mike stepped out, surprised to see them. Zenith sheepishly waved to him while Jonas lowered his head, knowing that Mike already knew what they did. Alanna informed him that they claimed to be his friends. He nodded and thanked her. When she left, he pointed inside the room. Zenith entered, followed by Jonas.

Mike looked up and rolled his eyes. Margot was pleased to see them but then asked, "Weren't you inside the shuttle?"

Zenith stammered before admitting that they stepped outside for some fresh air. Mike immediately asked, "You did secure the shuttle, didn't you?" Both lowered their heads, embarrassed by their failure. Mike grew flustered and informed Margot that he was going back. She reminded him that he might offend Jackson if he left without discussing it with him. Mike sat down and covered his eyes in frustration. Margot stared at them with her hands on her hips.

"Nobody's around to bother the shuttle," Zenith mumbled. "Only the creatures and they're probably guarding it." Mike grit his teeth at her and said no more. He stood on the balcony and stared out at the valley below.

Margot knew better than to bother him when he was in a mood like this. Instead, she sat with Zenith and Jonas and inquired about their progress on the database. Zenith was excited as she revealed how they discovered all the signatures in the data log and how she set up the shuttle's computer to ping each signature to identify its location.

Margot suddenly turned pale as she listened. Zenith and Jonas then realized that they did something terribly wrong. "Those pings you sent out can be interpolated to identify the source," explained Margot, "especially if multiple sources belong to Kronos." Now Zenith understood what she did. She apologized and admitted that she only wanted to find the location of the other bases for Mike.

"Where are the portable drives now?" questioned Margot.

Zenith lowered her head and replied, "I left them on top of the console."

Now Margot covered her eyes, hiding her disappointment in them. Finally, she reiterated their mistake. "You left the drives on the console with the shuttle unsecured and you were captured, leaving the shuttle open for anyone to enter to take the drives and, as an added measure, you programmed the shuttle to ping all the Kronos' locations listed in the log."

Zenith nodded, humiliated by her ineptitude. Jonas spoke up in her defense, explaining that they were left alone for a tedious task with no consideration of their feelings. Margot stood up and got in Jonas' face. "Kronos likely already sent at least one team to find that shuttle and retrieve the information from the database," she informed them. "They will likely come hunting for us as well, endangering these people."

Zenith became teary-eyed, knowing their poor judgment just created a disaster. Jonas placed his arm around her, hoping to console her. Margot sat down and buried her face in her hands. Mike entered the room from the balcony and noticed the saddened looks on their faces. "What did I miss?" he asked, knowing it was bad.

Margot stood and approached him. She placed her hands on his arms and suggested they speak with Jackson about securing the shuttle immediately. Mike glanced at Zenith and knew right away what happened. He ordered her and Jonas to stay put and promised there would be consequences if they did anything else without his approval. He stormed out of the apartment, followed by Margot.

Alanna met them in the courtyard between the buildings and inquired if something happened that displeased them. Mike informed her that they needed to see Jackson immediately and that something important had come up. She led them to Jackson's building and instructed them to sit. They waited for what seemed like hours. Mike paced the floor wondering what the delay was about. Just as he was about to leave, Jackson entered, grim-faced.

"We have a problem," he announced in a somber voice. "Several ships are approaching this region. It appears your ship is broadcasting a repeating signal that is drawing them." Jackson then informed them that the ships appear to be both Federation and Kronos, coming from different directions.

Mike acknowledged the problem and requested permission to return to the shuttle immediately to try and mitigate the damage. Jackson sent Alanna to assemble a team of the creatures to escort Mike and Margot. Jackson urged them to keep the ships away from his facility if possible. Mike promised to do his best and then departed. Margot attempted to reassure Jackson and mentioned that Mike is a great strategist and would likely solve this. He bade her to be safe and then left the room. Margot hurried after Mike.

When they drew near the shuttle, the creatures disappeared into the trees around them. The sound of voices at the shuttle caught their attention. Three armed men wearing black uniforms stood guard outside the shuttle. Suddenly pulse fire erupted from the trees opposite Mike and Margot. Two men emerged from inside the shuttle. One shouted, "I got the drives! Let's get out of here!"

A Kronos patrol ship descended on the area and fired at the Federation troops in the trees. Two Federation ships arrived and fired on the patrol ships. The creatures emerged from the trees and pursued the Kronos personnel through the forest.

"Now's our chance!" shouted Mike. He rushed to the shuttle with Margot trailing to cover him. Once inside the shuttle, Margot secured the hatch and Mike placed it in 'startup' mode. Immediately, he took the shuttle into cloak mode. As soon as startup diagnostics completed, he piloted the invisible shuttle away from the area.

The Federation and Kronos ships battled with all sustaining damage. While Mike watched the battle on the monitor, Margot promptly identified the program that Zenith implemented to send pings for each signature in the log and terminated it. "The program is shut down, Mike." Margot announced. "They can't track us."

Mike guided the shuttle into the upper atmosphere and idled there while watching the battle unfold. Margot sat next to him and, sensing his stress level, attempted to calm him. She explained what Zenith had hoped to do and that she meant well. Mike was upset that they disobeyed his instructions and now they lost the drives.

The battle below ended with Federation personnel from their last two ships boarding the remaining Kronos ship. Shortly after, the three ships departed away from the planet's surface, much to Mike's curiosity. "Why didn't the Feds finish them off?" he thought aloud.

Margot suggested he forget about them and return to Jackson's facility in the shuttle. He agreed and returned to the surface. Margot made contact and requested permission to dock at the facility. Jackson instructed them to enter the bay through a cave in the side of the mountain beneath the buildings that overlooked the valley.

Jackson and Alanna waited anxiously in the large underground bay for the shuttle to dock. The shuttle settled down in a corner berth and shut down. The hatch opened and Mike emerged, followed by Margot. He wore a look of dejection as he approached Jackson. Margot seemed disinterested in his mood and kept her distance until she reached their hosts.

Jackson congratulated them on a successful outcome and suggested they discuss things over dinner. As they walked toward an elevator, Mike expressed his apologies for the danger they put Jackson and his people in. Jackson didn't seem bothered by it but did express his concern that, no matter what, Kronos and the Federation would always be a threat to them. In spite of that, he believed that the colonies needed to accept that and work together to improve their worlds.

When they reached the dining facility located behind Jackson's official business building, Zenith and Jonas stood in the corner away from the table, like two school kids being punished. Jackson invited everyone to take a seat at the table while Alanna directed three servant girls to serve wine, followed by an appetizer soup. No one spoke until Jackson proposed a toast to Mike and his crew. Everyone raised their glasses and acknowledged him.

As they sipped from their glasses, Mike opened the conversation by offering to leave and never return to avoid putting them in any further danger. Jackson informed him that it wouldn't be necessary. He then revealed that he spoke with the other trade leaders who were agreeable to meeting over expanding trade opportunities. He revealed that the captain of the *Blue Eagle* apparently played her cards well with Cabistero on Tandenar and has his blessing to conduct trade among the colonies - along with the taxes he expects to receive from it. In addition, the *Blue Eagle* would be arriving in a few days with the trade leaders.

Despite the good news, Mike explained that they lost something very important from inside the shuttle. Jackson nodded to Alanna who left the room. He mentioned that his creature friends, the Nairobis, brought back something they took from the soldiers. Mike's eyes widened as he hoped it was the portable drives. Alanna returned and handed three of them to Jackson.

"These must be very important although I can't imagine leaving them unprotected as they were," he remarked.

Mike explained that it had information that both Kronos and the Federation wanted. Unfortunately, two of the drives were missing. Jackson then informed him that the Federation contacted him and requested a meeting with Mike over some missing property. "It sounds like these may be gone soon as well."

"We don't need them anymore," blurted Zenith. Mike glared at her, indicating she should shut up. He then inquired when they would arrive.

"Lieutenant Tieg will be here later this evening," Jackson informed them. "This could be an opportunity to get both the Federation and Kronos out of our way."

Knowing that Zenith copied the information to the shuttle's database, Margot added, "We might be better off without the drives if it guarantees our safety."

Jackson handed the drives to Mike and commented that he believed that Mike would find a way to make this new trade venture work. Mike was thankful and then tasted his soup. He was quite pleased thus far with the accommodations *and* the food. The servants returned with what appeared to be roast beef and vegetables that Mike was unfamiliar with. They enjoyed the meal and focused on conversation not business related.

After dinner, Mike retired to the apartment. He was still upset with Zenith and Jonas over their disobedience and the loss of two of the portable drives. Margot remained with them and questioned Zenith about the logs and what she learned from them. She was elated when Zenith revealed that they knew the general location of the fourth Kronos base. Jonas pointed out that it's possible they could narrow down the location of the fifth and last base by isolating all the departing ship reporting signatures to their destinations. They were sure that could be established by the progressing points of location of each ship in relation to the time stamp. Incoming ship signatures weren't likely to help as direct correspondence between the station and the ships was limited to simple yes or no answers based on generic pings, one or two, just like Zenith used.

Alanna joined them and announced that Lieutenant Tieg had arrived and was on his way to the dining facility. She offered to summon Mike and meet them shortly. Margot thanked her and walked to the facility. She advised Zenith and Jonas to keep their mouths shut unless Mike asked them for something specific. Both were embarrassed and offended by their treatment. They knew they screwed up but they always did a good job for Mike and this was excessive in their minds. Margot sensed that and suggested that they be patient with Mike. Once everything was taken care of on Terran, she would make sure he got over his anger with them.

Inside the dining hall, the servants directed them to their seats and served them glasses of wine. Jackson entered with Lieutenant Tieg and they took their seats. Tieg commented to Margot, "So, we meet again? Where is your partner?"

"He'll be here any minute," she replied curtly.

As if on cue, Mike entered with Alanna and took his seat. "Nice to see you again, Lieutenant," Mike said politely.

"It seems you misled us about accessing the Kronos database," he responded. "That wasn't nice."

Mike admitted that it wasn't worth the trouble and he should have given it to them when Tieg requested it. He apologized for losing two of the drives to the Kronos mercenaries. "What is on those drives that is so critical to the Federation?" he asked Tieg.

Tieg smiled and countered, "What's on them that you were willing to risk your life to take the whole database?"

"Touché, my friend." Mike raised his glass and proposed a toast to the end of the database. He reached into a leather bag attached to his belt and retrieved the three drives. He slid them across the table to Lieutenant Tieg. Tieg smiled and echoed his toast. Everyone seemed pleased with the outcome and enjoyed their wine.

Lieutenant Tieg then inquired what Mike was up to in the star system since he wasn't likely to leave. When Mike smiled and stared at his glass, Margot knew he had something up his sleeve. To play along, she queried Mike if he wanted her to relate their plans or if he preferred to handle it.

"I got this," he replied. Mike then explained that he wanted the database to see if the Kronos base would make a good trading hub, now that the Federation had control of it. He felt that it would be a neutral site that would keep all the trade leaders of the colonies happy. Then he explained that Tisch sent him there to help them re-establish their trade routes. In return, the *Blue Eagle* would run the long route between the hub and Archimedes-9 as they had no interest in returning to Taurus.

Lieutenant Tieg was interested in his story and inquired what they would do for protection. Mike suggested that they could work out an arrangement with the colonies to provide supplies to the Federation personnel on the hub in return for their protection, if required. Margot then asked Lieutenant Tieg if he expected Kronos to return to the area again and why they didn't destroy their remaining ship earlier.

Jackson was amused by the back-and-forth inquisition by the two parties and considered how it would benefit him. He gestured to the servants to bring more wine and plates of diced cheese.

Lieutenant Tieg then inquired if Mike still needed the drives for his research. Mike declined, hoping that he could trust Tieg to arrange a suitable atmosphere for the traders to conduct business instead. That being the case, Mike admitted that he no longer needed anything from the database. Satisfied, Tieg changed the topic to Mike's experiences with his brother Jorgan on Taurus. They talked until late in the evening and drank plenty of wine. Finally, Lieutenant Tieg announced he needed to return to his ship and crew. He promised to return in a few days for the trade meeting to affirm the Federation's responsibility to the traders. Satisfied with the outcome of their conversation, Tieg shook hands with everyone and departed.

Jackson surprised Mike and commented, "That's not really why you wanted the database, is it?"

Mike explained that it was personal between him and the leaders of Kronos and he hoped to find the location of their last two bases. He confessed that he enjoyed the simplicity of life on Terran so far as well as their fine cuisine. Margot added that they were tired of the fighting and preferred a different lifestyle.

Jackson was pleased to hear that and invited them to stay as long as they wished, whenever they wanted to. He then kidded that Mike should go easy on the youngsters. Mike sighed as he glanced at Zenith and Jonas. With that, Jackson retired for the night. Alanna instructed the servants to provide them with whatever they needed. Exhausted from all the excitement, Mike and Margot returned to their apartment.

Zenith asked one of the servants what Alanna's capacity was at the facility. She answered that Alanna was Jackson's daughter. Zenith then suggested to Alanna that they 'hang out' and get to know each other better. Alanna offered to have lunch with her before their departure and then retired for the night.

Mike sat on the bed and pondered what transpired in the dining facility. He was still upset about losing the portable drives and the disobedience shown by Zenith and Jonas. Margot stood in front of him with her hands on her hips and a grim expression. She chided him for being childish and stubborn toward his crew, including her. He leaned back and flattened on the bed with his arms out. Dejected, he had nothing to say.

Margot undressed and shoved him over so she could get into bed. Mike realized he needed to resolve this issue with Margot before it festered into something worse. He sat up and stared at her.

"Something you want to say?" she inquired.

"Yeah," he replied humbly. "I'm sorry."

Margot sat up with her legs folded in front of her and her hands supporting her against the bed. "When we went back to the shuttle, I shut down the program that sent the pings out to the signatures in the logs. Didn't you wonder how that program was running if the drives were missing?" Mike thought for a moment and then urged her to continue. "Zenith copied the database onto the shuttle's computer system. You don't need the drives, you idiot."

Now Mike was embarrassed. Not only was he wrong but he vented continuously on Zenith and Jonas for losing the drives, never thinking to trust that she went above and beyond to save the database and search for the potential locations of the Kronos bases. "I guess I screwed up, too," he confessed.

Margot then surmised aloud that both the Federation and Kronos would leave them alone, thinking that they no longer had the information on the database. "Fortunately," she began, "Jackson's creatures interrupted the Kronos mercenaries so only the drives were taken. They likely had no time to investigate the shuttle's computer."

Mike responded by voicing his displeasure that the youngsters didn't listen and put themselves in danger because of it. Also, by initiating the program to identify signatures from the log, Zenith put everyone in the colony in danger. Margot reminded him that they are inexperienced and meant well. She encouraged him to use this as a chance to teach them how to be better. Mike relented and promised to take care of it in the morning. He laid down and closed his eyes.

Margot took exception to him going to sleep and reminded him that this was like a honeymoon suite on a beautiful mountain. She suggested he behave as such. Surprised, Mike rolled toward her and was about to kiss her but hesitated. "Is this another trick to keep me from coming up with new ideas?" he whispered to her.

"We can stop right now, if you like," she replied and waited patiently for his answer.

"Nope, I'm good," he said and kissed her hungrily. They snuggled under the covers and enjoyed their night.

The *Blue Eagle* arrived on Terran and docked inside Jackson's facility next to Mike's shuttle. Tisch exited with eleven of the trade leaders and was greeted by Alanna. She led them into the dining facility where Jackson waited anxiously for their appearance. Wilmer and Shannon entered a few minutes later after shutting down the ship. Tisch was disappointed when she didn't see Mike or Margot. Standing behind her, Alanna noticed her concern and mentioned subtly that their friends were on the way.

Jackson invited them to sit and enjoy dinner with them. The servants brought in ewers of wine and water for the guests. Just as Tisch was about to open the conversation, Mike and Margot entered and greeted their friends.

When they finally took their seats, Jackson stood and thanked everyone for coming. He revealed to them the intentions that Mike proposed on Tisch's behalf. Tisch was impressed and yet surprised that Mike would do something as constructive as this to help her. Jackson expressed his displeasure that Cabistero chose not to attend.

One of the leaders commented that he was likely concerned about losing his control of the colonies and their trading revenues. Tisch informed them that she met with him and he was anxious to know what transpired at the meeting. Mike requested that she reserve her judgment until she heard all the facts. She suspected that Mike wouldn't disappoint her but he was up to something more than the obvious, once again.

Jackson proposed a toast to their new trading proposal and promised to give the leaders adequate time to assess their plan. The leaders of the colonies turned to Gundor and Filson to lead the negotiations. Filson mentioned that the number one issue was security. If the colonies bought into this trade pact and Kronos returned, they would all pay a heavy price. In addition, Lazaro was likely still around and he was a Kronos officer, even if he was rogue.

Tisch deferred the question to Mike, hoping he had the answers to this issue. Mike feigned a surprised expression and then rubbed his chin as if in deep thought. He turned to Jackson and suggested he bring in their guest. The leaders looked surprised, wondering who would be summoned in regards to security.

Tisch whispered to Wilmer, "And here's where Mike ruins the moment." Wilmer chuckled and glanced at the rest of the crew. Wilmer knew better than to doubt Mike and waited patiently. Jackson nodded to Alanna, who then left the room. Mike assured them that this plan was well thought out and provisions were made to ensure the colonies were not taken advantage of.

When Lieutenant Tieg entered the room behind Alanna, Tisch covered her eyes in frustration. She hoped to be free of any military or warring factions and to conduct business without any drama.

After Lieutenant Tieg introduced himself, Mike mentioned immediately that the Lieutenant was the brother of Major Jorgan Tieg, their *close* friend, on Taurus. The leaders looked concerned and seemed apprehensive over the Federation's involvement. Jackson gestured for him to take the seat next to Mike. Tisch glared at Mike, indicating her displeasure over their involvement with the Federation. Mike smiled at her with his usual teeming confidence that drove her crazy.

Mike stood and walked around the room, enjoying the attention. He related how the Kronos base was now under control of the Federation. He then revealed how circumstances have placed Kronos on the defensive, thus requiring them to withdraw their forces from the region. Mike then explained that he and Lieutenant Tieg discussed how to proceed in assisting the trade partners. He nodded for Tieg to speak and then sat down.

Lieutenant Tieg expressed his understanding of their apprehension over the Federation's involvement. He reminded them that both the colonies and his forces are a long way from home and need to trust each other if they are to succeed. Although he doubted that Kronos would return, there was always the possibility that the tide of the war could turn against them and that Kronos would attempt to reclaim their base. There was also the possibility of pirates moving into the area once word got out that Kronos was gone.

Filson inquired as to what the cost would be to them for the Federation to protect them. Lieutenant Tieg then turned to Mike for further explanation to answer their concerns about payment. Tisch folded her arms and smiled sarcastically at Mike. She was eager to hear him talk his way through this issue.

Mike suggested that the former Kronos base be a neutral site for everyone. All trading could be conducted there. Each colony would be given an area of its own, commensurate with their needs and their products. The colonies would elect a council to manage the station. The Federation would report to them unless they were summoned by their superiors to go elsewhere. They would only intervene in law enforcement when directed by the council. In return, the colonies would provide food and a modest stipend for the Federation personnel, since they were already on the Federation's payroll. Then he added that Federation personnel would not be seen on the trading floors when on duty. They would only appear if off-duty for leisure and on personal business, like trading.

The leaders nodded to each other in agreement. Gundor suggested that, instead of a stipend, they provide all military personnel with a reasonable discount on purchases at the trading platform. Tieg was amused by the idea and agreed that it would benefit everyone and maintain the simplicity of their arrangement.

Mike then announced that once the colonies established themselves on the base, the *Blue Eagle* would be their link to Archimedes-9 and Taurus. Logistically, this would maximize the *Blue Eagle's* availability to travel back and forth from the base to Archimedes-9. He reminded them that most of their trading capital was natural resources which were rare on the main hubs. The leaders were delighted over the idea. He then requested that Tisch take over to answer questions about her role with the *Blue Eagle* in helping them and why she would do this.

Tisch was stunned that Mike would show her this kind if respect. She stood and spoke with the leaders, relating her expectations and how this could elevate their living standards. When she finished, everyone was satisfied and a pact was created for all to sign. Lieutenant Tieg then announced that they were free to come to the station and inspect the areas that would be assigned to them.

Margot then inquired about the Kronos ship that was allowed to escape. Tieg smiled at her and explained that they spared their lives in return for future information so they could all co-exist in peace in the Nigus star system. The crews on those ships were happy to avoid the war and make the most of their assignment in the Nigus star system. Then he mentioned that he also had a spy on board so it was in their best interest to let the ship go. Satisfied with his response, she said no more. They arranged for the leaders to visit the base the next morning and plan the establishment of their trading posts.

Mike and Margot excused themselves and returned to their apartment. The others remained and enjoyed Jackson's hospitality. Once inside the apartment, Margot congratulated Mike on the success of such a complex plan with so many different people involved. When she went out to the balcony alone and remained for several moments, Mike sensed that something bothered her. He joined her and placed his arm around her waist. "What's wrong?" he inquired, concerned about her.

Margot turned and faced him. She shook her head, feigning disappointed and reminded him of the criticism she would receive over his ideas. "Tisch is going to think I'm inadequate in bed with you," she complained. "If our sex was good, then you wouldn't be thinking of all this stuff." Mike chuckled and assured her that he'd handle the comments. She giggled and they kissed.

The next day, the *Blue Eagle* arrived at the old Kronos base along with Mike's shuttle. The leaders were excited over the opportunity and the fact that the Federation assumed the risks of an attack by allowing them to trade there on the base instead of at their own colonies. It appeared to be a win-win for everyone.

While Lieutenant Tieg's men escorted Tisch and the colony leaders around the proposed trading area, Mike met with Tieg. He questioned Tieg about the possibility that Kronos had a spy among his men. Tieg believed that his team was vetted thoroughly but recognized that, if he could plant a spy among Kronos' crew, then it was possible that they did the same. They discussed how valuable the Nigus star system was to both the Federation and to Kronos. Personally, Tieg didn't see any value at all and preferred to be closer to home. Mike pointed out that it appeared to be a staging base for future operations and, until recently, was unknown to everyone.

Mike questioned the progress that the Federation was making with their portal technology and if they would provide one for transportation to and from the Nigus system. Tieg admitted that it was above his paygrade and that General Lennox was the only one who would have that answer.

Lieutenant Tieg was eager to hear more about Mike's experiences with his brother Jorgan on Taurus. The two men went to the cafeteria and drank tea while Mike related all that happened since he first met the older brother. Tieg was amazed at what they had to overcome on Taurus.

Mike was pleased with the friendship that developed between them and believed he could trust him.

Tieg surprised him and inquired about the module. Mike knew it would come up eventually but didn't expect it so soon. He admitted that they had it and how they used it, but also that it degraded and was no longer reliable. He confessed that he hoped his cooperation and success with the Federation would lay the groundwork for long-distance trade, not just between the Nigus system and Archimedes-9, but for all future routes. Tieg offered to recommend the portal for Mike when he made his next contact with Federation Headquarters. He also complimented Mike on the arrangement he offered with the leaders of the colonies and the Federation. He felt it would be good for the moral of his men while deployed out there.

Tisch entered the cafeteria with Margot and the crew. They joined the men at the table, wondering what new ideas Mike was conjuring up now. The Lieutenant thanked Mike once more and excused himself.

Mike immediately took the opportunity to apologize to Zenith and Jonas. He also emphasized why it was important to take certain measures and what could have happened. Then he admitted that his main concern was that Kronos could have taken them prisoner and used their lives for leverage against him. Zenith was pleased that he acknowledged her efforts and the success that she did have and assured him that they would never disobey an order again.

Sensing their focus on him, Mike turned his attention to Tisch and Margot. He leaned back in his chair and waited for more criticism from the women. "Go ahead. Give it to me," he said with a pained expression.

Tisch responded, "I'm proud of you, Mike."

Margot then added, "But I'm obviously not doing enough to occupy your mind at night."

Mike explained to the women that these ideas don't originate at night, but on the fly as their situations change. Margot mentioned her concerns that he was going to burn out at some point. She compared his ability to strategize and execute at this level to Marina's but Marina continued to pay a heavy price for that, particularly in leading a lonely life. Mike assured both women that he hoped this pact would lead to a normal life for all of them in the very near future.

"I have a hard time believing that you can walk away from your obsession with Kronos without achieving some degree of satisfaction," commented Tisch.

Mike laughed hysterically at her and reminded her that he was responsible for Kronos losing that base to them. "I would like to figure out where the last two bases are and then turn it over to Marina's people, just to know that Kronos lost," he admitted. "I am content to walk away from the battle though." Everyone was relieved to hear that.

"So, what is the next step for us?" questioned Tisch.

Mike recommended that they relax for a few days and then discuss their plans to initiate trade between the new trade center and Archimedes-9. Again, everyone was pleased and hoped that Mike was serious about his intentions. When he got up and left the table, Tisch suggested to Margot that she do her duty before Mike ruined a good day. Everyone, including Margot enjoyed the ribbing about her and Mike at night.

CHAPTER 12

THE TRADE ROUTES

Mike and Margot departed in his shuttle for Archimedes-9. Tisch remained on Terran to set up contracts with the leaders of the colonies. Meanwhile, her crew enjoyed the downtime on Terran.

Tisch sat with several of the leaders in the conference room and discussed her future ambitions for the region, especially if the Federation installed a portal for their access to Archimedes-9. The time saved in transporting goods would open the door for the colonies to provide their own transportation of goods to and from Archimedes-9. They were pleased to know that they had the opportunity to conduct their own trading with Archimedes-9, if they chose to do so.

The leaders then suggested a name for their new trade center and recommended *Genesis* for a new beginning. All were in agreement. Tisch then requested a list of the items each leader sought to trade on Archimedes-9 and what they hoped to receive in return. The leaders promised to provide the list as soon as possible. It was important that they don't duplicate items unless necessary to maximize their selection of goods.

Suddenly, the room became quiet. Tisch realized someone entered behind her and caught everyone's attention. She turned and was surprised to see Cabistero standing in the doorway. He approached them, dressed in a robe and turban with dark glasses.

"Ah, Captain Mallory!" he greeted her. "It seems you've taken matters into your own hands." Tisch didn't respond, feeling caught like a thief in the night.

Jackson stood up and informed him that he was only welcome if he was willing to join their new trade union. Cabistero laughed sarcastically at the idea that he would forego the profits he enjoyed. He warned them that there would be consequences for their actions unless they were willing to pay a privilege tax to him, amounting to an insane forty-percent of their sales, not their profits.

Determined not to be intimidated, Tisch informed him that he stood to gain more by joining their union than by opposing it. She also warned that, if he chose to create problems, he would have to deal with Mike Colby, who was already Kronos' worst nightmare. Cabistero pointed a finger at Tisch and shook his head in disbelief. Without another word, he left them.

The leaders grew concerned and questioned Tisch about what support Mike would have, should Cabistero attempt to disrupt their business. She reminded them that the Federation presence on *Genesis* would deter any aggression by him. Wilmer added that Cabistero may not be aware of the fact that Kronos has left the area and the Federation controlled more than just the base.

Filson voiced his concerns about the safety of their ships, transporting goods to and from their colonies to the station. Again, Tisch reminded them that, between Mike and the Federation's presence, they had nothing to fear. She promised to have Mike handle Cabistero as soon as he returned from Archimedes-9.

Tisch rolled out the latest information she had from Rebecca's people and opened the floor to questions and comments. Everyone was pleased with the outcome of the trade agreement and the creation of Genesis as a trading center for the colonies. Tisch reminded them that Mike and Margot were responsible for making that happen by removing obstacles that hindered trade previously.

The meeting ended and the leaders dispersed to meet with their merchants. Jackson requested that Tisch join him for a walk to discuss Cabistero's appearance.

Jackson explained to Tisch how Lazaro, despite being a Kronos officer, ran his own operation through Cabistero and likely did not want his side-business known to his Kronos superiors. He only had two cruisers, which may have been recalled after their encounter with Lieutenant Tieg's ships over the database drives.

Tisch then questioned him on Cabistero's resources and was surprised to learn that he had cooperation from several dangerous pirate groups with over a dozen fast-attack patrol ships. His success in throttling trade among the colonies was the speed that the patrol ships could strike and then vanish. No one was really sure where they were based at. She assured Jackson that Mike would have a plan, using the Federation's resources, to handle the pirates. In the meantime, she was assuming the risks in leaving the protected area around Genesis to travel back and forth to Archimedes-9. Jackson informed her that he would send out scouts to find out where Cabistero's crews were based at.

"Could his crews hide out on Tandenar without anyone's knowledge?" Tisch questioned. "It seems that he rarely leaves the planet, as far as I can tell from my visit there."

Jackson felt that was a strong possibility but there weren't any sightings to back it up. The two shook hands and Tisch returned to the *Blue Eagle*.

Zenith and Jonas sat with Alanna on a balcony, overlooking one of the several beautiful valleys on Terran. Alanna related how the colonies were formed and then abandoned by the Federation. Jonas inquired about what dangers still existed for the colonies, now that Kronos was gone.

Alanna frowned and then revealed, "Cabistero is going to be a problem." She then explained how the man was able to control several pirate groups after Kronos came. She feared he would summon them to ruin any trade pact that wasn't controlled by him. She also revealed that there was another man named Lazaro, who profited through Cabistero's monopoly on trade in the star system. Lazaro exerted his influence on any of the groups, pirate or merchant, that chose to resist his puppet Cabistero.

Zenith related some of Mike's accomplishments and assured her that there were few teams in the universe that could handle obstacles like this better than Mike and Margot. Jonas revealed that the two also were part of an alliance against Kronos that would surely back them, if required. Alanna hoped that their presence would make a difference and keep the peace as well. Zenith excused herself and returned to her apartment.

Alanna took Jonas by the hand for a tour of their kingdom. He was impressed with how they developed new technologies to improve their lifestyle while maintaining the equipment they brought with them when they started the colonies. Jonas took a liking to Alanna and considered staying on Terran. He felt that his relationship with Zenith had already run its course as she had different goals than he did. Zenith felt obligated to remain as part of Tisch's crew, while he was aware that he was a temporary replacement for Mike.

Wilmer and Shannon arrived and sensed Zenith's sadness. Shannon questioned her and was surprised to hear of her troubles with Jonas. Wilmer suggested she be patient and see how things played out. Sometimes passing whims aren't always what they seem to be. Zenith appreciated their words of encouragement and walked with them.

Once the contracts were completed and the requested return goods were identified, Tisch rounded up her crew and departed for Sargassa.

Mike piloted the shuttle to Archimedes-9 with Margot seated next to him. Margot questioned him if he was serious about leaving the fight to Marina and her alliance. He admitted that, since he became involved with Margot, he realized that he had too much to lose. She was stunned by his response, never expecting that she played a part in his decision. After initiating the autopilot function, she climbed onto Mike's lap and kissed him hungrily. Just as they got comfortable, the transmitter beeped.

Mike groaned, "Who could that possibly be?"

"Better answer it," kidded Margot. "It could be Kronos calling to surrender." They laughed as Mike acknowledged the call. A gruff voice announced that he was approaching a Federation portal and he should yield for an inspection. Suspicious, Mike glanced at Margot.

"You are welcome to inspect us," he replied. "Who is your commanding officer?"

"Major Trent," the man replied.

Mike requested a meeting with him upon completion of the inspection. The man responded, "I am Major Trent. You can speak with me at my quarters." Mike sighed as he sensed another stubborn officer, much like Jorgan Tieg when they first met. He wondered if all Federation officers were like that or if he was just lucky enough to meet the few.

Margot suggested that they go back or use the module to teleport past them. Mike felt that this was the most direct approach to reach General Lennox to meet and discuss the control of the portal by the military.

The shuttle approached a large Federation vessel and was instructed to dock inside. Six uniformed troops accompanied by Major Trent waited as Mike and Margot exited the shuttle. They were armed and wary of their visitors. Mike suggested that they relax as he was a friend of Lieutenant Tieg *and* Major Tieg as well. The men didn't seem to care.

Trent was a strange sort in Mike's eyes. He was short, but broad shouldered; bald but with a mustache and goatee'. Mike immediately ruled out an upper-cut if they fought due to Trent's height or lack of.

"Follow me, Colby," he ordered and exited the transport bay. Mike gestured politely for Margot to go first and he followed. The soldiers were close behind.

When they entered Trent's quarters, he directed them to sit. Mike and Margot wondered what his deal was. Margot sensed the testosterone build-up between the two men and decided to take charge of the situation.

"Excuse me, Major," she began. "How long has the portal been in operation?

Sitting at his desk, Trent turned on a monitor and operated a keypad. "Not long. It's the first one," he replied. "We were warned that you'd be coming through some time soon."

"Good news travels fast," Mike quipped.

"Your reputation precedes you and it's not all good," he responded.

"Is this the standard procedure for ships passing through a portal?" asked Margot.

The monitor showed the emblem of the Federation. Trent faced them and explained, "We're still ironing out the details. This is my call for now."

"How many portals are in operation?" Mike asked.

Trent stared him down and replied, "That's on a need-to-know basis."

The monitor beeped and a stone-faced, blond-haired woman stared at them. Mike was startled by her grim demeanor but Margot spoke eagerly. "Good day, General. I hope we aren't interrupting you."

Mike chimed in sarcastically, "Yes, your inconvenience was our main concern."

General Lennox replied. "I thought I'd hear from you sooner, Colby."

Trent mentioned that Mike wished to speak with her about the portal. Margot was silent and turned to Mike, indicating that it was his show.

"How are the portals being implemented?" Mike questioned Lennox.

"Forget the portals, Colby. Do you know the location of the last two bases yet?"

Mike was impressed by her directness. He mentioned that they were working on it and hoped to have answers soon. General Lennox looked disappointed and then inquired why he was concerned about the implementation of the portals.

"The module we used to travel long distances is shot," he explained. "We've set up a trade union among the colonies in the Nigus star system and will be transporting goods to and from Archimedes-9 until they are able to handle their own transportation."

Lennox informed him that there will be a fee for using the portals to cover the Federation's cost. Mike was disappointed and reminded her that long-distance hauling was new and would take some time before it was profitable.

"You can always get your module repaired and then avoid the portals, Colby," she responded sarcastically. Mike considered that he might have to do that.

Margot interceded and reminded her that they were working covertly for Marina to obtain information about Kronos. Then she added that it was Mike who discovered the third base and helped the Federation gain control of it.

"And I'm hoping he'll solve the location of the remaining bases," Lennox hinted to them.

Mike grew impatient and pointed out that the Federation patrol took the drives with the Kronos databases from him, which hindered their search. Lennox leaned close to the monitor and stated that the drives were a ruse and there was nothing on them. Mike and Margot glanced at each other, both knowing that wasn't the case and Zenith might have had something to do with that.

"What support can we expect from the Federation as far as protection for the freighters who traverse from the Nigus to Archimedes-9?" Mike inquired, curious.

"When they are in range of the portal, we will intercede on their behalf," Lennox answered. "Beyond that, they're on their own."

Mike requested that she suspend the idea of fees for using the portal for now as his shuttle and the *Blue Eagle* are likely the only ships that will be using it. Trent stared back at the monitor, waiting for her response.

"Very well," she answered. "For now."

"And if I get you the locations of the remaining bases?" he pressed.

Margot kicked him in the shin and glared at him, sensing he was pushing his luck. Lennox smiled and responded, "I'll think about it."

Mike thanked her and assured her that he'll give her the locations of the remaining bases as soon as he identifies them. Lennox nodded as if she expected that response but didn't believe him. The monitor went blank and the Federation symbol returned.

"Satisfied, Colby?" Trent asked.

"Well, it's not the warm welcome I expected from the Federation but it'll have to do, I suppose," he quipped. Then he added, "If Kronos returns to claim their base, you do realize that you will be outnumbered significantly."

Trent chuckled and then replied, "Kronos is licking their wounds. I'm sure they're circling the wagons at their last two bases, wherever they are. It's their last stand."

Mike shook his head in disbelief and warned him not to underestimate them. Trent called for his men to escort Mike and Margot back to their ship.

When they secured the hatch to the shuttle, Mike mentioned to Margot that he needed to get the module fixed as soon as possible. He wasn't comfortable with the Federation's handling of the portals and how the other shippers would respond if they had to pay a fee to use it.

The journey was boring and uneventful so Mike left the piloting to Margot. He studied the module and contemplated what was more valuable – the module or their cloaking ability. Margot was disappointed that Mike was obsessed once again with his strategies for whatever the challenge of the day was. She tried to speak with him but he was focused on a printout of the coordinates projected by Zenith of arrivals and departures of ships from one of the unidentified Kronos bases.

Finally, Margot had enough. She placed the shuttle on autopilot and went to their cabin. When she returned, she wore a string bikini that she purchased on their last visit to Archimedes-9. She hoped to use it during some pool time but that never happened.

Mike turned to her and smiled when she posed against the navigation console. "I think it's time for a break," he remarked. "You look ravishing." Margot didn't reply but returned to the pilot's seat. "What are you doing?" he asked, baffled. "I thought that was an invitation?"

"No," she replied, disinterested. "I just wanted to be comfortable up here... all alone... by myself."

"Well, come join me," he suggested.

Margot lost it. She chided him about his obsession to solve all the mysteries of the universe. Then she informed him about how he ignored her through most of the trip, leaving her feeling like a lone ghost on an abandoned space station.

Mike's eyes widened and he jumped out of his seat. "Margot, you're a genius!"

"What the hell for? Giving you a thrill in my bikini."

"No," he replied excitedly. "We're going to Niems!" He hurriedly took the copilot's seat and programmed the coordinates for the Archaenean space station.

"Have you lost what's left of your friggin' mind?" she shouted at him.

"You'll see," he responded confidently. Margot stormed off to their cabin, bristling over his insensitivity.

Mike realized that he hurt her and had better address the issue quickly. He entered the cabin and requested, "Can we talk?" Margot sat up and stared at him with a look of scorn. "Look, I'm sorry," he uttered humbly. "I promise to try harder."

"How much harder?" she quipped, trying to hold back a smile.

Mike sat next to her and embraced her, prepared to kiss and make up. Margot pushed him away and stood over him. "When I see results, then you'll get some of this," she declared, posing in several sexy positions.

"You're kidding, right?" he asked sarcastically. Margot smiled and returned to the flight deck.

"Women," grumbled Mike, not expecting Margot to hear.

"You can sleep by yourself as well, your Highness," she replied, mocking him.

Mike rolled his eyes and groaned. He sat next to her in the copilot's seat and tried singing to her. She responded by donning a headset. Next, he tried romantic overtures like nibbling her ear lobe, kissing her thighs, belly and neck and then posing comically in the same positions she used to torment him. Hoping for a thaw in her attitude, Mike was disappointed when she returned to the cabin and changed back into her flight attire.

"How long is this going to go on?" he asked, growing more concerned.

"I don't think we can fix this," she answered. "I'm done."

Mike pleaded with her several times but Margot wasn't backing down. Then Mike asked if he should be concerned with their working relationship, hoping to salvage something.

"When we get to Taurus, I'll arrange for Marina to get you a new partner. That should allay your fears."

Mike retreated to the cabin and cried. He realized how, once again, he neglected those who cared about him until it festered into hurt feelings. After hours of feeling sorry for himself, he returned to the flight deck and sat next to Margot. He apologized and explained the importance of repairing the module. He then promised to expedite their trip to Taurus so she could leave. Margot thanked him but maintained her focus on the controls, ignoring his presence.

The *Blue Eagle* came upon the portal and was quickly surrounded by four Federation cruisers. Zenith summoned Tisch to the flight deck, just as Major Trent contacted them. Tisch arrived and inquired why they were being stopped. Trent informed them that a search must be performed and then they would be allowed to pass. He also mentioned that Mike obtained a temporary waiver on the fees for using the portal but he couldn't guarantee how long it would be in effect. After the soldiers completed their inspection, the *Blue Eagle* continued on its way.

Tisch sat silent on the bridge in her captain's chair and pondered what the Federation was up to. The portal was a surprise but the fact that they were going to charge freighters to use it was absurd.

"How do you think Mike convinced them to suspend the fees?" questioned Zenith. Wilmer and Shannon listened anxiously as Tisch pondered. "Mike must have had something for leverage to get them to waive them," she responded.

"If they charge for the use of their portals, then that would ruin everything we're trying to build here," fretted Wilmer.

"I know that," grumbled Tisch. "We're going to need help from Rebecca to handle this."

Shannon offered to contact Mike and get his insight to the issue. Wilmer paced the deck, wondering what the Federation was thinking in doing this.

Zenith informed everyone that they were clear of the portal and would be arriving shortly on Archimedes-9. After several attempts, Shannon received no response from Mike or Margot and ceased trying. Tisch attributed it to the distances and the portal.

Mike's shuttle docked on Niems without incident. Margot remained seated while Mike retrieved the module from the rear of the shuttle. He paused at the open hatch and asked her to join him. She declined and remained seated on the flight deck. Mike felt lost without his partner and love. He now understood what she felt and knew he had to change his ways now. There were too many damaged friendships over his zealousness to conquer every issue that confronted them.

When he entered the space station, he waited for Denia to address him. After several moments, he continued up to the control room and sat down. There was still no sign of or a response from the Archaenean curator. The silence forced him to consider what his life would be like without Margot. Soon, he found himself in tears, fearing that he lost her forever.

The dim lighting flickered and grew bright as the main power came on. Denia's voice from behind, rattled him. "Why have you returned?" she asked.

Mike wiped the tears from his eyes and held up the module. "Can you help us?" he requested. "The module isn't functioning properly."

Denia walked around and stood in front of him. She took the module from him and studied it briefly. "This cannot be repaired," she informed him. "I will give you another." She left the control room through a hatch and entered into a stairwell.

Mike again thought about Margot and his heart broke. His eyes filled with tears as he recalled how she spoke to him on the shuttle. He hurt her badly and she had enough of it. A hand touched his shoulder and scared the daylights out of him. He turned and stared at Margot like a frightened child.

"You look like you saw a ghost," she commented, unsympathetic.

Mike stood and placed his hands on her hips. His voice trembled as he spoke to her. "Margot, I am so sorry. Please don't leave me," he pleaded.

"Come on, Mike. You don't need anyone," she reminded him.

"None of this matters, if I don't have you in my life," he confessed. "I'll do whatever you want. You can call all the shots from now on. Just give me another chance."

Margot stared at him with no emotion. She knew better than to expect an alpha male to change. It was his nature to be in charge. Before she could speak, Denia appeared with two new modules.

"We trust you, Colby, to do the right thing with these," Denia advised him. "Don't disappoint us."

Mike offered to return the modules to her after Kronus was defeated. Denia told him that it wouldn't be necessary if he was responsible with them. She handed him the modules and then stood in front of Margot. "You suffer much sadness," she mentioned. "I can only assume it is out of love or lack of that you feel this."

Margot was surprised by her remark. "It's complicated," she replied.

"It's really simple," Denia countered. "Love is unconditional, even among the many other races of the universe."

Margot felt Denia probe her mind and then was able to see into hers. Denia showed her how many partners she lost due to their responsibilities to the universe. She then allowed Margot to feel the emotional strain and the loss she felt over those duties.

Mike wondered what they were doing and suspected there was communication between them. He looked away, knowing that he must take Margot back to Taurus for a new partner. Suddenly, he felt as if nothing mattered. The trade routes didn't matter. Kronos didn't matter. Taurus didn't matter. There would be others to handle those matters. It didn't have to be him.

Denia wished them well and vanished. Mike followed Margot to the shuttle and closed the hatch. She turned to speak but he held his hand up for patience. Mike informed her that he would take her to Taurus or where ever she chose to go. After that, he would seek employment with Korick at the old Empire station. He admitted that he lost control of everything and announced that he was done. Then, after apologizing for the pain he caused her, he suggested that they get going. Stunned that he gave up, Margot wasn't sure what to do.

Mike installed one of the new modules at the rear of the shuttle and programmed it for Taurus. He stowed the second unit, assuming it was meant for the *Blue Eagle.* When he returned to the flight deck, Margot already started the shuttle and departed the station. Mike figured that she couldn't get away from him fast enough. Every time he glanced over at her, tears formed in his eyes. He wanted to remember all the good times they had but then he'd be haunted by the fact that he ruined it. The silence between them was killing him but there was nothing more he could do.

The *Blue Eagle* docked on Archimedes-9 and Rebecca arrived in the transport bay with several procurement specialists. Tisch exited first and was greeted with a hug from her. The crew followed and waited for instructions. Rebecca immediately noticed that Mike and Margot were missing.

"Anything I should know about with the dynamic duo?" she kidded.

Tisch suggested they discuss it over drinks after they perform the cargo swap. Rebecca instructed her team to work with Tisch and provide any assistance she required. She inquired if everything was alright with all her personnel. Tisch nodded and replied, "As far as I can tell, everyone is happy. I thought Mike and Margot would be here in the shuttle, but I guess he had other ideas."

Rebecca quipped, "That's what scares me. Mike's always up to something, despite Margot's best efforts." The two women laughed giddily.

The procurement specialists had no trouble fulfilling Tisch's requests for materials and supplies in return for the goods she brought from Genesis and Sargassa. Wilmer took charge of the loading of the new cargo and secured the ship when they were finished. The crew then proceeded to the pub for food and drink.

Rebecca and Tisch discussed everything that happened during the *Blue Eagle's* journey, including the issue with fees for the portal. Rebecca was surprised and promised to look into it. Tisch reminded her that it would take time before trade in the Nigus region became profitable for the other colonies. While the portal was necessary, fees or taxes could take away any initiative for the colonies to develop their own shipping facilities to handle trade with Archimedes-9.

Tisch requested a break in the schedule for the crew to rest and relax before returning to Sargassa and then *Genesis*. She hoped for Mike to return to handle the issue with the portal before it affected her plans.

CHAPTER 13

HOME AND AWAY

On Taurus, Julian was anxious when he heard that Mike's shuttle had just docked. Gemini was on a vacation with Dax and Sara was recently released from the infirmary and resting in her apartment. So, this was Julian's show for now.

Mike opened the hatch and stepped aside, realizing this could be the last time he sees Margot. She paused and stared at him with folded arms. "You know, Mike, the problem with you isn't our work," she started and then hesitated. "It's with how you handle it."

"I'm so sorry. I was always so focused on winning the game and surviving that I lost myself," he confessed. "It's not worth it when you lose your friends and the woman you love."

Margot explained that they both had much to think about and neither should make a rash decision. Mike felt a glimmer of hope and asked if she would promise not to leave without speaking to him.

"Do you think I want to do this?" she asked, venting her frustration.

"Please, Margot. I can't lose you. You mean everything to me."

"Then maybe you should show it," she chastised him.

Mike took her hands in his and got down on one knee. He reached into his pocket for a small box with a diamond ring inside. Opening the box, he proposed to her. "Margot, I swear I will put you before all else and never neglect you again, if you would be my wife."

Margot was surprised to see the ring and gestured for Mike to stand up. She tried to contain her emotions and fumbled for the right words. Finally, she replied, "I will, but if you ever let me down again, I'll cut your balls off. I'm not kidding."

Mike was elated and joked, "As romantic as that sounds, I'll take that as a *yes*."

"Of course, you jackass!" she blurted and kissed him. Mike placed the ring on her finger and she embraced him tightly.

They exited the shuttle and were greeted by Julian with hugs. Mike immediately noticed a small silver cross on a chain around Julian's neck.

"When did you turn to religious symbolism?" Mike inquired, curious.

Julian chuckled and answered, "It seems that, despite my denial of fate and morality, I have found my faith."

Mike was dumb-founded. "How the hell did you do that? I can't believe it."

"A wise person taught me the value of life, trust in humanity, and in love."

Margot teased, "Well, I certainly hope it wasn't Mike." Julian admitted that Mike pointed him in the right direction and he followed it. She looked shocked.

Julian escorted them up to the executive conference room and ordered dinner for them. When they were all seated, Mike proposed for their first order of business that Julian find them a minister to marry them. Julian chuckled and then made a call. "It's funny that you bring this up," he mentioned, "because it coincides with something I wanted to discuss." Mike and Margot glanced at each other, curious as to what he meant.

The door to the conference room slid open and an attractive, dark-skinned woman dressed in a light blue gown in heels and wearing ornate earrings entered.

"This is Deidra," Julian announced. "She is my wife."

Mike was both impressed and awed. This wasn't the Julian he knew when they first met on the *Blue Eagle*. Margot suspected that there was a story behind Mike's expression but was silent and smiled.

Julian took her hands in his and kissed her cheek. "These are my friends Mike and Margot," he informed her. "They would like to be married."

Deidra responded pleasantly, "I'd be honored to perform your service,"

"And I'd be honored as well," Mike replied. "I still can't believe someone restored Julian's faith in humanity!"

Julian and Deidra sat at the table across from them. Julian commented, "I wondered how long it would take for the two of you to consummate your relationship in wedlock."

Mike glanced at Margot and then back to Julian. He replied humbly, "It's a good thing Margot is forgiving and understanding or we wouldn't be here today."

Margot nodded and then congratulated Julian and Deidra on their marriage. She commented how she feared Gemini would corrupt him with her lust for greed and power.

Julian snickered and informed them that Gemini, too, has become a better person. He revealed that Dax has convinced her to be part of the corporation's success instead of just overseeing it. Her role was now expanded from bitching to participating. Amused by his comment, Mike was then disappointed to learn that they wouldn't be seeing Gemini this trip.

Julian inquired as to why Mike and Margot chose to get married without their friends on the *Blue Eagle* on hand. Mike responded that they had all been through a lot and this seemed appropriate. He assured him that they'd be celebrating at a later date, though.

Julian turned to Margot for her thoughts on the wedding. She explained that, due to Mike's desire to be the center of attention, she feared what he might do if they had a big wedding. Then she revealed how Tisch and her crew expected her to occupy Mike so he wouldn't come up with new and crazy ideas. Julian and Deidra enjoyed the banter and Margot smiled at Mike. He knew he deserved it and it was another reminder of how he often forgot about those around him in his quest to chase those wild ideas.

The four of them enjoyed a delightful seafood meal together before discussing business. Julian was impressed with how much Mike and his friends accomplished, particularly in locating and converting the third Kronos base into a trade center. He was disappointed to hear that the military was already looking to profit off of the portals and wondered if Marina or her rebel alliance could help with that.

Mike questioned Julian about Sara and her recovery from the attack. Julian informed him that Sara's days in the field with GSS were over and she was limited to administrative work due to lingering ailments, particularly with her heart. The conversation turned to the wedding plans and how long they planned to stay on Taurus.

The door beeped and slid open. Sara entered, looking as sharp as ever but in civilian clothes. Mike and Margot stood to greet her. "I heard that there was trouble in the station again," Sara joked and hugged them. "I should have known it was you, Michael."

Julian invited her to join them and poured a drink for her. Mike expressed his sorrow for her leaving GSS and offered to help her in any way. "Is the *Blue Eagle* hiring?" she teased.

Mike surprised everyone and answered that they very likely would need someone to coordinate security matters with business matters in the Nigus star system as he was limiting his role to just following orders and doing grunt work. He also pointed out that, if Margot was recalled by Marina, he would be joining her. Margot was floored by his remark. She realized how much she did mean to him now.

When Sara learned of Mike and Margot's wedding, she laughed and then quipped, "Maybe you can do something to occupy his mind at night, Margot."

Everyone burst into laughter except Mike, that her comment matched those of everyone else on the *Blue Eagle*. Margot raised her glass in a toast to lasting friendships, glancing at Mike with a sly grin. Everyone joined him and echoed his wish.

That evening, Mike and Margot were wed and everything seemed right for a change. They spent the next two evenings in an elaborate suite, arranged for by Julian and Deidra.

When they appeared for breakfast on the third day in the executive conference room for a farewell meal, Mike looked fatigued and tired, while Margot was enthusiastic and giddy. Julian, Sara and Deidra grinned, knowing that Margot did *occupy* his mind very much so since the wedding.

Mike excused himself to use the restroom and left the conference room. Sara congratulated Margot on a job well done and urged her to keep up the good work. The three of them enjoyed the humor, albeit at Mike's expense.

Unaware of two men standing nearby with their eyes on him, Mike entered the Men's Room. He was relieving himself when a female voice startled him. "Well, Mr. Colby. It's about time we had some face time."

"Excuse me," he replied, unsure of who it was. He finished and turned around. "Who are you?"

Darra stood, leaning against the wall, fingering a dagger. "You don't know me but everyone at Kronos, including myself, know all about you."

Mike wasn't concerned and suggested that they carry on the discussion someplace other than the Men's Room. Darra approached him and placed her dagger against his neck and inquired, "Where is Marina?"

Unintimidated, Mike shrugged his shoulders and replied, "Marina doesn't tell anyone where she was, is or going to be. That's why she is so elusive."

Darra sighed and then asked, "Where is the *Blue Eagle*?"

Mike chuckled at her and answered, "I don't work for the *Blue Eagle* or its captain."

Darra turned away with her head down. Mike knew better than to let his guard down. Suddenly, she turned and attempted to cut his throat. Mike blocked it and slammed her against the wall. "There's a hefty bounty on your head, Colby," she mentioned. "Someone wants you alive. Otherwise, you'd be dead."

"I doubt that," he responded, confident. Then she caught him by surprise. She dropped to the floor and elbowed him in the groin, doubling him over. Before he could react, she rolled on her back and kicked upward, striking him at the bridge of his nose with both heels in her boots. Mike staggered backwards and fell to the ground unconscious. She summoned the two men from the corridor to drop him in a trashcan and carry him back to her ship.

Deidra related how she and Julian met on the elevator and it was love at first site. Margot then told them of her first interactions with Mike and how she fell for him right away. Sara complimented Margot for finally finding a way to slow him down. Julian then commented that Mike was gone a while and that he should check on him.

"I hope I didn't kill him," Margot kidded, growing concerned. Julian excused himself and left them.

When he passed two men in plain clothes, pushing a trashcan, he became suspicious and hurried to the Men's Room. Memories of how he and Wilmer once kidnapped Gemini crossed his mind. He entered the Men's Room and found it empty. His worst fears were realized. The elevator display indicated that the men exited on the ground floor.

Rushing back into the corridor, Julian sounded the emergency alarm and contacted Major Tieg. When he returned to the conference room, the women waited anxiously for him to speak.

"Mike's been kidnapped," he announced. "Tieg's been notified. Stay here until you hear from me." Julian hurried out of the room. Deidra assured Margot that they'll find him.

Margot grew panicked and uttered, "I can't even trust him to take a leak without getting into trouble." Sara and Deidra knew she wasn't joking and sat with her, their hands on her shoulders in support.

Julian stepped off the elevator and met Major Tieg on the ground floor. Tieg informed him that a small schooner just left on an unscheduled departure. Ironically, Julian thought to himself, *What would Mike do*? Then he ordered Tieg not to contact them but track them. He hurried back to the elevator.

In the conference room, Margot fretted as to who would kidnap Mike, especially there on Taurus, when no one knew they were coming. Sara suggested that it was a random opportunity by pirates. After all, there was a bounty on Mike's head.

"But Korick's men are the pirates and they are loyal to him," Margot countered.

"Then Kronos must be involved somehow," she responded.

Julian burst into the room and ordered Margot to get to her shuttle and follow the tracking coordinates Tieg sent to her. Sara followed her out of the conference room and to the elevator.

"This could be a big opportunity," Julian commented to Deidra. She looked baffled until he explained, "I'm sure Kronos is behind this. They want Marina and they want the *Blue Eagle*. Mike is a lesser target but possibly with knowledge of the locations of both."

"But how is that an opportunity?" questioned Deidra.

"If they are behind this, then they are likely to take him to one of their remaining two bases. The shuttle can cloak and follow them."

"What if they kill Mike?" she asked, still trying to understand his logic.

"Why risk getting caught if they wanted to kill him. They want information or leverage."

Now wide-eyed and understanding him, Deidra commented, "I didn't realize you were so smart."

"I learned to ask myself: What would Mike do?"

"Uh-oh," Deidra uttered. "Am I going to have to keep you busy at night, too?"

Julian chuckled and responded, "Gosh, no. His mind is out of control all the time. Mine is just occasionally out there." The two of them laughed.

The women prepared the shuttle for departure. Sara requested that the transport supervisor not announce their exit for security reasons. Margot placed the shuttle in 'cloaked' mode and navigated away from the station. Major Tieg sent them additional tracking coordinates tracking coordinates, allowing them to lock onto the ship before it left the region.

Julian contacted them and urged them not to give away their position. He promised to arrange support for them once they reached their destination. Sara understood and convinced Margot to be patient.

Julian then contacted General Lennox from the communications center and informed her of the situation and the potential. He suggested that they take no action until Margot and Sara confirmed their destination. In the meantime, he would update her on the most recent coordinates of Mike's shuttle. He returned to the conference room and poured drinks for himself and Deidra.

Deidra sat with him and asked, "What's next?"

Julian sipped his drink and replied, "We sit back and let this play out. It's the Mike Colby show now."

"Why do you say that?"

Julian smiled at her and explained, "You have no idea how determined he is to take down Kronos. I expect he'll be taken to the fourth base and do something crazy to find out the location of the last base. While he's doing that, Margot will likely sneak onto the base to help him. Shortly after, the Federation and the rebel alliance will arrive and finish the job."

"You have this all figured out," she remarked.

"Nope," he replied confidently. "I have Mike figured out." They tapped glasses together and sipped.

Tisch sat with Rebecca in her office and discussed the potential for the trade routes in the Nigus system. She expressed her concerns about the Kronos officer named Lazaro and Cabistero's pirates interfering with their ship. Rebecca agreed it was a concern and offered to speak with General Lennox about providing additional support along the routes.

"You do know that Lennox will expect some form of payment for the use of the Federation's portals," Tisch reminded her.

"I expected as much. The haulers involved in joining the long-distance operation are already developing a contingency to cease all trading if that happens. That means the Federation's outposts get no supplies, equipment or troop rotations."

"Ah, like a labor strike," remarked Tisch.

"Exactly. They need us as much as we need them."

"Have you been able to get in touch with Mike or Margot?" Tisch asked with a note of concern in her voice.

Rebecca frowned and reluctantly gave her the story of Mike's abduction as she heard it. She warned her not to interfere or use the *Blue Eagle* to rescue Mike as this was now the concern of the Federation and the rebel alliance. Tisch feared for their safety and paced the floor. Rebecca urged her to focus on the transportation of cargo and she would update her as soon as she had something of value to tell her. Tisch thanked her for her hospitality and left to prepare for departure. She was relieved that everything appeared under control by others, leaving her to focus on her ship and crew.

When she boarded the *Blue Eagle*, Tisch commented to Wilmer that she hadn't seen much of him and Shannon lately and questioned if everything was okay. He and Shannon smiled at each other and he replied, "We're just capitalizing on quality time."

Tisch noticed that Jonas was missing and questioned Zenith about his absence. She knew they were having issues but hoped they'd work things out. Zenith replied somberly, "Jonas is staying to work out some things. Basically, he's dumping me and moving on."

Tisch apologized for bringing up the issue and expressed her hope that there were better things down the road for her. She admitted that things were rather boring without Mike and Margot around. She enjoyed

Margot's friendship and Mike kept her on her toes for the unexpected. She did enjoy piloting her ship again as Geezer was gone and Zee was taking on the cooking duties in addition to piloting the ship.

As they pulled away, Wilmer inquired if anyone had heard from Mike or Margot. Tisch relayed what Rebecca told her about Mike being involved in a security issue. Wilmer grew suspicious and questioned what kind of security issue would press them to leave Taurus in a hurry and not contact the *Blue Eagle*. Tisch reminded them that it proved there are still threats present and they needed to be alert.

They reached the portal in a day and were surprised by the cooperation they received from Trent's men. They waived the inspection and signaled them through. Wilmer commented that this was too easy.

"Don't complain," warned Tisch. "We've had more than our share of obstacles. I'll take this any day."

A few days later, they arrived at Sima's facility on Sargassa. Shannon attempted to make contact several times to let them know they were arriving but received no answer. "Wilmer, when we set down, you'd better check out our communication system," she complained. "This is ridiculous. No one answers when I send out a contact signal."

"Yeah. Yeah," he grumbled from the navigation station.

The *Blue Eagle* set down on the landing pad and, except for Zenith, everyone else stepped out. Everyone was anxious to see the forests and wildlife surrounding the facility and things appeared normal thus far. The broken windows had been repaired and a new door installed in the entry way. The communication equipment was intact on the roof and the antennae weren't damaged.

Tisch opened the door and was immediately greeted by twelve men with pulse rifles pointed at her. They wore shabby, old militia uniforms and each had scraggily hair, a beard and a mustache. They rushed out and circled Tisch's crew before they could retreat inside the ship.

"What the hell is going on here?" shouted Tisch.

One of the men punched her in the mouth. "You'd best shut your yap, Missy, if you know what's good for you."

Zenith approached the hatch and saw the man strike Tisch. She hurried to the comm/nav panel and sent out an SOS, hoping to reach a Federation vessel.

Six of the men commandeered the *Blue Eagle* and lifted off into the sky with Zenith hidden on board. Tisch couldn't believe that they walked into a trap like this and even worse, she lost the *Blue Eagle*. The remaining men escorted them inside and locked them in a room on the second level.

"Well, that went well," groaned Wilmer. Silent, Tisch sat down and cried.

Shannon attempted to console her but to no avail. "I'm the worst captain there ever was," Tisch uttered between sobs.

"Don't worry, Tisch. Mike will rescue us," Shannon assured her.

Tisch cried again and muttered, "Mike was kidnapped on Taurus. He's not coming."

Wilmer rubbed his temples and paced the floor. "Well, Zee is still on board. Maybe she can do something," he mentioned.

One of the men unlocked the door and targeted Tisch with his rifle. "Where is Marina?" he asked.

Tisch was stunned that he would ask her that. "How the hell should I know?" she replied angrily. "Marina isn't part of our group. We're only space truckers."

The man laughed at her. Cabistero will appreciate that beautiful ship you donated to him. I'm sure he'll enjoy the transport module as well. Tisch was baffled at first but then realized they thought Mike's module was installed on board her ship. She summoned her courage and mocked him. "You buffoons have got to be the worst pirates in the universe."

"And why is that, missy?" he challenged.

"Because the module isn't on my ship," she informed him. "Neither is the cloaking device, you idiot."

"Then what's so special about that ship?" he asked, wondering if they just made themselves a target without the protection they thought they had with the *Blue Eagle* in their possession.

Tisch laughed at him and replied arrogantly, "The only thing special about that ship was Mike Colby and when he finds out what you morons did, he will come looking for you."

Wilmer then added, "And this isn't the *Blue Eagle*, you fool. It's the *Rising Phoenix*." The man grew nervous and slammed the door on his way out.

"Good thinking, Wilmer," Tisch complimented him.

Shannon suggested that they don't say anything else to the men. Tisch agreed and suggested they listen for anything the men might say that could help.

The *Blue Eagle* arrived on Tandenar and docked inside a cave. Several tunnels migrated from the cave and were filled with the spoils collected over time by Cabistero's men. Among the loot were fancy pieces of furniture, musical instruments, jewelry, and communications equipment pillaged from the colonies. Unfortunately, there was no one to sell their loot to, rendering it worthless.

Cabistero waited anxiously as his men exited the ship. The leader approached him with a grave expression. "We have the greatest ship in the galaxy!" exclaimed Cabistero. "What could possibly paint that goofy look on your face, Dazz."

Dazz placed his hands in his pockets and answered humbly, "It doesn't have the module or the cloaking technology on it."

"Says who?" Cabistero shouted at him.

"We received word from the boys on the ground that the prisoners told them it wasn't on their ship. They also claim that it isn't the *Blue Eagle* but the *Rising Phoenix*. We checked all the control systems anyway and there isn't any mode for teleporting. There was a switch for cloaking but it wasn't connected to anything."

Cabistero's face turned red and he clenched his fists. "Do you know what this means?" he shouted at Dazz.

"Yeah. It's not the *Blue Eagle*," Dazz replied and took a step back, but too late. Cabistero leaped on him and beat him unmercifully. He repeatedly called Dazz a moron and incompetent as he pummeled his face. When he ceased the assault, Dazz lay motionless with blood streaming from his face and pooling on the ground.

Cabistero boarded the *Blue Eagle* and searched for himself. Eventually, he gave up and accepted the fact that they had the wrong ship. When he exited the ship, he was surrounded by Federation soldiers and his men were placed in handcuffs. He swore and kicked at the ground in anger.

Lieutenant Tieg approached the group and inquired to the whereabouts of the crew. Cabistero laughed and swore at him. Tieg smiled, realizing he had some leverage over the prisoners. Tieg asked once more and still Cabistero refused to speak.

Zenith emerged from inside the *Blue Eagle* and informed Lieutenant Tieg that they were captive on Sargassa. Tieg thanked her and complimented her on her bravery and smart thinking.

"Take them away," he ordered his men. "Long-term lockup."

Cabistero shouted, "You can't do this to me!"

"Of course, I can," replied Lieutenant Tieg. "You won't be going back to headquarters either."

"What does that mean?" Cabistero asked, growing more concerned about his fate.

"It means you will be staying out here on the base for a long time. Probably forever. I imagine no one will know or care either."

Cabistero panicked as he and his men were escorted away. He had no allies now to help him. "Wait! We can work something out!"

"Too late," remarked Tieg, seemingly bored. He took one of his pilots and returned the *Blue Eagle* to Genesis as a gesture of good will toward the trade union.

When they landed at the docking facility on Genesis, Jackson waited to greet the crew but was stunned to see Lieutenant Tieg instead. "What's the meaning of this?" he shouted.

"The crew was kidnapped and the ship stolen. We recovered the ship but we're still searching for the crew."

"How am I to believe this?" Jackson asked, suspicious. Then Zenith approached and confirmed what Tieg had told him.

Lieutenant Tieg pointed to the cargo bay. "I imagine that whatever cargo they were hauling is still on board the ship. I leave it in your hands until they are able to return for it."

Lieutenant Tieg extended his hand in friendship. Still surprised, Jackson warily shook hands with him. Tieg suggested that he accept this as a gesture of goodwill and cooperation in creating a successful trade union. Jackson nodded and then grinned, wondering if they really were on the way to successfully implementing trade with all the colonies again.

A dozen Federation soldiers marched past them with Cabistero and five of his men in handcuffs. Jackson noticed and waited for an explanation from Tieg.

"They will be placed in long-term lockup with no chance of parole or release," Tieg informed him.

"I am grateful for your help, Lieutenant."

"Oh, and the cave they led us to on Tandenar has a plethora of valuable items in it," Tieg mentioned. "I suggest you send a reclamation team to collect them. I imagine they belong to the colonies." He smiled and then followed after his men. Jackson was amazed at their good fortune since the *Blue Eagle* arrived.

Tisch paced the floor in a panic. Wilmer and Shannon studied their confines and pondered a way out. Then Wilmer figured it out. The door had three hinges with hinge pins. The room wasn't meant to be a jail cell but a storage room. He anxiously wiggled the middle pin until it came out.

"What are you doing?" asked Tisch.

Wilmer explained how they can escape by removing all three pins. Shannon understood and rushed to help him. They used the removed pin to force the bottom pin out and then the top one. Tisch and Shannon held the door in place while Wilmer shimmied it off the hinges.

"We have to put the door back in place," Wilmer instructed them. "We'll use it to trap at least one of them."

To restore the door, Shannon unlatched the hasp in the corridor. The latch was designed to hold a lock but none was used; the rotating latch thus served to lock them inside but not inhibit access from the corridor.

With the door now opened, they placed it back on its hinges and pinned it. Shannon opened the door to the room on the opposite side of the corridor for them to hide. Wilmer directed Tisch to hide in a room further up the corridor as their backup. He and Shannon hid in the opposite room and waited for someone to check on them.

A short while later, one of the men came down the hall and peered in the room. Seeing it empty, he shouted for help. Wilmer and Shannon burst out of the other room and tackled him. Shannon took his pistol and knife from him and Wilmer knocked him out with a solid punch to the forehead. They shoved the man's unconscious body into the room but left the door open.

Halfway down the hall, he and Shannon hid in another room. Two of the men rushed down to see what the yelling was about. Wilmer and Shannon crept out of the room and followed them. When the men found their pal inside the first room, one of them entered to help him. Wilmer held his pistol against the other man's head. Shannon took his pistol and marched him inside the room as well.

"Drop your weapon and back away," warned Wilmer as he and Shannon targeted the armed man with the pistol. He dropped the pistol and backed to the rear of the room. Wilmer shoved the other man after him. Now with three pistols and three men locked in the room, they had a chance. Shannon went to the end room to give Tisch a pistol.

Someone shouted from the top of the stairs for the men to respond. Then there were two more voices. Shannon hid with Tisch, ready to intercede if Wilmer was caught.

The men crept down the stairs and paused. "Give up now and we'll let you live," shouted one of them.

Wilmer hurried into the nearest room and closed the door. The men entered the corridor with pistols ready to fire. Down the corridor, one of the trapped men beat on the door and caught their attention. The others approached cautiously, knowing that Tisch's crew couldn't have gone far.

Wilmer waited inside the door and listened carefully for their footsteps. Then he heard something strange – heavy breathing. He turned on his pen light and screamed. Sima and Creeg had been asleep but they too leaped up, shrieking.

"What the hell?" shouted Wilmer. The men in the corridor stopped outside the door, wondering what happened.

Creeg approached Wilmer and inquired, "What are you doing here?"

Wilmer held one hand over his heart and panted. "What do you think?" He then reached for the door but it had closed and locked.

While the men laughed at Wilmer's misfortune, Shannon and Tisch approached from behind. Each woman placed the barrel of her pistol against a man's head and ordered them to drop their weapons. The third man targeted Shannon and taunted, "Or else what?"

Shannon immediately fired a pulse of energy into his forehead and killed him. "Or else that," she answered. The other two promptly dropped their weapons and put their hands over their heads.

When Tisch unlatched and opened the door, she was surprised to see Sima and Creeg standing next to Wilmer. They hurried out and then Shannon prodded the two men inside the room. Anxiously, she latched the door.

Creeg inquired how Wilmer learned to scream with such a high pitch in his voice. The women chuckled as Wilmer looked flustered. "I had no idea you were in there," he grumbled. "I disguised my voice so they'd think it was one of the women."

"And a wonderful woman you were," Shannon teased. Now Wilmer knew how Mike felt, being the butt of the women's jokes.

"We are so glad to see you," Sima announced, relieved to be free of their captivity.

"I wondered how long it would take for Mike to rescue us," commented Creeg. "But I see you are capable of such action without him." Everyone laughed at his jest.

Tisch commented, "I'll take that as a compliment."

"Do you have some use for these thugs, Sima?" inquired Wilmer.

Sima smiled deviously and responded, "I have pets who require feeding. I'm sure they'd appreciate it."

"You have my blessing to do whatever you like with these dirt bags," Tisch quipped.

Concerned, Shannon asked, "What do we do about our ship?"

Wilmer suggested they take the pirates' ship and go back to Terran for help. Tisch agreed and expressed her hope that they would hear from Mike soon. She realized how much she relied on him in times like this.

"Perhaps we're learning to function without him," Shannon commented. "Not that he isn't important, but we need to take care of ourselves sometimes."

Tisch patted her shoulder and praised her for her smart assessment. "I've often thought that but then something would prove that I still needed him," she admitted. "Now I see that my crew is just as capable with or without Mr. Colby."

"He'd be proud of us," Shannon added.

"I suggest we find our ship before we get ahead of ourselves," advised Wilmer.

Taking his hint, Tisch ordered them to the pirates' patrol ship. She told Sima and Creeg of the success she had obtaining the goods they requested but would have to return with them when she finds her ship.

Once everyone was on board, Tisch initiated the hatch closure. Sima and Creeg bade her farewell as the hatch closed. Tisch and Wilmer stared at the controls, baffled by the small ship's operation. Shannon pushed past them and took the pilot's seat. She expertly operated the controls and started the ship's engines.

"You know how to fly one of these?" questioned Tisch.

"Sure do," Shannon replied confidently. "I just have to figure out the navigation so we can get to Terran."

Tisch instructed Wilmer to scan through the ship's database for anything that might be helpful.

Wilmer glanced at the monitor and announced, "We have the previous location - Tandenar!"

"Contact Lieutenant Tieg and relay the information to him. Hopefully he'll help us."

Before Shannon could establish contact with him, they received an incoming message. Wilmer gestured for silence and acknowledged the incoming signal.

"This is Lazaro. I need to speak with Cabistero," he requested.

Wilmer responded, "We're on our way to pick him up as we speak. Can I help you with something?"

"I'm returning with both of my cruisers and I'll meet him on Tandenar."

When Wilmer acknowledged the message, the transmission ended. He turned to Tisch, wondering what she would choose to do.

"Contact Tieg. Tell him to meet us on Tandenar. We're going after Lazaro and my ship." Shannon immediately initiated contact and informed the Federation communications officer this was a priority one message for Tieg. The officer responded and thanked her for the information, not mentioning that they were already aware of the base on Tandenar.

"Yes!" shouted Shannon. Tisch chuckled over her enthusiasm. "They're going to regret messing with the *Blue Eagle*!" she added.

Wilmer inquired, "So do we have a plan for this?"

"We're in one of Cabistero's ships. That should be enough to get us on the ground. We have weapons, so we can fight."

Shannon suggested, "What if we abandon this ship and commandeer one of the Kronos cruisers? When they investigate our ship, we overtake theirs."

"Theoretically, it could work," commented Tisch. "They'd never expect us there."

"And if the *Blue Eagle* is there, we'll take both," Shannon added. "Screw those shitheads."

"The cruiser can be a present to the trade union!" suggested Tisch. "They'll appreciate it, especially since that evens things up against Lazaro."

Wilmer inquired humbly, "Does anyone want to know what I think?"

Both women replied giddily, "No!"

Tisch ordered Shannon, "Get us to Tandenar in a hurry!"

Darra was eager to deliver Mike to her Kronos superiors and collect her bounty. Her hubris ended when the transmitter beeped and Carl Klingman spoke. "You said that Marina was dead, Darra."

Darra suddenly looked frightened and replied, "She is. I'm sure of it."

"She has cost me a lot of money in mercenaries and you know how I feel about failure," he reminded her.

"I'll handle it, Carl," she assured him. "I've never failed you before."

"We'll discuss it soon enough," he responded and ended the transmission.

"Shit!" screamed Darra.

Mike awoke in a cabin, surprisingly with no restraints. Still dazed, he stumbled to the door and entered the main cabin. The cobwebs in his head began to clear and he recalled his encounter with Darra in the Men's Room on Taurus. The door to the flight deck opened and Darra emerged. "Well, it's nice of you to join me, Colby."

Mike still couldn't believe she knocked him out and he still wasn't sure how she did it. Everything happened so fast. "So, how much is Kronos paying you to deliver me?"

Darra laughed at him and then replied, "I'm not doing this for Kronos. I'm doing this for revenge against Marina for killing two of my sisters."

"And that has what to do with me?" he inquired, curious.

"All in time," she answered confidently. "All in time."

Mike stepped toward her but she held her hand out for him to stop. "Try anything stupid and you may not get up next time," she warned. "Sit down and enjoy the trip."

"Where are we going?" he asked, "not that it matters."

Darra informed him that there were some people who wished to speak with him. She mentioned that they weren't very happy about his interference in their operation. Then she strolled over to him and suggested, "If you tell me where Marina is, I won't deliver you to Kronos' base."

Mike suggested that she start at Marina's home. He was pleasantly surprised when Darra slipped and responded, "I'm tired of Yord. I have an apartment with a view of the palace and I know she hasn't been there for quite some time."

Mike suggested that she hang out at the pirate haven on Zim and wait for her to show. She laughed and replied, "Those people are all her allies. I know what they did to my friend Borath, so why would I go there?"

Now Mike was amused. She became irritable over his pleasure about Borath's fate. Mike asked her, "Did you know that it was me who killed him, not once, but twice."

"What are you talking about?" she shouted, now angry.

"I killed him on Zim and then sold his cyborg body to a woman on Sargassa." He then explained what happened when she used his cyborg parts in another body. Darra was impressed.

"I knew there was something different about him. He was too…," she considered her words and then finished, "…too damned good."

"But not as good as me," he remarked sarcastically.

"Last chance," Darra offered. "I'm going to request authorization to land and I have to tell them why."

Mike grinned and informed her that it was her last chance to work something out. Once she turned him over to Kronos, she might never find out where Marina is. Darra smiled and returned to the flight deck. Mike searched the cabin for anything useful but found nothing. The ship was a bare-bones schooner, meant to be disposable. He hoped that any of his friends were smart enough to track or follow them.

Rebecca spoke with Julian on Taurus and then General Lennox at Federation Headquarters from her office on Archimedes-9 about the portals. Then she learned that Mike's abduction could be a prelude to something bigger by Kronos. Lennox informed both that she was preparing a plan to handle both Mike's situation and any Kronos activity in the Nigus region.

Rebecca recommended they include Marina, if possible, in case this is their opportunity to take down Kronos upper tier of management and end them for good. Lennox then assured her that they'd work out the details on the portal usage later.

Julian then mentioned that Margot and Sara were trailing Mike's kidnappers in his shuttle, which happened to have the ability to cloak. He expressed his hope that it would lead them to one of the two remaining Kronos bases. Lennox thanked them for the information and promised to make contact with Marina.

When the pirate patrol ship neared Tandenar, Tisch scanned the surface for any activity that would indicate the *Blue Eagle's* presence. Shannon used the short-range sensors to do an infra-red scan to locate any underground facilities. She piloted the ship slowly into the outer atmosphere, while Wilmer attempted to contact Cabistero for permission to land.

"That's strange," Tisch remarked. "No response."

"I don't like this," mumbled Wilmer.

Tisch noticed significant activity near one of the mountains in an isolated area. "I've found something!" she announced, excited. There were a large number of people on the ground and appeared to be moving cargo from a cave into three freighters.

Shannon focused the sensors on the same area, particularly on the side of the mountain. "I've got something, too!" she blurted. "There's a lot of tunnels inside that cave. It's some kind of network."

"Find a secluded place for us to land," instructed Tisch. "No one seems to know or care that we're here."

The patrol ship glided closer to the surface and approached a smooth landing spot. Suddenly three Federation cruisers dropped down from the sky and surrounded them. "Uh, Tisch. I think we have a problem."

Tisch joined her and studied the monitor. She toggled to close-range cameras and was surprised to see that the ships were Federation vessels. "Wow! Those are Tieg's ships," Tisch shouted. "That was fast."

Then the transmitter beeped. Shannon acknowledged and was stunned when one of the Federation officers demanded they surrender or be blown out of the sky. She explained who they were and why they were there. The officer was wary of a trap and ordered them to land and shut down all systems. She willingly complied.

"They must think we are Cabistero's men," Wilmer remarked. "We're lucky they didn't shoot first."

"Relax, Wilmer," urged Shannon. "It'll be fine." Wilmer rolled his eyes. This wasn't how he and Mike handled things. Or was it?

Once the ship was on the ground and all systems powered down, Tieg's men on the surface surrounded the ship, while the cruisers targeted them from the sky.

When Tisch emerged with her hands out to show she wasn't armed, the soldiers stood down. Wilmer and Shannon followed her as she sought out Tieg.

Numerous people carried an interesting variety of items from the cave and loaded them into the three freighters. Tisch and her crew wondered what was going on. When she saw Tieg, she called to him. He gestured for her to be patient. A moment later, Jackson appeared from the cave and the two men approached her.

"What the heck is going on?" blurted Tisch.

"You're a little late for the party," teased Jackson.

Tieg explained how they captured Cabistero and his pirates thanks to an SOS from the *Blue Eagle*.

"Damn! Zee came through for us," Wilmer remarked, proud that she handled the situation so well.

"That's my girl," replied Tisch.

He then revealed that the cave held a massive trove of valuables that had been confiscated from the colonies over the years. Jackson informed her that, thanks to Lieutenant Tieg, all the valuables have been turned over to them.

"Have you found the *Blue Eagle*?" she asked anxiously.

Tieg replied, "She's safe and sound, as well as her cargo, too. We moved her to Genesis to protect the cargo until you were available to disperse it."

Tisch was elated. She then revealed that Lazaro was on his way with two cruisers. Tieg assured her that they would take care of him. Then she inquired about Mike's status. Tieg revealed that they hadn't heard anything but were confident Margot would be in touch soon.

Tisch asked Jackson if he cared to have the pirate patrol ship as a present from Cabistero. He graciously accepted her gift and planned to use it if any of Cabistero's ships remained in the area. Tieg promised to root out the remainder of them, especially since they no longer had a leader and would likely attempt to flee the area. Tisch and her crew then boarded the patrol ship and returned to Genesis, anxious to have the *Blue Eagle* back in their possession.

When they arrived, they were greeted by all the merchants and their families. Tisch instructed the crew to begin unloading the cargo for them. They gathered around her, anxious to hear about her mission. Everyone cheered when she announced a successful and promising trade with Archimedes-9.

Zenith joined her, holding the manifest of the cargo. Tisch hugged her tightly and thanked her for pulling a 'Mike' in the heat of battle. Zenith was pleased that her efforts to prove her worth paid off. She then turned her attention to the cargo off-load.

As each crate, pallet and box was off-loaded, Zenith called out the vendor who ordered it. The cargo was successfully transferred inside the station to each vendor's booth. Many of the merchants took the time to thank Tisch personally and for honoring her word about protecting them. She reminded them that Lieutenant Tieg was a big part of this and can be trusted as a friend.

Alanna emerged from the crowd and instructed them to dine with her. She mentioned that Jackson would be joining them in a little while. Zenith noticed the look on Alanna as she searched for Jonas. When Alanna questioned Tisch about Jonas' absence, Tisch informed her that he stayed on Archimedes-9 to address certain issues. Zenith felt her heart break but then realized that she and Tisch were two of a kind. Neither meant for love.

Tisch noticed Zenith's sad expression and placed her arm around her shoulder. Zenith smiled and commented, "I guess it's you and me and the *Blue Eagle*."

The two of them entered the *Blue Eagle* and shared a drink in the galley. Tisch gazed at Zenith, admiring her for her ability to step up and solve problems in the heat of a crisis. Zenith noticed and inquired, "I sense that you want to say something."

Tisch smiled and pondered for a few moments. Finally, she spoke up. "I've been considering the business model for the ship to be successful and I think I need a partner."

Zenith agreed that it would be a smart move. She then asked if Tisch thought Mike would be suitable. "Why would you ask that?" Tisch responded, curious as to her loyalties. Zenith then stunned her with something she never expected to hear.

"Just my opinion but it seems that Mike couldn't be a partner to Gemini and, thus far, he hasn't been able to function as a partner for you. You need someone who can think like you and be your other half, not your competition. They'd also have to be able to speak up and give their opinion on things; kind of like a devil's advocate at times."

"And you have someone in mind?" asked Tisch, growing more interested in Zenith's responses.

"I don't. It's hard to imagine someone sharing the *Blue Eagle* with you," she revealed. "This is your baby and nothing will ever change that."

Tisch then had a smug look on her as she realized something. "You know Zenith, I think you'd be a great partner."

Zenith giggled and replied, "That's funny. Can you imagine me and you…?"

"I'm serious, Zee. You've contributed a lot to our success, especially in solving the unusual, which we've had a lot of." Zenith stared at her, waiting for the punchline of a joke. Tisch wasn't laughing, though. "You saved all of us and you saved my ship."

"You're serious?" Zenith asked, still not believing Tisch was serious.

"Yes, I am," responded Tisch. "I think we'd get along just fine, working together." Zenith leaped onto Tisch's lap and hugged her, crying with joy.

Wilmer and Shannon stopped outside the galley and stared at them, wondering what they missed. Tisch stood and informed them of her decision. Wilmer and Shannon were pleased and congratulated Zenith.

Tisch nodded and replied, "I guess this is our destiny... you and I."

"So far," Zenith quipped. "Who knows what's around the corner for us."

"Amen, sister."

CHAPTER 14

THE CHASE

As Margot piloted Mike's shuttle closer to Darra's schooner, the two women plotted how they were going to rescue Mike. Both agreed that they could follow the schooner into the base's transport bay while still cloaked. Margot ordered Sara to remain on board due to her weakened state, but Sara was reluctant to let her enter the base alone.

"We have to let the Federation know where we are," Sara reminded her.

Margot contemplated what Mike would do. She gestured for Sara to be silent for a few moments while she thought. Then she replied confidently, "I have a plan."

Sara kidded that she was beginning to sound like Mike. Margot retorted that her plans were always better than Mike's.

Amused, Sara teased, "Maybe Mike needs to do more to occupy you at night." Margot laughed and welcomed that suggestion.

While Margot operated the computer near the hatch for several moments, Sara folded her arms on the flight deck and waited patiently for her big revelation. When she returned, she directed Sara to follow the schooner into the transport bay and dock as close as possible to it.

"What will that accomplish?" questioned Sara.

"The shuttle is emitting a pinging that should attract everyone within receiving distance," she explained. "The Kronos command will hear it and think that the schooner is a trap. They will force the schooner to leave immediately or risk exposing their location."

"And what do we do in the meantime?" questioned Sara.

"Sit back and see how this unfolds."

They monitored the schooner on the long-range monitor as it approached the Kronos base. The women were ecstatic that they now knew the location of the fourth base. Sara positioned the shuttle toward the schooner until they were nearly beneath it.

The bay doors opened and the shuttle glided in, while hiding beneath the schooner. Once inside, the shuttle veered into the next empty dock.

On board the schooner, Darra argued with the transport supervisor on the transmitter. He refused her admission to the facility and requested she leave immediately. Unsure of why she was suspected of emitting the tracking signal, she checked all the systems and found nothing. Again, the transport supervisor warned her to depart immediately. Darra had no choice but to leave. With no place to go, she panicked and set a course for the base now called Genesis.

Mike sensed her fear and inquired what her problem was. Then she considered that there was a device on Mike's body. "Stand up!" she screamed at him. "Are you wearing a tracking device?"

Mike chuckled, knowing that his friends were nearby. "Nope. I don't wear trackers in the Men's Room," he kidded. "It's a distraction."

Darra retrieved a scanner from a locker and checked Mike from head to toe. Frustrated, she threw the scanner at the wall and shattered it. Mike inquired why she was so upset about being denied access to the Kronos base. She grabbed Mike by his chin and replied angrily, "Because, if there is a tracker on my ship, then Marina and the Federation know where I am."

"But I thought you wanted to find Marina?" questioned Mike. Darra spun and karate kicked him in the head and knocked him out.

A sleek Calamaari cruiser, called the *Reaper*, streaked across the galaxy and followed the tracking signal. On board was Marina and her confidant Kat. Kat was an exotic beauty with dark skin and platinum-colored hair. Both women wore hooded cloaks and donned daggers for weapons. Each kept a pulse pistol holstered to her belt on the back side. Marina piloted the cruiser, while Kat monitored the tracking signal.

"Looks like the signal changes direction after a brief stop," Kat commented.

"Find out where that ship stopped," Marina instructed her. "Then we'll resume following the trail."

Kat repositioned the long-range sensors to the coordinates where the signal changed direction. A large image appeared on the monitor. She activated the cameras for the sensors and was stunned. "Marina, we found it! The fourth Kronos base!"

Marina leaned over, staring at Kat's monitor, and grinned. "Notify Lennox that it's their baby now. We're going after Mike." Kat happily relayed the message via transmitter.

Mike came to on the floor and rubbed his jaw gingerly. "Damn, that bitch hits hard," he groaned. He got up and entered the flight deck. "Get out of here!" shouted Darra.

Mike sat down nonchalantly and warned her, "If you hit me one more time, I will spank your ass bare-bottom and I won't stop until you cry like a baby."

Darra drew a dagger from her belt and held it to Mike's neck. Mike swatted it away and grabbed her by the throat. The dagger fell to the floor, under her seat. "I warned you," he uttered and dragged her into the main cabin.

Darra attempted to scissor-kick him but with no luck. He rammed her head into the bulkhead and choke-slammed her to the floor. Darra was dazed and lay still. Mike undid her pants and slid them down to her knees. She tried to resist but her head still spun. He lifted her up and over his knee as he sat down in a chair at the navigator station.

"Let me go or I'll kill you, you son of a bitch!" she screamed.

Mike spanked her repeatedly until she cried for him to stop. He ripped two cables out of the electrical panel, not concerned with their function, and tied her wrists and ankles together. After another series of profanity-laced threats at him, he ordered her to shut up. When she threatened to kill everyone he cared about, he lifted her over his head and slammed her to the floor. Darra tried to move but her ribs were badly injured. With her pants still down around her knees, blood seeped from her mouth and forehead.

Mike entered the flight deck and attempted to contact the *Blue Eagle.* Unfortunately, no one was on board to take his message. He then tried to contact his shuttle. To his surprise, Margot responded. When she revealed that they were still in the transport bay of the Kronos base, Mike instructed her to turn off the beacon and wait until he returned before doing anything.

Margot was elated and hugged Sara. "I can't believe that was him!" she cried as she shut down the program for the beacon.

Sara was somber and shook her head. "How does he keep doing this," she muttered. "I thought we could humble him by saving his ass."

"I don't care!" she exclaimed. "So long as he's safe."

"You know Margot, you've got to do something with him. This is ridiculous."

"I have an idea that might work since we're married now," she informed her.

"Oh, no!" Sara uttered, feigning fear. "Not the C-word!" Margot nodded and affirmed that it was her intention to use the threat of children to slow Mike down. "I never took you for that kind of girl!" kidded Sara.

"If this doesn't work, then we're all doomed to be part of Mike's fantasy universe forever."

"Please don't fail us, Margot," Sara pleaded. "I've had enough adventures in my life, thanks to Mr. Colby."

"Me, too." The women high-fived and then focused on the monitors for any activity in the bay that would endanger them.

As the schooner neared the Kronos base, Mike considered that he should have Darra contact them instead of him. He left the flight deck and sat down in front of her. She lay on her side, still tied and hurting. "I hope you'll at least have the courtesy to screw me, since you left me on the floor with my pants down."

"Sorry. That's not gonna happen," he replied, amused by her request. "I would like to discuss a proposition with you."

Darra reluctantly listened as Mike offered to arrange a meeting between her and Marina if she would help him. He added that, while he didn't have direct contact with her, he had sources that also had sources that could get a message to her. In return, he wanted her to speak with the transport supervisor to get permission to dock inside the base.

"Why do you want to go inside the base so bad?" she inquired, curious. Mike explained that he had some things to settle with Klingman.

"Jack or Carl?" she questioned him.

Surprised that there were two of them, he figured that they both had to be dealt with. Then Darra revealed Jack's condition as a result of Sima's machine malfunctioning. Jack was more like a seal than a person. Carl was the quiet psycho who was more dangerous.

"Do we have a deal?" Mike asked.

Darra snickered and replied, "I'm more than happy to help you get yourself killed. You'll never get near him and he's very good at traps. He'll snare you."

"Sounds like you know him well."

"He doesn't tolerate failure. You should have seen how he made a mercenary named Antwan suffer." She then revealed the fate of Antwan's family due to his failure. Mike was amazed at how cruel someone could be. Darra continued and boasted about how Antwan's wife was now her whore on Yord. When she revealed how she made the pornographic films of the two of them and sold them to cover some debts, Mike realized how screwed up she really was. Warily, he lifted her and carried her onto the flight deck and set her in the copilot's seat.

"One more thing," she mentioned. "How about a good shagging? I haven't had a guy in a while and I could use a little work on my plumbing." She spread her legs as wide as she could, hoping to coerce him to satisfy her.

Mike shook his head in disbelief and repeated, "That's not gonna happen. Are we doing this or what?"

Darra sighed and groaned, "It was worth a try." She contacted the transport supervisor and informed him that the issue with the beacon was resolved and she needed to pick up some parts for her ship. She assured him that it was a short visit and she'd be leaving immediately after her procurement. The transport supervisor gave her the okay but warned her that she'd be arrested if the beacon became an issue again.

Mike docked the schooner without incident and then untied Darra. He looked away as she pulled up her pants. "There aren't many gentlemen left in the universe, Colby. It's nice to meet one, even if you did spank my ass. Damn, that hurt, too."

Mike inquired where she wanted to meet Marina. She suggested he surprise her. "Then you might want to hang around and I'll get you an answer as soon as I finish with these fools."

Just as he was about to exit the hatch, Darra called out to him, "You're wasting your time. The Klingmans aren't here."

"I expected as much," he replied. "The Federation is waiting to hear from me in case they were. It seems they want them alive, assuming I don't kill them first."

"I'll stick around in case you need a ride and... information," she informed him.

"As a courtesy, I suggest you leave immediately before the Federation blows this place to pieces."

"We will meet again," she warned.

Mike nodded to her and left the schooner.

Margot spotted him on the monitor. "There he is, Sara!" She opened the hatch and called to him. With the shuttle still cloaked, all he saw was her head sticking out of the hatch. He hurried inside and closed the hatch. Margot hugged him tightly and cried. Mike kissed her hungrily and insisted that this wasn't his fault.

"Don't worry about it," she replied and they kissed again. Sara smiled at them from the flight deck.

"Why don't you two get a room?" a voice from the rear of the shuttle startled them. When they turned around, Marina and Kat stared at them from under hooded cloaks.

"How did you get here?" asked Mike, amazed to see them.

"We followed the tracking signal," answered Kat. "The Federation will be here shortly so I suggest we let them handle things for now."

"There's someone in the schooner next to us that wants to meet you. I believe she's a friend of yours named Darra."

Marina checked the outside monitor and saw that the bay just depressurized and the gates opened for the schooner to depart.

Marina complained, "I came all this way to find out what ails that bitch. I guess she'll have to wait for another day. We have more important things to deal with right now."

Margot and Sara anxiously started the shuttle and left the bay, trailing the schooner. Mike mentioned that it was about two of her sisters that Marina killed. Marina smiled and recalled that Fiona and Willow had a third sister that must be Darra. Now she could look forward to defeating the last of the psychotic litter of bitches.

"What can you tell me about the remaining plans for Kronos?" Mike inquired. "I'd hate to cross you again, Marina?"

Marina touched the bruises on his face from Darra and commented, "You should really consider retirement." Mike groaned in frustration.

Marina nodded to Kat, approving the revelation of some of the details of their plans. Kat explained that they are reserving the rebel forces for the attack on the fifth base. This allowed them to keep their existence a secret, while reducing the possibility of a spy warning them. In addition, they wanted to capture the Klingmans before the Federation for other reasons.

Margot returned from the flight deck and inquired, "So, you were able to transport inside the bay from your ship, just by knowing where we were."

"Of course," she replied. "It did require a little magic to deal with the station's hull and gates."

"Oh, and congratulations, Margot," said Marina somberly. "Thanks for inviting me to the wedding."

Margot was embarrassed and responded, "It was a spur of the moment thing. I'm sorry."

"Relax. I'm glad for you," Marina replied. "Not sure why you did it, but I'm glad."

Mike frowned at her but she continued, "Only kidding Colby. You and your team did well." Kat stood by her, ready to transport back to the *Reaper*.

"Will we see you again?" asked Mike.

"Of course," she replied with a smile. In a flash, she and Kat were gone.

Sara pointed out that the gates were open and they should leave while they had the chance. "Get us out of here," Margot ordered her. "Take us to Terran."

Then she led Mike by the hand into the rear cabin and closed the door. From the flight deck, Sara glanced back through the open door and shook her head. "They're both insane," she mumbled to herself. The shuttle pulled away from the station as other Federation ships arrived.

Sara accepted an incoming signal and Major Tieg's face appeared on the monitor. "Glad to see you are leaving in time," he remarked.

"It's all yours, Major," she replied.

"Thanks for all your help. You and your friends did an outstanding job." The transmission ended.

Sara smiled and thought to herself, *Yes, we did.*

The door to the cabin flew open and Mike stormed out, wearing only his boxers. Margot called, "Come back, Mike. I was only kidding."

Sara looked back, stunned, and asked, "What happened?"

Mike waved his hands in the air and complained, "She wants to get a house and have lots of kids and two dogs!"

Sara laughed as she recalled the threat of the C-word - *Children.*

Margot came out in a thong and a lace bra and embraced Mike. She insisted that she'll wait for those things so long as he was a good husband. Sara thought, *Damn! She even looks good to me. That lucky guy.*

Sara checked the long-range sensors and was surprised to see three Federation ships and the *Reaper* escorting them back to Terran. She was amazed by the interest they created in the Nigus star system.

Focusing the sensors and cameras aft, she watched as the Federation vessels pounded the base relentlessly until all that remained was a battered, twisted mass of metal. She pondered where her future would lead her and considered that she could be effective running security for the colonies or even the Federation. Her heart limited her activity to desk work but, after her last battle, she was fine with a peaceful location and only petty criminals to deal with.

CHAPTER 15

THE SWEET TASTE OF SUCCESS

When the shuttle landed on Terran, a great festival was in progress to celebrate the first long-distance trade between the colonies and Archimedes-9. The pirate patrol ship already had painting on it and was named *Li'l Eagle* in honor of Tisch's ship and crew. Sara eagerly departed the shuttle, followed by Mike and Margot.

Tisch and Jackson approached them and congratulated them on their role in making the first successful long-distance trade. Then Sara suggested that Mike and Margot had some news for her. Tisch placed her hands on her hips and stared at them. "Margot, I was counting on you to keep him under control. What happened now?"

Margot shook her head, feigning despair, and replied, "I was desperate and out of options. I married him."

Tisch was stunned and turned to Sara. Sara nodded and kidded how Margot used the C-word to tame him. Tisch laughed hysterically. "You mean that's all it took - the threat of parenthood?"

Margot smiled and kissed Mike's cheek. "I'm sure you'll see a big difference in him from here on out." They were amused as Mike was quiet.

Jackson then requested that Sara join him to discuss an important item. No one thought anything of it as the two left the table.

Marina and Kat sat at one of the tables and drank ale. Tisch suggested to Mike and Margot that they join her and her friend for an update on the war. Marina introduced Kat as the strategist behind her plans. Pleased by Marina's perception of her, she shook hands with everyone.

When she held Mike's, she hesitated and grew concerned. Mike noticed and questioned what was wrong. "You play a dangerous game, Mr. Colby. Beware," she warned.

Marina glanced at Margot and Tisch, fearing what Kat saw. The women suspected Kat had special powers, particularly since she was allied with Marina and was unique in her appearance. It seemed wise not to question her warning.

To break the tension, Margot teased, "Here that, Mike? Don't piss me off."

Mike was unaffected by their words and questioned Marina about the last Kronos base and if they had any idea where it might be. Marina suggested he focus on his new life with Margot and let them handle it. Tisch reminded Mike of his pledge to walk away from all this, so he changed the topic to the portals. Marina then relayed a message from General Lennox. "You owe her the location of the fifth base before she'll commit to discussions with you."

Mike groaned and replied, "How can I find it if I'm out of the game?"

"You have a way of figuring things out," Marina complimented him. "I'm sure that, between you, Margot and your friends, you'll solve the mystery if we don't."

Tisch emphasized that their focus would remain on the trade routes and continuing their development. Marina encouraged her that their progress was vital for a lot of reasons. She saw it as a way to unite the distant sectors and bring peace to the region.

When Zenith joined them, Tisch introduced her to everyone as her new partner. Mike was surprised and impressed. Zenith immediately inquired about the locations of the first two bases and requested their coordinates. Marina agreed to send them to the *Blue Eagle* and wondered why. Zenith only answered that it was a hunch.

The Tieg brothers Jorgan and Bartholomew approached and thanked them for their assistance. Bartholomew informed them that the Kronos base was destroyed and that it housed a significant amount of the Kronos forces. Jorgan explained that their success was based on Kronos not knowing that they were coming. He thanked Margot and Sara for that. Bartholomew then praised Mike for his ingenious plan to get kidnapped by the infamous Darra. Mike wasn't sure if it was a compliment or a jest. The confused expression on his face led everyone to a bout of laughter.

Tisch inquired about Lazaro and his cruisers. Major Tieg informed them that the cruisers fled the region and were pursued by two of his vessels. He doubted that they'd be coming back.

Mike recommended that Marina seek out Antwan's wife on Yord and see if she knew anything. He revealed what Darra mentioned about the apartment overlooking the palace. Marina then related the story of how Carl Klingman punished Antwan and sent the kids to be sold off as slaves. "We took advantage of that and procured the children," she announced proudly.

Kat mentioned that there were few buildings that had an upper view of the palace to search for Antwan's wife. With the return of her children, they had no doubt that Tia would be cooperative.

Marina then inquired as to what their immediate plans were. Tisch announced that they would stop at Sargassa to deliver some items to Sima and Creeg, then proceed to Archimedes-9. After that, she wanted to make a return trip to Taurus to discuss their progress with Gemini. She then indicated that Mike would likely want to coerce Gemini into providing additional staples for the ship – like rum and beer. Again, everyone had a good laugh while Mike shook his head in disbelief.

"The disrespect I get for all my accomplishments," he complained. "It's just not right."

Margot kissed his cheek and reminded him of the rewards he got as well. He sighed and relented that things would never be the same. After a brief hesitation and several stares, he added that he was happy and grateful for the adventures he had with all of them.

"You'd better keep your wife happy, Colby," warned Marina. "Don't make me come back and kick your ass."

Margot responded, "I'm sure he'll be a good boy. Little boys want their candy. Right, Mike?" she whispered in his ear.

Mike smiled at her and replied, "I love candy."

Wilmer and Shannon arrived, holding hands. Tisch teased, "I suppose you two were studying the operation of the onloading system."

"What?" blurted Wilmer. "Why would we do that?"

Tisch answered bluntly, "With Jonas back on Archimedes-9, and with Zenith promoted to partner, you and Shannon will need to step up your game." Wilmer and Shannon glanced at each other, with the feeling they got the short end of the stick by losing two crew members on the loading detail.

"But what about Mike and Margot?" Wilmer asked, hoping for some support from his friend. Mike patted him on the shoulder and assured him that they'd help – when they were on board. Wilmer knew what that meant and groaned.

Jackson, Filson and Gundor greeted them and congratulated them for accomplishing what many believed was impossible. When Mike complimented Jackson on the name for his new patrol ship, Jackson thanked him for handling the early negotiations for Tisch. Jackson's expression changed to one of cheer to a more somber tone. "There is one thing I need to inform you of," he announced. "I've asked Sara to stay on as my security officer."

Jackson looked beyond them at Sara and nodded to her. She joined them and explained, "I'm not ready to hang it up for a sedentary life yet."

Mike expressed his concerns for Taurus since GSS just lost the best security officer in the universe. Sara blushed and hugged him. He whispered in her ear, "I still think I married the wrong sister." They two chuckled and then Mike shook Jackson's hand. They congratulated Sara and wished her well.

"You will come stay with us during your stops in the colonies, won't you?" Jackson asked Mike. "I'd enjoy hearing more about your adventures." Everyone shook their heads with fear in their eyes.

Teasing, Margot interjected, "Mike leads a boring life. There are no adventures."

Mike lowered his head and remarked, "Yeah, my life was boring and lonely. I even had to be blackmailed into marrying the love of my life. Man, I need a drink."

"And Margot did a great job of it, too," Tisch added giddily.

When the festival ended, everyone retired to their apartments. Zenith returned to the *Blue Eagle*, pondering over the Kronos database. She was sure that the location of the last base was there somewhere. She was startled by a man's voice from the hatch.

"Hi, Zenith. Want some company?"

Zenith was surprised to see Kai from Tandenar standing there. "What are you doing here, Kai?"

"I'm the new leader on Tandenar and I heard you aren't in a relationship anymore."

Zenith invited him to sit with her. The two talked until the early morning hours and developed an attraction for each other. She confessed that she had obligations to Tisch and the *Blue Eagle* so she wouldn't be staying.

Kai explained that his new role would keep him very busy as well, but hoped that she would come to see him whenever they were nearby. Zenith explained that they would be the sole long-distance hauler for a while, depending on the outcome of the portal issue with the Federation so she expected to be by regularly.

The next morning, Mike moved the shuttle into the *Blue Eagle's* cargo bay while the others boarded. Jorgan entered the bay and approached him. He informed Mike that several portals had been established to enable them to reach Archimedes-9 and Taurus in reasonable time. Mike thanked him and then asked if Bartholomew was the only reason he participated in the attack on the Kronos base and then visited the colonies.

"I was ordered by General Lennox to observe and evaluate the operation you set up, regarding the Federation's interaction with the trade union."

"She doesn't like me very much," Mike commented.

"It doesn't matter. She respects you," he replied. "The model you've established on Genesis could be the ideal foundation for the Federation to interact with the traders."

"How so?" Mike asked.

"If the portals are erected in the location of key trading points, then we could arrange for the merchants to support the Federation presence, just like on Genesis. If this is acceptable to the merchants, then I'm sure the General would be willing to forego any taxes or fees. It's a win-win for everyone."

"That would be great," admitted Mike. "But it won't be easy. It'll take a lot of work to get everyone to buy into this."

Jorgan patted his arm and responded, "You got us this far. I'm sure you'll get us the rest of the way."

Mike appreciated his confidence in him. Jorgan mentioned that he expected Mike to join him for a drink when he returned to Taurus. Mike agreed and then the two shook hands. He was pleased with the support and watched proudly as Jorgan departed the *Blue Eagle*.

Margot came down to the cargo bay to see what was keeping Mike. "Is everything okay?" she asked, curious.

"Everything is wonderful he replied, smiling. He embraced her and kissed her passionately.

"I have to ask you something, Mike?" she mentioned, looking somber. "Do you really feel that strongly against having kids?"

Surprised by her question, he responded, "No, just not yet. I feel like I have to make the universe a safe place to raise a family. That means no Kronos. No Empire."

"The universe, huh?" she kidded.

"Well, maybe not the whole universe. Just our part of it."

"And that's it?" she pressed.

Mike pondered and then answered, "We have to define who we are. Is this what we want to do for the rest of our lives or is there something else?"

Margot was pleased with his response. "Perhaps someday we'll have all the answers. Until then, your ass is mine," she reminded him and led him by the hand to their cabin.

The *Blue Eagle* arrived on Sargassa in short time thanks to the first of the new portals installed by the Federation. Creeg and Sima waited anxiously with four of their technicians who returned from hiding in the mountains to join her again.

Tisch and Zenith exited from the ship while Wilmer went to work unloading supplies for the facility. Wilmer was surprised when Mike assisted them with the cargo.

"Did you think I forgot you?" Mike kidded.

"Well, yeah. It's been a while since we did anything together." They looked across the bay and noticed that Margot and Shannon were conversing and laughing giddily.

"I guess we're handling the cargo by ourselves," Mike commented.

"Sure does. I guess we should get used to it," Wilmer suggested. They tapped knuckles as a sign of their camaraderie and resumed offloading the supplies. Once the supplies were removed, they loaded ten grafting machines and ten nano-generators. When the cargo bay was secured, they returned to the bridge where Tisch and Zenith were anxiously waiting to move on to Archimedes-9.

"What took you guys so long?" Zenith inquired, teasing.

"A little help would have been appreciated," Wilmer commented. Margot and Shannon entered and embraced their men. Shannon took the pilot's seat and initiated start-up procedures.

"Looks like you guys are doing just fine," Tisch commented.

"Are they complaining?" Shannon asked, looking disappointedly at Wilmer.

"No, but…" he started, but was interrupted.

"Mike mentioned that you two never get to spend any time together," Margot reminded him. "This seemed like the perfect opportunity for the two of you to be a team, just like the old days. Right, Mike?" Mike realized that Margot used his own words against him. She was much smarter – and cunning - than he gave her credit for.

"Nothing to say, Mike?" teased Tisch.

"Nope," he replied. "I'm just enjoying life."

Everyone laughed, satisfied with the relaxed atmosphere void of drama.

"Why don't you boys go have a beer or two?" suggested Tisch. "You earned it,"

Mike and Wilmer hurried off the bridge and went to the galley. Wilmer searched the corridor to see if the women followed and then closed the hatch while Mike took a bottle of rum and two glasses from the cabinet. They sat down at the table furthest from the hatch and Mike poured the rum into the glasses. They raised their glasses in a toast.

"To the women!" exclaimed Mike. "Our bane and our booty!"

Then they were horrified to hear Margot's voice over the intercom. "Is that what I am to you, Colby? Booty."

"Oh, shit," blurted Mike.

Then they heard Shannon's voice. "Are you boys unhappy with your booty?"

They stared at the intercom and saw that the switch was taped in the depressed mode. Mike stared at Wilmer and groaned, "They set us up."

"Yeah, they did."

Then Mike replied, "I wouldn't trade your cute little booty for anything or anyone else in the universe, Margot."

The two men became concerned when there was no reply. They glanced at their glasses and proceeded with the toast. They tapped them and then drank heartily. Mike quickly filled them again. "I think we're going to need a lot more than this?" he remarked.

"Any chance we can get more from Gemini?"

"Screw Gemini!" Mike exclaimed. "I'll talk to Julian."

The hatch unlatched and started to open. They stared at each other, wondering how much trouble they were in. They tapped the glasses again and chugged the contents. Margot and Shannon entered, wearing sexy lingerie and slinked onto their laps. Margot took the bottle of rum and filled the two glasses. She and Shannon drank half and then handed the remainder to the men.

Mike and Wilmer weren't sure what to think. Instinctively, they finished off their drinks. The women then seduced them with slow kisses and rubbed against them affectionately.

"Are we going to do this here or would you boys prefer the privacy of your own cabins?" Shannon inquired.

"I'm fine, either way," Margot remarked.

Mike and Wilmer were speechless. They anxiously lifted the women and carried them off to their cabins.

Tisch and Zenith were alone on the flight deck. Zenith piloted the ship while Tisch entered the coordinates for the portals she received from Major Tieg. She paused to consider that the two of them were alone on the flight deck.

"This job can get pretty lonely at times," Tisch remarked.

"I've realized that for a while now," Zenith responded. "Sometimes it's a good thing."

"Are you okay with this?" Tisch asked, concerned.

Zenith smiled at her and countered, "Are you?"

"I think that's why I needed a partner. Sometimes I feel like I gave up too much for the *Blue Eagle*. I see everyone finding love and it hurts sometimes."

"You mean Mike?" Zenith asked.

"Yes, I mean Mike," answered Tisch. "I'd do the same thing if I had it over but I can't help but wonder."

Zenith went to Tisch and embraced her in a friendly hug. "Don't worry," she said compassionately. "We'll be just fine. We have friends everywhere we go and we have each other."

Tisch then commented that making her a partner was the best move she could have made. Zenith thanked her for not giving up on her when she supported Mike instead of her.

The *Blue Eagle* docked on Archimedes-9 for a cargo swap. Rebecca was anxious to see them and met them in the pub. While Tisch related the progress in establishing the trade routes, Rebecca noticed the diamond ring on Margot's finger. At the end of Tisch's briefing, Rebecca inquired if Mike or Margot had something they wanted to tell her.

Mike smiled at Margot and allowed her to announce their marriage. Rebecca sighed with relief and commented that she would sleep better, knowing that Mike had someone to keep him occupied. Margot affirmed that Mike was indeed occupied and things should be much quieter for the *Blue Eagle*, at least for a little while.

Mike informed her of the fate of the fourth Kronos base and hoped that Kronos' capabilities were limited over the recent loss. Rebecca admitted that she didn't trust Kronos and was sure they were up to something. Mike promised to keep her informed if they discovered anything new.

Rebecca was excited over the arrival of the additional medical equipment and the natural resources that were delivered by Tisch. Only half of the machines were for Archimedes-9, while the other half were for Taurus. Tisch assured her that more were coming. Rebecca revealed that she hoped to have one of each machine installed at every main station or depot over time. She then provided Tisch with a list of items that were sorely needed and hoped she could deliver on her next visit. The two women shook hands and Rebecca left them.

The next day, the *Blue Eagle* set out for Taurus. Everyone was gathered on the flight deck, discussing their return to Taurus. Wilmer requested that Shannon and Margot assist with the cargo swaps in the future. He felt it was a burden for him and Mike to do it alone. Tisch looked to Mike for his thoughts on the women's participation.

Mike questioned the women about what they were doing while he and Wilmer were busting tail with the cargo. Shannon placed her hand on Wilmer's cheek and revealed that she and Margot were discussing new ways to please their men.

"Is that a problem, Mike?" asked Margot.

Mike glanced at Wilmer who shook his head. He was more than happy with Shannon's zest for creativity in the cabin. Mike responded, "Margot, you don't need to be creative. I love you just the way you are." Everyone groaned at Mike's kiss-up act.

The transmitter beeped, catching their attention. Zenith acknowledged the message and activated the video accompanying it. Carl and Jack Klingman's faces appeared on the screen.

"Mike, I think these are friends of yours," uttered Zenith. Mike stood in front of the monitor, anxious to hear what they had to say.

"Well, Colby, it seems you've created quite a problem for us," stated Jack.

"That's funny, Flipper," taunted Mike. "I think I'd be the least of your problems right now."

"We will come for you one day," warned Carl. "And when we do, we'll start with everyone dearest to you first, especially that cute little blonde you're married to."

Jack added, "She'd fetch a nice price on the market and I'm sure we'd have plenty of buyers."

Mike grew impatient and his temper began to flare. "Isn't this what started the whole thing, you dumb asses?" he replied. "You and your Empire assholes couldn't stay out of my business."

Jack reminded him that it was the module he stole that started this feud. Carl reiterated his warning and mentioned that there were two assassins out there who were paid well to put an end to him and his friends. Mike quickly thought about who he was referring to.

Margot eagerly jumped in and informed them that Borath was permanently erased already and Darra was next on their list.

Jack and Carl glanced at each other with concern. Carl muted the transmission and asked Jack, "Is that true about Borath?"

Jack responded, "There were rumors but nothing to substantiate them."

Carl's face turned beet red. He screamed at Jack, "You friggin' idiot!"

Jack was stunned by his brother's outburst. Then Carl drew a dagger from his belt and stabbed Jack in the chest several times. Everyone on the *Blue Eagle* watched in horror at Carl's vicious attack on his own brother.

Finally, Carl finished. Jack lay slumped over in the chair, covered in blood. Carl unmuted the transmission and regained his composure. "I don't tolerate failure or anyone who accepts it," he said somberly. "The days of the *Blue Eagle* and its crew are numbered. I'm coming for you." The transmission ended.

Tisch asked Mike, "Should we be concerned?"

Mike was hesitant and then suggested they stay alert at all times, not to underestimate Klingman's influence around the galaxy.

The *Blue Eagle* approached Taurus and prepared to dock. The transmitter beeped once more, making everyone nervous. Zenith acknowledged it and was relieved to see Marina's face.

"Is Colby available?" Marina asked.

"Right here," he replied as he stepped in front of the monitor.

"We have Antwan's wife. She was quite grateful to be reunited with her children."

"Anything useful?" he asked.

"Nothing until we informed her that we'd reunite her with Antwan. Watch this."

A video then played on the monitor. Tia waited alone in a room, dressed elegantly. Antwan entered and pleaded for forgiveness. He proceeded to blame Mike for everything that went wrong.

Mike commented, “Damn! And I thought we were friends.”

Tia revealed everything that was done to her because of him. She made him watch the sex video that Darra distributed of the two of them. Antwan cried and swore he'd get even with Mike.

“No, you won't, Antwan. This is your doing, not this guy Mike who you're obsessed with.” She drew a stun gun and zapped him repeatedly until he lay paralyzed on the floor. Then she took a small knife out and dismembered his genitalia. After placing it in a bag, she commented, “No one will ever humiliate me again.” Three men entered the room and lifted him upright. “He's all yours,” she announced. The video ended.

Marina appeared again and informed them that Antwan was sold to a sex slave operation and, without his genitals, he was of no use to women. So, you know what's left for him?”

Mike chuckled and remarked, “He always had a thing for men, especially me.”

“We were able to withdraw the video from the galactic server for her. She was very appreciative.”

“What did you learn?” questioned Mike, eager to know.

“Don't worry about it,” replied Marina. “Just take care of my girl and let me handle the rest.” She thanked them again for their help and ended the transmission.

Margot teased, “You heard her.” Mike groaned once more, disappointed to be sitting on the bench during the last stages of the war with Kronos.

The *Blue Eagle* docked on Taurus. They had quite the welcoming committee when they disembarked from the ship. Gemini was especially anxious to greet them. Tisch requested that they finish the cargo swap before rejoicing but Gemini was adamant about celebrating their success.

While waiting for the elevator, Gemini asked Mike, "What do you know about labor relations?"

Mike cringed as he knew where this was going. "I, uh. Not much."

"Well, you'd better learn quick. This long-distance hauling is a whole new animal that needs taming and I need you to tame it."

"But…" he began and moaned. Margot kissed his cheek and assured him that she'd be there to help him.

Everyone laughed as Mike realized his troubles were only beginning. There was still one more Kronos base out there. Carl Klingman was determined to kill them. General Lennox will be an obstacle for him with anything to do with the military. And now, he's caught in the middle of how the long-distance hauling is going to be controlled. Mike suggested, "Can I have some of that fine rum, Gemini? I think I'll need it."

Gemini giggled at him. "There is no more. You took it all."

Mike rubbed his eyes with a pained expression. "It's gonna be a bad day."